SEALED WITH A KISS

A SMALL TOWN CHRISTMAS ROMANCE

EMERALD LAKE, BOOK 1

LEEANNA MORGAN

"Now I know I've got a heart because it is breaking."
- Tin Man -

L.Frank Baum. The Wonderful Wizard of Oz

ABOUT THIS BOOK

Fans of Pamela Kelley and Robyn Carr will love this small-town, feel-good, Christmas romance!

John Fletcher is used to living his life on the edge. He's a former Navy SEAL and the owner of one of the most successful security companies in America. When his daughter asks for the one thing he can't give her, it breaks his heart.

Rachel McReedy isn't impressed with John Fletcher's money, fast cars, or jet-setting lifestyle. What she cares about is Bella, his eight-year-old daughter. She might not have had the type of life Bella has, but she knows what it's like to be left on her own. Rachel is determined to show John the error of his ways, but she isn't prepared for what she's about to find.

Discover the magic of Montana in *Sealed With A Kiss*, the first book in the Emerald Lake series. This book can easily be read as a standalone. All of my series are linked, so if you meet a character you like, you could find them in another book. For news of my latest releases, please visit leeannamorgan.com and sign up for my newsletter. Happy reading!

Other Novels by Leeanna Morgan:

Montana Brides:
Book 1: Forever Dreams (Gracie and Trent)
Book 2: Forever in Love (Amy and Nathan)

Book 3: Forever After (Nicky and Sam)
Book 4: Forever Wishes (Erin and Jake)
Book 5: Forever Santa (A Montana Brides Christmas Novella)
Book 6: Forever Cowboy (Emily and Alex)
Book 7: Forever Together (Kate and Dan)
Book 8: Forever and a Day (Sarah and Jordan)
Montana Brides Boxed Set: Books 1-3
Montana Brides Boxed Set: Books 4-6

The Bridesmaids Club:
Book 1: All of Me (Tess and Logan)
Book 2: Loving You (Annie and Dylan)
Book 3: Head Over Heels (Sally and Todd)
Book 4: Sweet on You (Molly and Jacob)
The Bridesmaids Club: Books 1-3

Emerald Lake:
Book 1: Sealed with a Kiss (Rachel and John)
Book 2: Playing for Keeps (Sophie and Ryan)
Book 3: Crazy Love (Holly and Daniel)
Book 4: One And Only (Elizabeth and Blake)
Emerald Lake: Books 1-3

The Protectors:
Book 1: Safe Haven (Hayley and Tank)
Book 2: Just Breathe (Kelly and Tanner)
Book 3: Always (Mallory and Grant)
Book 4: The Promise (Ashley and Matthew)
The Protectors Boxed Set: Books 1-3

Montana Promises:
Book 1: Coming Home (Mia and Stan)
Book 2: The Gift (Hannah and Brett)

Book 3: The Wish (Claire and Jason)
Book 4: Country Love (Becky and Sean)
Montana Promises Boxed Set: Books 1-3

Sapphire Bay:
Book 1: Falling For You (Natalie and Gabe)
Book 2: Once In A Lifetime (Sam and Caleb)
Book 3: A Christmas Wish (Megan and William)
Book 4: Before Today (Brooke and Levi)
Book 5: The Sweetest Thing (Cassie and Noah)
Book 6: Sweet Surrender (Willow and Zac)
Sapphire Bay Boxed Set: Books 1-3
Sapphire Bay Boxed Set: Books 4-6

Santa's Secret Helpers:
Book 1: Christmas On Main Street (Emma and Jack)
Book 2: Mistletoe Madness (Kylie and Ben)
Book 3: Silver Bells (Bailey and Steven)
Book 4: The Santa Express (Shelley and John)
Book 5: Endless Love (The Jones Family)
Santa's Secret Helpers Boxed Set: Books 1-3

Return To Sapphire Bay:
Book 1: The Lakeside Inn (Penny and Wyatt)
Book 2: Summer At Lakeside (Diana and Ethan)
Book 3: A Lakeside Thanksgiving (Barbara and Theo)
Book 4: Christmas At Lakeside (Katie and Peter)
Return to Sapphire Bay Boxed Set (Books 1-3)

The Cottages on Anchor Lane:
Book 1: The Flower Cottage (Paris and Richard)
Book 2: The Starlight Café (Andrea and David)
Book 3: The Cozy Quilt Shop (Shona and Joseph)
Book 4: A Stitch in Time (Jackie and Aidan)

CHAPTER 1

*R*achel parked her car outside her friend's apartment. For the entire ride across town, she'd been thinking about the envelope sitting on the seat beside her, the exciting news that would bring a smile to Annie's face.

For the last couple of months, Rachel had been helping a group of friends who'd started The Bridesmaids Club. They gave donated bridesmaids' dresses to women who couldn't afford to buy their own.

Most weeks, at least a dozen dresses were sent to her friends, packed in boxes, bags, and anything in-between. Sometimes she helped with the dress fittings, but her main job was to sort through the letters they received. She made appointments for the bridesmaids to see the dresses and contacted the people they couldn't help.

Nearly a year ago, a letter had arrived from a little girl called Bella. Rachel's friends had spent weeks trying to find her, but it wasn't easy. With no return address and no last name, the glittery card with sparkling jewels had become their mystery card. The only clue to where she lived was the Bozeman postmark on the envelope.

Bella's big, round handwriting made them smile, and her request had touched their hearts. She didn't want a bridesmaid's dress. She wanted a bride for her daddy.

Rachel picked up Bella's envelope. She was almost positive she'd found the little girl they'd been searching for.

Stepping out of her car, she headed toward Annie's apartment. The cold October wind tore through her coat and left her shivering on the doorstep. They were lucky it hadn't started snowing. Montana's weather could be unpredictable at the best of times but, during the fall, they could have four seasons in one week.

Annie opened her front door just as Rachel was about to knock. "Tell me you have good news."

"What's happened?" Closing the door behind her, she stared at the boxes scattered around the living room. Annie was getting married the following weekend. After lots of careful planning, she was determined not to get stressed or give in to the last-minute pre-wedding nerves most brides seemed to develop.

Annie ran her hands through her hair. "Dylan's mom is driving me insane. She doesn't like the table favors we've chosen. I knew we should have waited until next April to get married. Why did I want to have a short engagement?"

"Because you love Dylan and couldn't wait to be his wife." Rachel glanced at the tulle and ribbon bags they'd filled two nights before. "What's wrong with peppermint creams? I thought Dylan's mom liked peppermint."

"So did I, but she's found a company in Vermont that makes maple toffee crunch brownies. One of her friend's daughters got married last weekend. The brownies were the most delicious thing she'd ever tasted. They come in individual boxes, gift-wrapped with ribbon, to match the theme of the wedding."

"But this is Montana, not Vermont," Rachel said carefully. She didn't want to get between Annie and her mother-in-law but, with one week left before the wedding, it wasn't the time to be changing anything.

"Precisely. But is she listening to me? No. Dylan called her this morning, but she's determined to have the brownies. She called the company and they can send enough boxes to us by Friday. She even offered to pay for them. What am I going to do?"

Rachel took off her coat and scarf and left them on the back of a chair. "What difference does it make if you have the brownies?"

"Nothing, if they arrive in time. We could give the sixty bags of peppermint creams to someone else. But it's the principle that counts. Dylan and I have spent months getting everything ready."

"Do you want my advice?"

Annie nodded. "You're the sanest person in the room at the moment."

"Go with the brownies. No one will be worried if they don't get peppermint creams."

Annie moved two pairs of shoes off a chair and sat down. "I suppose you're right. It's just so annoying."

"Welcome to the world of families. Dylan's mom probably had the best of intentions when she mentioned the brownies."

"If she'd had those same intentions two months ago, it would have been better," Annie grumbled.

"I have some news that's better than the brownies."

Annie frowned. "Did you find the animal costumes from last year's Christmas play?"

"I don't think we'll ever see them again. A teacher must

3

have left them in a box somewhere. This is more exciting than lost costumes." She waved Bella's envelope in the air. "Do you remember this?"

Annie looked closely at the brightly colored envelope. "Is that Bella's card?"

Rachel nodded and smiled.

Annie's eyes widened. "You've found her? How did you do that? We spent weeks searching for her."

"The reason we couldn't find her is because she's home-schooled. Her dad travels around a lot with his job. She has a tutor who goes with them when they need to leave Montana."

"Does Bella's dad really need a bride?"

"I don't know. I haven't spoken to him."

Annie grinned. "I'd like to hear that conversation."

"You can if you want to."

"Let me guess…Molly, Tess, and Sally didn't want to go with you?"

Rachel really hoped her friend took pity on her. "Molly's getting ready for another exhibition, Tess is baking like crazy for a Halloween party, and Sally's busy teaching."

"Sounds like it's you and me, then."

"Only if you can spare the time," Rachel said quickly. "I know Bella's last name, but I don't know where she lives or what her father's name is. If it takes more than a few days to find him, you'll be well and truly on your honeymoon."

Annie walked across to the kitchen. "Bozeman isn't a big city. It shouldn't take too long."

"I hope you're right." Pulling the pretty card out of the envelope, she re-read the message. *Dear Bridesmaids Club. Can you please help my daddy find a bride?*

Bella's words had brought back so many unhappy memories, that she had to find her. After weeks of searching through every public record she could get her hands on, she'd almost given up. Then, amazingly, Bella had walked into Rachel's classroom.

Hopefully, finding the little girl's father would be easy.

The hard part would be telling him his daughter was looking for a mom.

JOHN FLETCHER STARED at the release form in front of him. He'd been working with the Department of Defense for the last year, creating a prototype drone that would change the way surveillance operations were carried out around the world.

The drone had passed the field tests and they'd provided all the information the Special Ops Unit wanted. Now all he had to do was sign on the dotted line and his bank account would be millions of dollars better off.

"Are you going to keep staring at the contract or sign it?" Tank, his friend and one of the former Navy SEALs who worked with him, wasn't known for his patience off the battlefield. But leave him in the middle of an alligator-infested swamp, and he could stay still for hours.

"Did Connor encrypt the schematics?"

"All done."

"And Sam sent the files through to Tanner?"

Tank focused his flat stare on him. "What's wrong?"

John wasn't going to admit he'd had misgivings about this project long before they'd started the design phase. Tank didn't need to know about the conversations he'd had with top-ranked officials in the Department of Defense or the issues that kept him awake.

He picked up a pen and signed the contract. "Make sure this leaves here today. I don't want it getting into the wrong hands."

Tank slid the document into a brown envelope. "It's safe with me."

John didn't believe anything was safe. He'd learned a long time ago to listen to his instincts, and his instincts were screaming at him to be careful. "Take Connor with you. He knows his way around the Pentagon."

Tank didn't bother saying anything. The look he sent him said it all.

"And don't spend too much time in Virginia. I have another job for you."

Tank grunted. "Middle East or Europe?"

"Neither. Texas. A senator needs an escort to New York City in three days' time."

"I'll call you when I get back. Try to get some sleep tonight."

Tank left and John sat back in his chair. He turned toward his first-floor window and looked across the garden.

Fletcher Security was based in a historic building on the outskirts of town. It had been built in the 1860s as Montana's first flour mill. When he'd bought the property, it was derelict and in serious need of repair. Over the following two years, he'd rebuilt most of the interior, keeping as much of the character as he could, and recreating the rest.

No one seeing the red-brick building would know what went on inside the property. He provided high-risk security services for clients around the world. He'd gathered together an elite group of men and women, mostly ex-military, all dedicated to their roles in his company. Their list of clients, past and present, was impressive.

John didn't advertise—he didn't need to. Word of mouth traveled faster than an ad in the New York Times. The uber-rich of the world knew how to find him. What most people didn't know was the other side of his business. The side that had been giving him sleepless nights for the last few weeks.

Developing state-of-the-art surveillance software was a side product of what they did. Out of necessity, they'd had to look at other ways of keeping track of their clients and their property. When Samantha Jones joined his company, she'd quickly slipped into the role of Technical Development Manager. She had a PhD in electrical engineering from one of the most prestigious universities in the world and a mind that was never content with the word 'no'.

Sam pushed the limits of whatever project she was working on, and the drone was no exception.

The phone on his desk rang and John reluctantly answered it. He'd told his secretary not to put any calls through unless they were urgent. Apart from World War III breaking out or anything to do with his daughter, he was hoping to have a few hours to work on another project.

"What is it, Gloria?"

"Sorry to bother you, but a Rachel McReedy is here to see you. It's about Bella."

The hair on the back of John's neck stood on end. "What's happened?"

"I don't know."

He ran through Bella's schedule for the day. She'd still be at home. Her ballet class didn't start for another hour and the people looking after her would have contacted him if something was wrong. He'd made sure nothing concerning his daughter turned into a life or death situation. Ever.

He glanced at the folders on his desk. "Send her through, but warn her I don't have a lot of time."

He walked toward his office door. Whatever his visitor had to say would have to be quick. He had a project plan to work through and clients he needed to contact.

If he finished early, he'd meet Bella at her ballet class. Tutus and pink tights had to be better than worrying about surveillance drones. And a lot less dangerous, too.

~

RACHEL JUMPED as the big wooden door in front of her opened. Apart from dark hair, the man walking toward her looked nothing like Bella. The little girl she'd met had big brown eyes, olive skin, and mahogany curls.

She wondered if she'd found the right person. The form she'd seen had definitely been signed by a John Fletcher. There was only one John Fletcher living in Bozeman, and he was standing in front of her.

"Hello, Mr. Fletcher. My name is Rachel McReedy. I have something I need to talk to you about."

His cool blue eyes held her gaze as he shook her hand. "I have a conference call in five minutes."

Rachel nodded. Five minutes was better than nothing. For the last few days she'd been trying to make an appointment to see him. The staff at his home had told her he wasn't available and she couldn't get through to his secretary. Out of desperation, she'd driven to Fletcher Security's head office, hoping he'd be able to see her. With only three days left before Annie's wedding, she was on her own.

John held open his office door. "Come in."

She tightened her hold on her bag. "Thank you for seeing me."

He pointed to a chair in front of his desk. "You're welcome. What did you want to discuss with me, Ms. McReedy?"

"Rachel…you can call me Rachel."

He sat down and looked closely at her. She wished she'd worn something a little more business-like. Her 'Welcome to Hawaii' T-shirt didn't make her feel confident. She'd pulled it on after an over-excited student splattered her with paint.

But she wasn't here to make a good impression. She was

here to help Bella's dad understand his daughter a little better.

She cleared her throat and unzipped her bag. "I'm a teacher at Bozeman Elementary School. Your daughter, Bella, spent time with my class last week."

"Was there a problem?"

Rachel shook her head. "Bella is a wonderful little girl. I enjoyed working with her."

"Why are you here, then?"

Rachel wondered if the frown plastered across his face was permanent. He didn't seem like the type of person who smiled a lot. Bella's dad was completely different from the happy little girl who'd visited her school.

"Ms. McReedy?"

She blinked and yanked her mind back to the man sitting in front of her. "Sorry." She took Bella's envelope out of her bag. "As well as teaching at Bozeman Elementary School, I help a group of friends who have started The Bridesmaids Club. Have you heard of us?"

John was beginning to look irritated. "No. I can't say I have."

"We're sent pre-loved bridesmaids' dresses from all over the country. Women who need dresses contact us and take them for their own weddings. Everything is free. It's really rewarding making people's dreams come true."

Rachel smiled and John's frown deepened. She wouldn't let his grumpiness distract her from what she had to tell him. "About a year ago, The Bridesmaids Club received a letter from a little girl. My friends tried to find her, but they didn't have much luck."

"And you think my daughter wrote this letter?"

"Someone called Bella signed it."

"You have the wrong person. I can assure you, Bella doesn't need a bridesmaid's dress."

"It wasn't a dress she wanted."

John's gaze sharpened. "What did she want?"

Rachel had thought long and hard about how she'd break the news to Bella's dad. She could be incredibly diplomatic when she needed to be, but John Fletcher didn't seem to have a lot of time for diplomacy. So instead of telling him what the card said, she handed it to him.

"It might be better if you read the card."

John took the envelope out of her hand. He looked at the picture on the outside, then glanced back at her.

She didn't look down.

He pulled out the card and read the message. "My daughter wants me to get married?"

Rachel had a feeling the chance of that happening was practically zilch. He might be handsome in a rugged, outdoorsy sort of way, but his personality needed work.

"Or she could want a mom. She might be lonely."

John's face hardened. "I can assure you, Ms. McReedy, my daughter isn't lonely."

Rachel sighed. Coming here was an enormous mistake. "In that case, you have nothing to worry about. Thank you for seeing me. I'm sorry I kept you from your phone call."

John's scowl relaxed into an annoyed frown. "Anything to do with my daughter comes before my work."

"That's good to know." Rachel plastered a polite smile on her face and left his office. At least she could tell her friends Bella was no longer their mystery girl. It was just a pity John Fletcher didn't share his daughter's personality. If Bella was unhappy, there was nothing she could do about it.

Not today, anyway.

CHAPTER 2

*J*ohn glanced at his daughter. Bella was sitting on a kitchen stool, swinging her legs in time to some music. Her head was bent over a book, concentrating on the words.

He took a container of fruit salad out of the refrigerator and two bowls out of the pantry. "I met Ms. McReedy, today."

Bella looked up at him. Her absent smile told him she was still stuck somewhere in *Anne of Green Gables*. She frowned at the fruit salad, then glanced back at him. "The teacher from the school I'm going to?"

He nodded and Bella smiled. Her wide grin caught him off guard. She was so much like her mom that a sharp stab of grief made him forget what he was about to say.

He wished his wife was here to see how beautiful their daughter had become. Bella lit the room with her laughter and wide smiles. She was his beginning, middle, and end, and the only reason he'd been able to function after Jacinta died.

He cleared his throat and reformed the words inside his head. "Ms. McReedy said she enjoyed teaching you."

Bella leaned forward and rested her elbows on the counter. "I liked her, too. She's a fun teacher."

Her gaze followed him as he put a serving of fruit into each bowl. "She came to my office to see if I knew who'd sent her friends a card."

Bella took one of the bowls and waited for him to pass her a spoon. There was no flicker of recognition, nothing that told him his daughter knew what he was talking about.

He handed her a spoon, then took the envelope out of his briefcase. "Does this look familiar?"

The fruit on Bella's spoon dropped into her bowl. "How did Ms. McReedy get my card?" she whispered.

John pushed the envelope across the counter. "She helps her friends give bridesmaids' dresses to people who need them."

Bella nodded and moved the fruit around in her bowl.

"Is there anything you want to tell me?"

"Daisy sent us a postcard from Barcelona. I left it on the counter."

Daisy was Bella's tutor. Unfortunately for Bella and John, she'd called three nights ago and told them she wouldn't be coming back. The two-week vacation she'd first planned had turned into twelve months of traveling around Europe. John's housekeeper was filling in as a substitute tutor, but he needed to find someone more permanent.

He glanced at the postcard. "That's nice, but it's not what I'm meaning. Why did you ask The Bridesmaids Club to find a bride for me?"

Bella blushed and looked down at her fruit salad.

"Bella?"

"It was ages ago," she muttered.

He wasn't sure how to find out if his daughter was lonely. So he didn't. He carried his fruit salad across to the counter and sat on a stool beside her. "Mrs. Daniels said you're doing really well with your schoolwork."

Bella shrugged her shoulders.

John stabbed a piece of melon with his fork. "What did you do today?"

"We did some math and reading. Mrs. Daniels showed me how to make a chicken pasta salad and a huckleberry cheesecake. We're having them for dinner tomorrow night."

"Sounds great." He'd seen the weekly work plan that Daisy had left with Mrs. Daniels. His housekeeper had shown Bella a lot more than cooking skills but, if that's what Bella remembered the most, he wasn't too worried. He was advertising for a new tutor next week. With the money he was offering, he didn't expect to have any problem filling the position before Christmas.

"Ms. McReedy is nice." Bella glanced at him quickly.

He nodded and kept eating his fruit salad. Rachel McReedy hadn't been too impressed with the welcome she'd received in his office. Her blue eyes had flashed at him more than once, warning him he'd annoyed her.

"Will Ms. McReedy be my tutor?"

"She already has a job, so she can't help us. But she'll be at your new school when you start." He watched Bella pick through her fruit salad, looking for the strawberries he'd buried at the bottom of the bowl. "How did you find out about The Bridesmaids Club?"

"Mrs. Daniels read me a story from the newspaper about what they're doing. I went onto the Internet and looked at their website."

John stopped eating. "You found their website?"

Bella smiled and nodded. For the first time since he'd mentioned the card, her eyes lit up. "They have so many pretty dresses. They even have tiaras and petticoats. Mrs. Daniels said her granddaughter donated her wedding dress to The Bridesmaids Club. Mrs. Daniels' granddaughter found her husband on the Internet."

He almost choked on a piece of apple. He coughed, trying not to look as though he was worried about his eight-year-old daughter knowing about online dating sites.

He glanced at Bella. "Did you look at any dating sites?"

She shook her head and looked sad. "Mrs. Daniels said they're only for adults."

"You asked her?"

Bella nodded. John breathed a sigh of relief. "That's good."

"She told me she met her husband at a friend's wedding. I thought The Bridesmaids Club might know someone who'd want to marry you."

The fork in John's hand never made it to his mouth. He put the fruit back in his bowl and pushed the whole thing away.

He watched Bella closely. "I don't want to marry anyone. I'm happy living with my favorite girl."

"Mrs. Daniels said Mr. Daniels makes her happy every single day. Sometimes you don't look happy."

John didn't know what to say. He'd worked hard to provide a stable, loving home for his daughter. But sometimes, after Bella went to bed and the house was quiet, he felt the weight of the world on his shoulders.

His wife, Jacinta, had died six years ago. He'd been working in the Middle East when he'd been told the news. He returned home, unsure of what the future held. He didn't know Bella, didn't know how to look after a two-year-old who missed her mom.

A chance meeting with a senator had set him on the path he was on now. He'd started his own security company, quickly moving into high-risk, high-return contracts catering to the rich and famous. Over the next five years, he'd bought companies across America. Moving into international security operations seemed like the perfect fit. But with the fit came danger.

He'd created a successful security operation, but some days he wondered if it was all worth it. He could afford to give his daughter anything she wanted, take her anywhere in the world. But after ignoring his life beyond work and his daughter, he'd forgotten what it felt like to be happy.

He put his arm around Bella's shoulders. "I love you, sweet pea. Sometimes if I don't look happy, it's because I have things on my mind. I promise it's not because I'm sad."

"Pinky promise?"

He held out his hand. "Pinky promise."

Bella grinned and John's heart swelled with love. They wrapped their little fingers around each other and sealed their bargain with a kiss.

"Do you want to see the pretty dresses on The Brides-maids Club website?"

He couldn't think of anything worse, but he smiled at his daughter. Bella loved frilly, flouncy, dresses. He didn't know how or why it had happened, but it had. "Sure, I do. Finish your dessert first, and then we'll go into my office and use my computer."

Bella ate some more fruit, watching him with eyes that were far too wise. He needed to show her he was happy, that she didn't have to worry about him. And, more importantly, that he didn't need a wife.

Pretending to be the Dad Bella wanted wasn't hard. All he needed to do was work out what made him happy and stay clear of single women.

THREE DAYS LATER, John reminded himself this was what it felt like to be normal. He was standing in Charlie's Bar and

Grill, trying to look as though he belonged with the loud, over-excited crowd of business executives, cowboys, and college students.

He was thirty-four years old, but he might as well be one hundred. He felt uncomfortable and so out of his depth that he was almost ready to leave.

Dylan Bayliss, his friend and business partner, was getting married tomorrow. The bachelor party was supposed to be his last chance at freedom. But John knew how badly Dylan wanted to marry Annie. She'd changed him, helped him find a new normal in a world that didn't understand what it was like to be different. Dylan had been kidnapped and tortured by the Taliban, left for dead in the middle of Afghanistan. After what he'd been through, coming home was one of the most difficult things he'd ever done.

"How are you holding out?" Dylan stood beside John, looking almost as uncomfortable as he did.

"I'm nearly ready to leave."

"Yeah, me, too. You want to go outside?"

John didn't need to be asked twice. He followed Dylan through the crowded room, scanning the faces around him for anything out of the ordinary. The only thing out of the ordinary were the two men walking outside into single digit weather.

Once they were through the doors, Dylan led him across to a bench seat. "We'll be safe here."

John sat beside his friend. "You know we'll probably freeze to death if we stay out here for more than fifteen minutes?"

"Works for me. By that time, Annie would have found us and thought of some interesting ways to keep me warm."

"She's coming here? To your bachelor party?"

Dylan shrugged. "I couldn't see any way around it. There aren't that many options in Bozeman on a Friday night."

John took a sip of his soda. Even from the garden, the noise from the bar was loud. The music and laughter mixed together to create something he wasn't comfortable around. He pulled on his jacket, zipping the front together before his fingers went numb.

"You sure you're warm enough?" Dylan asked.

"You're just annoyed you didn't grab your jacket on the way out."

Dylan grunted. "Or it could have been that I saw where you were heading and decided to stop you from leaving. A jacket didn't seem important when I was inside."

John wasn't going to disagree with his friend. They'd known each other for too long. They'd been through too much to worry about what they should or shouldn't be doing.

He glanced back at the bar. He might be cold, but at least he could speak to Dylan without having to yell over the noise from everyone else. "Why are you having a bachelor party?"

"It sounded good at the time. I'm not getting married again, so I thought I might as well follow the wedding plan in Annie's book. Stupid idea. What's your excuse for being here with me?"

"I figured if you could be here, so could I. But I'm too old for this," John said with a grim smile. "I'm ancient compared to most of the people inside the bar."

Dylan's sharp bark of laughter made him smile. "You and me both."

John raised his can of soda in Dylan's direction. "Here's to ancient men who should know better."

"And to new beginnings that are scaring the living daylight out of me."

He watched his friend. "You're worried about getting married?"

Dylan shook his head. "I'm not worried about getting

married. I'm worried Annie will come to her senses and decide I'm not the man for her. Once she signs the marriage license, I figure I'm safe. But until then, I'm not taking any chances."

"She loves you," John said with a conviction he meant. "Annie won't change her mind."

Dylan rested his head against the back of his chair. "I hope not. What did you do with Bella?"

"Mrs. Daniels is on babysitting duties."

"Doesn't happen often." Dylan glanced across at him. "You looked comfortable in there. If I didn't know you as well as I do, I wouldn't have thought you were ready to leave."

"I'm good at pretending."

Dylan nodded. "Works for most of us. You should come to Pastor Steven's support group with me. The guys are okay, if you ignore Jeremy's smart-ass comments. It might help."

"I don't have post-traumatic stress disorder."

"Are you kidding? With what you were involved in and your wife's death, I'd say there's more going on inside of you than even you know. When was the last time you dated a woman?"

"About the same amount of time as you before you met Annie."

Dylan looked him in the eye. "Have you been on a date since Jacinta died?"

John focused on the can in his hands. "I've been too busy."

"I can't argue with that. You never stop."

"Bella sent a letter to The Bridesmaids Club. She wanted them to find a wife for me."

Dylan smiled. "I heard."

"Annie told you?"

"Finding the little girl who wrote the mystery card was the highlight of their year. They've been searching for Bella for ages. If they'd asked me, I could have told them I know a

SEALED WITH A KISS

little girl called Bella. But then you wouldn't have met Rachel."

"She might have preferred we didn't meet."

Dylan looked at him closely. "She wasn't impressed with your sophisticated charm?"

"It was in short supply on the day we met."

"You'd better find it again."

John's eyebrows rose. "Are they coming to your bachelor party, too?"

"Annie insisted they join us. Remember to watch them. No one's safe when they're in the same room together."

"I heard that." Annie walked toward them, smiling at her fiancé. She stood beside Dylan, keeping her hands warm in her jacket pockets. "Charlie said you'd come out here. Aren't you cold?"

Dylan pulled Annie onto his lap. "You can keep me warm."

Annie shivered. "You're as cold as a block of ice. Charlie's lighting the outdoor fire. It will be warmer than sitting in the garden."

Dylan held his fiancée close and kissed the side of her face. "I'm happy right here."

She patted his hand. "Two minutes of snuggle time and then we're moving to the patio. I don't want either of us getting sick before our wedding."

John glanced at the patio and frowned. Rachel and three other women were helping to tie the sides of the screens into place.

Even though he wasn't looking forward to seeing her again, he decided it had to be better than watching Dylan and Annie making out beside him. "I'll leave you to whatever it is you're getting up to."

"It won't be much," Dylan said with a sigh.

John walked toward the patio and tried to look as though

he was having a good time. But a certain blond-haired, blue-eyed woman chose that moment to glance at him.

Her eyes narrowed and her smile dimmed.

He knew, without quite knowing how, that she'd seen through the mask he'd worn to survive the bachelor party. He needed to leave. The sooner he went home, the better off everyone would be.

CHAPTER 3

*R*achel helped Molly pull the second to last screen down. Charlie, the owner of the bar, had almost finished another wall. The plastic would keep most of the chilly night air away from them and the stone fireplace would warm the patio.

Hopefully, the lovely atmosphere would distract her from thinking about John Fletcher.

As he'd walked toward her, he looked as happy to see her as she'd been to see him. Rachel was still embarrassed about the last time they'd met. She didn't normally act like a spoiled two-year-old, but there was something about his cool attitude that annoyed her.

Molly smiled at John. "I'm Molly. If it's some fine company and a little heat you'd be wanting, come this way."

He looked at Rachel.

Once Annie married Dylan, there were bound to be lots of times when they'd meet. If she didn't fix what they'd started, it would be even more difficult to apologize and get on with their lives. "You're welcome to stay. Charlie's bringing some food outside."

"I'm not sure that's a good idea."

She tried again. "I'm sorry about the other day. I don't usually barge in where I'm not wanted. I guess I was caught up in the search for Bella. I didn't consider that you might have other things to do."

John's face didn't soften, but his eyes lost their frosty glare. "I wasn't very welcoming, either."

Molly wiggled the plastic screen she was holding. "Now you're on speaking terms again, you can help me tie the last screen in place." Grabbing hold of John's arm, she pulled him forward. "I've heard Dylan speak highly of you. Would you tie the top string for us?"

John looked up at the wooden beam. A thick cord dangled from the edge of the plastic screen. He glanced at Rachel. "It looks like I'm staying. Do you think we could start over?"

Rachel held out her hand. "We can. It's a pleasure meeting you, John." He shook her hand and a warmth that had nothing to do with the outdoor fire, seeped into her bones.

"It's good to meet you, too."

Another zing of electricity replaced the first. When he wasn't in a grumpy mood, Rachel suspected he could be charming and incredibly dangerous.

Molly looked beyond the patio and sighed. "Would you do me a favor, John? Annie and Dylan will catch a cold if they stay outside for much longer. Before you tie this string, could you unlock their lips and send them inside?"

Before John was halfway across the backyard, Dylan and Annie ran toward them.

"No unlocking necessary," Annie said as she ducked under the plastic screen. "Even Dylan can't keep me warm out there."

Rachel ignored the blush on Annie's cheeks and tied the middle string. John wouldn't have trouble keeping a woman warm. Even a woman with ulterior motives who wanted to see how his daughter was.

After the screen was in place, she stepped back and smiled. They were here to enjoy the last single night of Dylan and Annie's lives. If she could do a little snooping and find out how Bella was, she'd be even happier.

John Fletcher didn't know a lot about her but, by the end of the night, Rachel was hoping to know a lot more about him.

JOHN WASN'T sure when he'd started enjoying himself. He was sitting beside Rachel, listening to the light-hearted banter bouncing around the table. Over the last hour, other friends had joined them, filling the patio with a buzz of laughter and happy conversation.

He'd met Tess and Sally not long after Charlie lit the fire in the big stone fireplace. They were part of The Bridesmaids Club and Rachel's friends. Dylan had been right—when Rachel and her friends got together, no one was safe. Their funny stories and good-natured ribbing brought a smile to everyone's faces, including his.

He leaned across the old wooden table and picked up another slice of pizza.

Rachel watched him as he bit into layers of beef, salami, bacon, and mozzarella cheese.

He swallowed what he was eating and frowned. "Is there sauce on my face?"

She smiled and shook her head. "I didn't think you'd eat pizza."

"Why not?"

She shrugged her shoulders. "You'll think I'm crazy."

He'd learned a lot about Rachel over the last hour. She

was impulsive, easily excited, compulsively happy, and able to be part of two conversations at once. There wasn't any room for craziness in her brain.

"Try me."

She looked at the pizza, then back at him. She leaned in close and her blond hair brushed against his arm. "You're rich," she whispered. "I thought you'd have a housekeeper making you healthy meals."

John grinned. Rachel wasn't joking. She honestly thought he wouldn't eat the same food as everyone else. What other people thought of his life had never worried him but, for some reason, Rachel's opinion made him laugh. "Everyone likes pizza."

Annie, the bride-to-be, pointed at her plate. "Everyone that's not getting married likes pizza. I feel like I've turned into a rabbit."

Rachel had told him Annie was on a strict diet. No amount of tempting could make her eat one spare rib or anything dripping with cheese. John had no idea why Annie was starving herself, but he'd never been very good at second-guessing the way a female brain worked.

A waitress brought out more plates of hot, spicy food, drawing a groan from Annie.

Rachel passed her the salad dressing. "This might make your dinner taste better."

Annie took the bottle out of her hand. "As long as I fit into my wedding dress, I'll be happy."

As the conversation randomly moved from one thing to the next, John relaxed, laughing more than he had in a long time. It felt good to be sitting with a group of adults who wanted nothing more from him than his company.

"I still don't know why your mom didn't like the peppermint creams," Sally said to Dylan. "It doesn't make sense."

"Nothing about my mom makes sense," Dylan said with a

smile. "I love her, but she changes her mind about every-thing. One year we were driving to Denver for a vacation. Halfway there, she changed her mind and we ended up in Texas."

"Did you have a good time?" Molly asked.

Dylan nodded. "My mom might change her mind, but she's fun to be around."

"That must make up for her spontaneous nature. What about you, John? Do you have any childhood vacation tales to share with us?"

He looked at Molly and took her question at face value. "We didn't go on many vacations. My parents preferred to stay at home on their ranch."

Rachel looked at him. "Are you from Montana?"

"I spent the first eighteen years of my life here."

"And then?"

John picked up his pizza. "And then I joined the military."

She watched him finish his slice of pizza. Dylan asked him a question and everyone joined in with their opinion about the latest scandal to hit the streets of Bozeman.

Rachel leaned toward him. "You don't like talking about yourself, do you?"

"It's easier not to." He'd learned the hard way not to speak about where he'd come from and what he did. There were lots of reasons why being a billionaire was great. There were other, less obvious ones, why it wasn't.

He'd been in enough situations to tell him when to be careful. And, right now, his internal radar was telling him to slow down and watch what he said. "You don't freelance as a reporter, do you?"

She shook her head. "No. I leave that up to Logan."

Logan was married to Tess, one of Rachel's friends. John had met him not long after he'd moved back to Bozeman. He was a reporter for *The Bozeman Chronicle* and a former war correspondent.

When John moved Fletcher Security's head office to Montana, it created a ripple on the information highway. Half the folks of Bozeman wanted to know all about the man who'd transformed the old flour mill into a security company. The other half couldn't care less.

Their first meeting had gone better than he'd expected. They'd come to an understanding, trading information like a game of poker. Logan wanted to know what he was doing and why he was doing it. John wanted to promote his company, not himself. The stories Logan wrote were focused on the public face of John's business and the jobs he was creating. The rest was left alone, filed away for another time.

John hoped that once people became used to seeing him around town, no one would care what he did. On the whole, keeping a low profile had helped keep him invisible, and he wanted it to stay that way.

Rachel nudged his elbow. "Well?"

"Well, what?"

"What happened after you joined the military?"

"I was stationed overseas for a while. When I came back, I started Fletcher Security. I built my business from nothing into what it is today."

"So you're just another country boy turned billionaire success story?" She looked impressively underwhelmed by the sketchy story he'd given her.

"You could say that. Although the billionaire part is fairly new."

"It must take time to get used to having so much money?"

He looked closely at her. "My life isn't much different to what it was three years ago. I reinvest most of my profits straight back into my business."

Molly tapped her dessert spoon against her wineglass. "I'd

like to propose a toast," she said in her lilting Irish accent. "To Dylan and Annie, two of the nicest people I've met. May your marriage be strong and true, tied together with bonds that will last all time." She raised her glass and smiled. "To Dylan and Annie. Slainte."

Everyone raised their glass to toast the nearly married couple. John glanced at Dylan. He looked so nervous it almost brought a smile to his face. Until he remembered why he was nervous. Annie meant everything to him. He'd given his heart and soul to her, expecting nothing in return. It was the kind of relationship Dylan never thought he'd find. The kind of relationship he didn't think he deserved.

John watched Rachel as Annie kissed Dylan's cheek. A gentle smile lit Rachel's face and her eyes filled with tears.

He picked up a napkin and handed it to her.

"Thanks." She wiped her eyes and smiled through her tears.

The wobbly breath she took told him more about what she felt than her words could have. She cared deeply about her friends and believed in love. It was a dangerous combination for a man who was trying to keep away from single women.

She left the napkin on her lap and turned toward him. "Was it hard to find a babysitter for Bella?" A soft blush skimmed her cheeks. "I know I'm changing the subject but, if I keep watching Annie and Dylan, I'll cry again. There are only so many tears I can manage before my face goes red and blotchy."

Her face was already red and blotchy, but she still looked beautiful. "Mrs. Daniels, my housekeeper, is looking after Bella tonight."

"Did you talk to her about the letter she sent to The Bridesmaids Club?"

John chose his words carefully. "She was worried about

me. She thought I was sad because I don't have a wife. And before you ask why I'm sad, I'm not. Bella thinks if I don't smile, I'm unhappy. I have to work on making sure I don't frown so much."

"You're doing it now."

"What?"

"Frowning."

John lifted his hand to his face and his frown deepened.

"You could always get Bella more involved with other children. Then she wouldn't have time to worry about you."

"She already does ballet class." A cheer rang out from inside the bar and John glanced over his shoulder. Another bride-to-be was walking past the window, dressed in a veil with a bouquet in her hands. It was just as well Bella wasn't here. She would have been grilling each of the brides about what their dresses looked like and how many bridesmaids they had.

"What about a different type of program?"

He turned back to Rachel.

She sat forward and rested her elbows on the table. "She could join a drama club—the local library runs a wonderful program."

The whole idea of Bella visiting Bozeman Elementary School was to get her used to being in a classroom. After Christmas she'd go to school, settle into life in Bozeman like any other child. He hadn't thought joining other after-school programs would be worthwhile.

"It might be too much."

"It's only once a week. It would give her another opportunity to meet children who'll be in her class."

"She's met you. That has to be just as important?"

"I won't be her teacher. I'm a substitute teacher at the moment. Jackie Reynolds will be looking after Bella's class."

John felt his frown deepen. When he'd met with the

school's principal, he'd been very clear about why he was sending Bella to school once a week. He wanted her transition into the local school to be as easy as possible. Part of that transition involved placing her in the classroom she'd be in after Christmas. Putting her in a classroom with a different teacher wasn't what he'd had in mind.

"Don't worry about Bella," Rachel said. "Jackie is a great teacher. I'm sure they'll get along fine."

His mind was working overtime and coming up with answers he wasn't comfortable with. Bella liked Rachel. His daughter needed a tutor for the next two months. If Rachel wouldn't be her teacher in January, he'd do everything he could to make sure she became Bella's tutor now. He didn't know what she earned, but it had to be a lot less than what he would pay.

Rachel glanced across the table and smiled at something Annie said.

He took a deep breath and ignored the warning buzzing inside his head. Spending more time with Rachel would be a big mistake. But his daughter needed a tutor and she was the obvious choice. If he could convince her to take the teaching job, Bella would be happy and he'd have one less thing to worry about.

CHAPTER 4

*R*achel was sitting at a table at Annie and Dylan's wedding reception. The newlyweds were dancing their first waltz of the night. She smiled as Dylan spun Annie into a very unwaltz-like move.

Their wedding ceremony had been beautiful. Pastor Steven had officiated, saying some of the loveliest words she'd ever heard. More than once, she'd glanced across the church at John, watching his reaction to the simple vows.

She'd thought about him and the card his daughter had made. Bella seemed happy around her dad. She smiled and laughed and did all the things a normal eight-year-old would do. But there must be something missing in her life for her to want to find a bride for her father.

Rachel hadn't worked out what was missing, and she wasn't sure it was a good idea to try. She'd enjoyed John's company last night—maybe a little too much. He'd seemed to enjoy talking to her, too, and had looked almost disappointed when she'd gone home with her friends.

But, with a wedding the next morning, and a bride who

was stressed, leaving Charlie's Bar and Grill early was the best thing she could have done.

"It will be our turn to dance soon." Tess sat in an empty chair beside Rachel. Her pale blue dress fell in soft folds around her legs. "Annie and Dylan are happy."

Rachel nodded. "It's been an amazing wedding. Has Logan decorated their car, yet?"

"He finished about ten minutes ago. I'm not sure Dylan will appreciate the tin cans and balloons attached to his rear bumper."

Annie and Dylan's get-away car was a Porsche. Logan had decided Dylan needed to start his married life in style. So he'd replaced Dylan's truck with a silver Porsche and made sure the hotel they were staying in had secure parking. Tomorrow morning, the newlyweds were flying to Ireland for their honeymoon.

The song that was playing ended, and Tess stood up. "Come on, twinkle toes. Let's find Jeremy so you can show everyone what a star you both are on the dance floor."

Rachel jumped to her feet. She loved dancing and, after a little bribery, Jeremy agreed to practice with her. After six weeks of intensive dance therapy, he'd perfected the waltz and foxtrot as much as he ever would.

Tess smiled. "Logan's walking toward us with Jeremy. Sally's already on the dance floor and Molly's putting down her camera."

Rachel looked at Tess and sighed. Her friend's extra height came in handy when she wanted to look around a crowded room. Rachel wasn't short but, at five-foot-six, her friends all towered above her.

As soon as Jeremy was close enough, he swung her into a turn. Her skirt billowed around them and she laughed at the cheeky grin on his face. "Are you ready to dazzle all the women here?"

"As ready as I'll ever be. Make me look good." And with that last remark, they were off. Jeremy stepped into the 1-2-3 pattern easily, waltzing his way around the dance floor like a seasoned pro.

Even though he looked relaxed, she could feel the tension in his shoulders and arms. "Enjoy the moment. You know what you're doing."

Jeremy's shoulders dropped a little, but he was still holding himself ramrod straight. "It's easy for you," he whispered. "Debbie Adams isn't staring at you."

"I take it Debbie is the girl you've been dating?"

"*Was* dating. She decided we didn't have a future."

Rachel could hear the disappointment in his voice. "I'm sorry. I know how much you liked her." Whenever Debbie's name came up in a conversation, Jeremy changed the subject and blushed beet red.

"It doesn't matter." He glanced at Rachel and sighed. "Okay. It does, but I'm trying hard to hide it. Will you do me a favor?"

"Is this on top of making you three batches of triple fudge brownies and a Christmas cake?"

"That was for taking dancing lessons with you. This is more important."

"You want a dozen cupcakes, too?" Rachel teased.

Jeremy shook his head. "No, but if you're feeling sorry for me, you could always throw some in. This is about Debbie. If you see her walking toward me, come and save me."

Rachel was having a hard enough time staying away from John. Keeping Jeremy and his ex-ladylove in sight, as well as John, would be a challenge. "You might have to dance with me more often."

Jeremy relaxed. "We'll be each other's decoy."

"What do you mean?"

"You've been watching the tall blond guy all day."

"I have not."

Jeremy snorted. "Of course, you haven't. The little girl with him is sweet."

"That's his daughter, Bella." John had sat in the front row of the church with his daughter beside him. Bella's attention had mostly been on Annie but, now and then, she'd grin at Rachel.

"I read a newspaper article about him a few months ago. John Fletcher is one wealthy guy."

"Money isn't everything," Rachel muttered.

Jeremy's shoulders tensed again. "Debbie alert on your right. I'm heading left." He did a quarter turn and started moving away from the dance floor.

"You'll have to get used to seeing her at some stage," Rachel said softly. "Bozeman is a small place."

"I'm good at hiding."

Rachel believed him. If Jeremy put his mind to something, there was no stopping him. "You can't hide forever."

"I don't need to. Debbie's leaving Bozeman next April."

"How do you feel about that?"

"I'm trying not to feel anything. Does that answer your question?"

Rachel smiled at someone she knew. "It does. And as long as you keep me away from John, I'll be your wingman with Debbie."

Jeremy stepped into a sharp quarter turn. "You gotta warn me sooner if you want to avoid someone. John was on his way over here. Hold on tight, we're about to move as fast as this song can take us."

And before Rachel knew what he was doing, Jeremy whisked them off the dance floor and straight onto a covered balcony. "Are you sure you haven't done this before?" she asked as he opened the door.

Jeremy pulled her outside and closed the door. "This is a walk in the park compared to what I've done."

She wrapped her arms around her waist. It might be a walk in the park for him, but it was winter. Snow was falling beyond the covered balcony and it was cold. If they didn't get back inside soon, they'd end up with hypothermia.

"We can't stay out here all night. We'll have t0—" Something tugged on her skirt. She looked down and gasped. A little girl with big, brown eyes, was staring up at her and shivering in the cold.

JOHN DIDN'T OFTEN PANIC, but his heart was thumping against his chest. Bella had been beside him the entire afternoon. She'd sighed when the bridal party walked down the aisle, straining against his hand as she'd tried to get closer. She hadn't stopped staring at Annie's lace and satin wedding dress all afternoon.

While he was talking to one of Dylan's relatives, Bella had slipped away. She'd disappeared into the middle of the reception venue as easily as a pat of butter melting on a hot skillet.

For the first five minutes, he wasn't too worried. Then five minutes stretched to ten and panic set in. He'd hurried around the room, peering under the tablecloths and behind the white fabric draped along the walls. He'd even checked the bathrooms, shocking an elderly woman as she'd come out of a stall. And he still couldn't find Bella.

He'd seen Rachel on the dance floor, drifting through the other couples with one of the groomsmen. As soon as she'd seen him, she'd disappeared. He didn't have time to wonder why she was avoiding him. His daughter was missing and he needed to find her.

He pulled his cell phone out of his pocket and hit speed dial. "It's me. Bella's missing. Watch all exits. Tell Tank to check everyone who's leaving the building."

He nodded at the quick response from Tanner and put his phone away.

"Are you okay?" John spun toward Dylan. His mind was still on Bella, thinking of all the things that could have happened to her.

"I've lost Bella."

"How long has she been missing?"

He checked his watch and tried to steady his breathing. "Twenty minutes." She could be out of Bozeman by now, heading toward the Canadian border in a truck, or sitting in a plane, ready to fly out of the country. He looked around the room, then back at Dylan. "Are you using any other rooms in the building? Maybe an audiovisual office or a storage room that isn't obvious?"

"Come with me." Dylan walked across the room. "The AV room is over here."

When Dylan threw the door open, the guy sitting in front of the sound system leaped out of his chair. "You nearly gave me a heart attack. What's wrong?"

John scanned the room. "Have you seen a little girl? She's eight years old." He held his hand at hip level. "Bella's about this tall, curly brown hair and brown eyes."

The AV guy shook his head. "No kids have been in here all day. Do you want me to call the front reception desk? They could keep an eye on everyone who comes and goes."

Dylan told him to make the call while John left the room.

Within seconds, he was back on the dance floor, weaving through the couples who were oblivious to what was going on. On the far side of the room, a white curtain billowed into the air. It was November and freezing cold. No one would have been outside unless there was another reason they were there.

He rushed toward the curtain and frowned as one of Dylan's groomsmen walked through the French doors. Rachel followed him.

For a split second, the skirt of her dress caught on the wind, hiding the child beside her. He didn't need to see the face of the person holding Rachel's hand to know it was his daughter.

He ran to Bella and hugged her tight. "Where have you been?" She was so cold, she was shivering. Taking off his jacket, he wrapped it around her shoulders. "Are you okay?"

Bella nodded. "I'm sorry, Dad. I went outside to watch the snow and the doors locked behind me. No one heard me knocking on the glass."

He picked her up and walked quickly toward the fireplace. Rachel and the groomsman didn't follow. He'd find them later and thank them.

"Don't worry about being locked outside. You're safe and that's all that matters." Sitting in a chair, he held her close. "I just need to call Tanner to let him know you're all right."

Bella nodded and leaned against his chest. After he'd spoken to Tanner, John breathed a sigh of relief.

A flash of blue silk caught his eye. Rachel was walking toward them with a blanket and a takeout cup in her hands.

She left the drink on the floor and shook out the fluffy blanket. "Wrap this around Bella. It will help keep her warm."

When the blanket was tucked around his daughter, Rachel handed Bella the cup. "It's hot chocolate. It will make you feel nice and warm."

Bella glanced at John. He nodded and she carefully took the drink out of Rachel's hands. "Thank you."

"You're welcome," Rachel said softly. She glanced at John and he saw the understanding in her eyes. If she knew why he'd panicked when Bella had gone missing, she wouldn't be so calm.

"Are you okay?" Rachel asked.

John nodded. "I am now. Thanks for finding Bella."

A red blush hit her pale cheeks. "It was lucky Jeremy and I were outside."

Disappointment dragged its heavy feet against John's heart. He'd never asked her if she was dating anyone. He didn't know her any better than most of the people in Bozeman. What she did with her personal life wasn't anything to do with him.

Her blush got a whole lot redder. "Jeremy was helping me to…" Her voice petered out. "Jeremy's talking to the manager about the door. The lock's broken. Bella couldn't get back inside." She knelt in front of Bella. "Are you feeling better?"

Bella nodded. "Dad's keeping me warm."

Rachel's gaze locked on his. "Dads are good at that. Do you need anything else?"

She shook her head. Her mouth popped open when Annie rushed over.

"Dylan told me what happened. Are you all right, Bella?"

Bella looked at Annie with such utter devotion that John almost smiled. She pushed the blanket away and slid off his legs. John took the drink out of his daughter's hands before it spilled over Annie's dress.

"You look beautiful." Bella's voice was soft and sweet. Her hand reached out and gently touched Annie's dress.

Annie smiled and held the skirt of her dress toward her. "My dress is made from champagne silk. My friend Emily made it for me. The lace came all the way from Italy. If you look closely, you can see little beads stitched in the pattern."

Bella's fingers ran across the lace.

John hoped like crazy her hands were clean.

Annie didn't seem to mind. She pulled her veil forward and showed Bella the silver thread was sewn along the edge.

"Did your friend make your veil, too?" Bella asked.

Annie nodded. "She's very clever. Would you like to try to catch my bouquet?"

Bella's eyes were glowing with excitement.

John opened his mouth to tell her he couldn't let her out of his sight. He knew she'd be disappointed, but he'd nearly lost her once and he didn't want to lose her again.

"I could hold her hand." Rachel caught his gaze and held it. "She'll be safe with me."

He glanced at Bella, then back at Rachel.

"*Please*, Dad. I'll be really careful. I'll stay with Ms. McReedy and I won't move from beside her."

"Okay, but we're going home after you've finished."

Bella held Rachel's hand. "Do you think I'll be able to catch the bouquet?"

Rachel smiled. "It depends on where you stand. If you want to catch it, you stand at the front of the group. If you don't want to catch it, you stand at the back."

Bella looked up at Rachel, a hopeful look in her eyes. "Where are we standing?"

"We'll go to the front."

A grin as big as the moon filled Bella's face. John didn't know where Rachel would have normally stood, or if she would have been there at all. But he was grateful for her thoughtfulness.

"I guess I'd better get a move on, then." Annie gathered the skirt of her dress in her hands and whispered something in Bella's ear.

Bella tugged on Rachel's hand and whispered something in *her* ear. Rachel nodded, then looked at him. "We'll be back soon."

John watched them move toward the dance floor. He

picked up the blanket and Bella's half-full cup of hot chocolate. Tonight wasn't as stress-free as he'd imagined.

Most weddings had moments when something didn't go to plan. And, most of the time, it didn't matter. But, in his case, if something went wrong, it could be deadly.

CHAPTER 5

*T*he next afternoon, Rachel passed Tess an envelope. They were sitting in Tess and Logan's loft, the space that had become the official Bridesmaids Club headquarters. "This letter arrived last week. Can we help the bride?"

Tess read the letter and nodded. "The bride lives in Bozeman and can come in next week for a fitting. The only thing I'm not sure about are the bridesmaids' dresses she wants. I have a feeling the Cinderella Collection dress went to another bridesmaid last Thursday."

While Tess checked their database, Rachel walked over to a rack of dresses. They'd divided the bridesmaids' dresses into four different collections. The Cinderella, Grace Kelly, Exotic, and Winter Romance Collections filled the room to overflowing with color and sparkle.

Of all the collections, the Cinderella dresses were Rachel's favorites. With big, puffy skirts and pretty beads, the bridesmaids' dresses were everything Rachel had dreamed about since she'd been a little girl.

She pulled a dress off the rack and sighed. "When Sally

gets married, I'm wearing this dress." Sally was one of their friends and another Bridesmaids Club organizer. Her wedding was supposed to be before Christmas, but they'd postponed it until March of the following year.

Tess looked up from her computer. "Isn't that the dress that arrived two weeks ago?"

Rachel nodded. The dress was made from a deep blue-green silk. With a full skirt and the loveliest sweetheart neckline she'd ever seen, it was romantic without being too gushy, feminine without being frilly.

Tess walked across the room and touched one of the sleeves. "It would look amazing on you. Why don't you take it home?"

Rachel shook her head. "It wouldn't feel right. What if someone else wants it?"

"We have plenty of dresses."

She bit her bottom lip. "Are you sure no one else will mind?"

"Of course, they won't."

"I'll bring it back after the wedding." Rachel held the dress in front of her and looked in the full-length mirror. Everything about the dress was so perfect she couldn't believe she'd be wearing it.

Tess pulled another dress off the rack. "You don't need to bring it back. Here's the dress one of our Bozeman bridesmaid's wants to wear."

Rachel draped her gown over a chair and headed back to the letter they'd been reading. "I'll find the other dresses and leave them in the closet for their fitting."

The next dress was from their Winter Romance Collection. With fur trim, capes, and full, heavy skirts, these dresses would have taken up most of the racks if they'd brought everything out.

While Rachel looked for the next dress on the list, Tess

hunted through the Grace Kelly Collection.

"Tell me how it felt to catch Annie's bouquet?"

Rachel ignored the teasing note in Tess' voice. She was determined not to spoil a perfectly good day by thinking about John Fletcher.

"I didn't catch the bouquet. Bella did."

"You were holding her in your arms. I'd say it was a combined effort."

"Maybe, but the bouquet never touched my hands." She lifted a dress off the rack and put it over her arm. After they'd caught the bouquet, Annie made a big fuss about her catching it with Bella. What she didn't bother telling everyone was that she'd told them to stand under the chandelier. The bouquet was aimed straight at them, cruising at supersonic speed toward Bella's outstretched hands.

Rachel glanced at the rack of dresses, looking for gown number forty-six. "Bella was happy."

"Was her dad?"

Rachel didn't know if John had been happy or not. She'd felt his eyes on her the entire time she was with his daughter. She'd met parents who were overprotective of their children, but he took it to a whole new level. "Do you think it was odd he kept Bella so close to him?"

Tess pulled another dress out of the Grace Kelly Collection. "I didn't notice what he was doing. But it's winter and it's been snowing. Bella was lucky you went outside. Otherwise, she might have been in trouble. While we're talking about last night, why did you go outside? It was freezing."

"Jeremy wanted to get away from his ex-girlfriend." Rachel picked up the dresses they'd taken off the racks and walked into their changing area. She hated stretching the truth, even if it was half true. But there was no way she'd tell Tess the other reason she'd been on the balcony.

Keeping her distance from John wasn't exactly a sensible

or mature thing to do. Bella seemed happy around her dad. He looked after her, made sure she was okay. It was easy to see they were close. If Bella was lonely, it didn't show. Her dad, on the other hand, was an entirely different matter. Rachel didn't know what to make of him.

By the time she left the changing area, Tess had put another two dresses aside.

"Has Logan told you anything about John Fletcher?" Rachel asked.

Tess picked up a pen and started crossing numbers off the list in front of her. "Only that he's incredibly wealthy." She put the pen down and looked at Rachel. "We don't need Logan to tell us about John."

"What do you mean?"

Tess walked across to her computer and started tapping on the keyboard. "John Fletcher is rich and gorgeous. There has to be something about him on the Internet."

Rachel stood beside Tess and watched pages open and close in quick succession. "You know what you're doing."

"I was a model. I used to live and breathe the media. The girls I lived with were obsessed with making sure their photos were featured on as many sites as possible." Tess pointed to the page she'd downloaded. "Here you go. It looks as though John Fletcher has been busy. He received the Businessman of the Year Award in New York City last month."

Rachel read the news article. "His wife died in a car accident. That must have been terrible."

"It's probably why he left the military," Tess said quietly. "Bella would have been a baby."

Rachel read the rest of the story. She felt sad when she thought about what he must have gone through. "How did he manage to raise Bella and start a company?"

"With a lot of hard work and help from other people. Did you know he's looking for a tutor for Bella?"

"And you're telling me this, because…?"

Tess rolled her eyes. "You're working odd hours as a substitute teacher. Your full time contract doesn't start for a couple of months. I'd bet you anything he'll be paying a better hourly rate than Bozeman Elementary School."

"I like my job. Even if he is paying more, money isn't everything."

"What about the deposit you're saving for your first home? You could save a lot more money if you worked for John. Besides, you like Bella. What's not to like about the job?"

"I'm not working for John Fletcher," Rachel said firmly. "He could choose anyone he wants to teach Bella. I don't even think he likes me."

Tess' eyebrows rose. "Are you kidding? He didn't take his eyes off you when you were holding Bella on the dance floor."

"He was watching Bella." Rachel picked up the two dresses Tess had put aside. "Just because you've found your happy-ever-after moment with Logan, it doesn't mean John is my happy-ever-after man."

Something must have come second in John's life when he was building his company. That something could have been his daughter. "I'm not interested in someone who thinks money is more important than family."

"You don't know if that's true. He could be a good guy."

Rachel looked at the dresses in her arms. "There's more chance that he isn't."

"What about Bella? If she's as unhappy as you think she is, then maybe you could help her."

"I don't think she's unhappy. And even if she is, the only person who can help her is her father."

Tess sat back in her chair. "Are you sure?"

Rachel knew The Bridesmaids Club helped women with

more than dresses. They'd changed people's lives with a little kindness and a helping hand. Bella was worried about her dad. The only person who could help Bella was John. A teacher with a soft spot for big brown eyes wouldn't be able to solve Bella's problems—and neither would The Bridesmaids Club.

She held the dresses tighter. "John needs to talk to his daughter. I can't help them."

Tess picked up the list in front of her. "I think you're being stubborn. Bella asked for our help and you're the best person for the job."

Rachel's eyes narrowed. "If you're worried about Bella, you could always help her yourself."

Tess smiled. "Nice try, Ms. McReedy, but I'm not a teacher. If anyone can help her, it's you. John Fletcher isn't the only person who needs to work out what's important."

Tess ignored the glare Rachel sent her way. Bella might be looking for a bride for her father, but Rachel wouldn't be helping her.

John Fletcher wasn't looking for a wife. He was trying to conquer his habit of frowning to make his daughter happy. The only other thing he needed to do was slide a teaching contract under someone's nose. With the money he'd be offering he could afford the best teacher in the entire country.

Before he knew it, he'd have a happy daughter, the perfect tutor, and a face that didn't get premature wrinkles.

It was a win-win situation for everyone.

JOHN SLOWLY LIFTED himself off the edge of Bella's bed and looked down at his daughter. Her long, dark lashes fluttered against her cheeks. She turned in her sleep, cuddling her favorite soft toy close to her chest.

They'd spent the day with his brother, sliding down a hill on his ranch, making snowmen and Christmas angels, and anything else Bella wanted to do. After more than one game of Scrabble and a dinner of homemade pizza, Bella arrived home tired, but happy. She'd pulled on her pajamas and crawled into bed, ready for the beginning of her favorite book.

John had read *Anne of Green Gables* so many times he could almost recite the whole story word-for-word. They'd only just made it to the end of chapter four before Bella fell into a deep sleep. He kissed the top of her head, pulled her blankets up so she didn't get cold, and tiptoed out of her room.

Halfway along the hallway, he reached down and turned the night-light on. The soft pink glow lit the way to the bathroom. It gave Bella a sense of security, an independence she wouldn't have had without it.

He looked at the book in his hand, then back at Bella's room. He didn't want to risk waking her up, so he took it into the living room and left it on the coffee table.

It was eight-thirty on Sunday night. Snow had been falling for the last four hours, coating everything with a deceptive picture-perfect veneer. Regardless of what they'd have to do tomorrow to dig their way out, it was the kind of evening he'd always enjoyed.

Part of that enjoyment came from his parents. He'd grown up in a Scrabble-crazy house. On nights like this, he'd played Scrabble with his mom, dad, and brother until they were ready for bed. They'd test each other's word-building abilities, double-check his mom's creative use of words with their favorite dictionary, and groan their way through the hundreds of three-letter words their dad could make.

But that was more than half a lifetime ago. If he'd been

able to look into a crystal ball and see what was in store for his family, he might have treasured those times more than he had.

He walked into the kitchen, poured himself a coffee, and looked through the window. Pitch black nothingness stared back. He turned the radio on, listened to the latest weather forecast, then turned it off when someone started singing about falling in love.

Stopping at the kitchen table, he picked up his new house plans. For the last twelve months, he'd been renting the home they were living in. He could have stayed with Grant in their parents' old home while he decided where he wanted to live. But he had a business to run and living forty minutes from town wouldn't have worked.

A month ago he'd bought a parcel of land overlooking Emerald Lake. With its amazing lakefront views, the mountains surrounding them, and the open fields in front of the building site, it was one of the most incredible places he'd ever seen. The three-thousand-acre development was split evenly between four owners. With only one house allowed per property, it was the kind of place he'd dreamed about for years.

His cell phone vibrated in his pocket. He pulled it out and answered the call.

"Did you arrive home okay?" Grant's voice echoed down the phone.

"It was slow. We made it through just before the road closed. Thanks for today. Bella loved it."

"Bella loves everything about the ranch." John could hear the smile in his brother's voice. "You should move out here over the Christmas break. We might get snowed in, but there are lots of things to do in this big old house."

"Thanks for the offer, but we'll be all right."

"If you change your mind, you know where I am. Did

Auntie Betty get in contact with you?"

Betty Fletcher was their dad's sister. Since their parents' death ten years ago, she'd become their main contact for what was happening with the rest of the family. She was the only person in three living generations who was interested in preserving the stories passed down from one family member to another.

John checked his phone. "Nope. What did she want?"

"She's ready to publish the book about our family history. Send her an email telling her how many copies you want."

"Do you think she included the story about Great Aunt Nellie's ghost?"

Grant laughed. "Probably. I haven't seen much of Nellie in the last few months. It must be too cold for her."

A gust of wind tore across the roof of John's home. The shingles rattled and banged, making him wonder if Great Aunt Nellie had heard them laughing.

"You still there?" Grant asked.

"Yeah. The weather's getting worse."

"It'll get a lot worse before the storm's over. Have you made the phone call you said you'd make?"

"Not yet." John had told Grant about Rachel, about the conversation he wanted to have with her.

"She'll be back at school tomorrow. You should call her now."

"It can wait another day."

"Bella needs a tutor. This weather will make her go stir crazy if you leave Mrs. Daniels in charge. Call the teacher tonight."

John rubbed the frown away from his forehead. "I know you're my big brother, but you should have grown out of bossing me around."

"I don't know who told you that," Grant scoffed. "Make

the call. You looked as though you could do with one less thing to worry about."

"Thanks."

"You're welcome. Let me know how you get on. If she says no, just add another zero or two to her pay." With that last cheerful comment, Grant ended the call and left John staring into space.

He'd negotiated multi-million dollar deals with the government, dodged bullets and bombs. Calling Rachel shouldn't have been the big deal it had become. But for some strange reason, he was worried she'd say no. And to be honest, he couldn't blame her.

He knew he could find someone else to be Bella's tutor. He had enough money to recruit the best teacher in the world. But no one's qualifications or work experience could replace the connection Bella had with Rachel. Since the wedding yesterday, Bella hadn't stopped talking about Rachel and the next visit to her classroom.

If he wasn't careful, Bella would start the Rachel McReedy fan club. Knowing how determined his daughter could be, he had a feeling it wouldn't take her long to get half the town registered.

He glanced at his phone, then hunted through the drawers under his coffee table for a pen and some paper. He needed to unjumble what was going through his head. Writing down why Rachel should tutor Bella would focus his brain and give him extra ammunition if she said no.

Tapping the pen against the table, he looked at the paper, then started writing. By the time he was halfway down the page, he felt a lot better. Rachel couldn't say no to the reasons he'd come up with.

Mrs. Daniels hit the list at number one. No matter how happy she'd been to step into the previous tutor's shoes, she had her own busy life. Bella needed to be taught by someone who knew what they were doing and he needed them to work from his home. He wanted Bella to be ready to start school with children her own age and not stand out as the girl who'd been homeschooled for too long.

There were other, less obvious reasons why Rachel needed to work for him. Money came in at number ten. Bribing someone wasn't the best way to start a professional relationship but, if Rachel wanted to play hardball, he had deep pockets.

He read through the list twice more. He'd come up with good reasons why she should teach Bella. But even with his list, she could still say no. She might even have a better list of logical reasons why teaching Bella wouldn't work.

He reached for his phone when it pinged. Someone had sent him a text. He glanced down at the number and wondered what his brother had forgotten to tell him. If he'd been less nervous, he would have laughed at what he read. *Call her.*

John texted a quick message back and waited for his brother to reply. Instead of a text, his phone rang.

"You're stalling for time," Grant said. "Find her number and call her."

"Mind your own business." John ended the call. His brother could be a pain in the butt sometimes. Occasionally, he was right. Like now, at nine o'clock on a Sunday night when most people weren't expecting to get a phone call asking if they wanted a job.

John frowned. He could at least find her number, organize himself so he didn't look as desperate as he felt.

He tapped the screen on his phone, and searched for her name on the Internet. She was the only McReedy in Bozeman. He saved the number in his contact list and left his phone on the coffee table. He'd call her tomorrow, make her an offer she couldn't refuse. Then wait for hell to freeze over while she decided what to do.

CHAPTER 6

*J*ohn parked his car outside Bozeman Public Library. The brick and glass building looked tall and imposing against the winter sky.

Someone had cleared a path to the front entrance. Snow rose on either side of the concrete, creating an icy channel that only the foolhardy or desperate were willing to navigate. He didn't have to think too hard about which one he was.

It had been a long time since he'd been in the library. He didn't know where he was going, or even if Rachel was inside. All he knew was that the drama club met here on Monday afternoons. He'd put two and two together and driven across town to offer her a job.

He stuck his hands in his jacket pockets and walked toward the library. The front doors opened and he stepped into the wide entranceway. A display of children's art on the wall in front of him drew him forward. He glanced to his right and saw a row of bookshelves and two large, comfy chairs.

He walked through the open doorway and stood at the side of the room. Tall steel columns supported the exposed wooden beams of the ceiling. The architect had softened the use of metal with wood, mixing the two components cleverly. It was a space people could spend time in and enjoy.

There were more chairs, a help desk, and lots of computers for people to use. But he wasn't here to look at the interior design. He was here to find Rachel.

"Can I help you?"

A woman in her late twenties stood beside him. She had the greenest eyes he'd ever seen. "I'm looking for the community room. Do you know where it is?"

She smiled and John realized he was frowning. "I haven't been here for a few years," he mumbled. It wasn't much of an excuse, but she didn't seem to mind.

"Don't worry. We're almost harmless."

He wasn't sure whether she was serious or joking. John looked at her name badge.

She held out her hand and smiled. "Erin Williams, Library Manager, at your service."

He shook her hand. "John Fletcher."

"Welcome to the library. Come with me. I'll take you to the community room."

Erin walked into the corridor he'd just come from. But instead of turning left, she kept going straight ahead. "Are you here to collect your child from drama club?"

John shook his head. "I've come to see Rachel McReedy. She recommended the club for my daughter."

"I don't think you'll be disappointed. It's a great way for the children to be creative and learn to work together." She held a door open for him. "They're rehearsing for their Christmas play."

He walked into the large room. Chaos surrounded him. In front of the windows overlooking the parking lot, a woman was listening to a group of children sing a Christmas carol. Their voices filled the room, bounced off the walls, and were being ignored by the other children.

"Rachel's over there." Erin pointed to the stage. "Enjoy drama club."

She left the room and John's gaze went back to Rachel. She had her back to him. Her arms were waving in the air and the children in front of her were following what she was doing. She stepped to the left. Half the kids stepped to the left, the other half stepped to the right. They bumped bodies, laughed, then untangled themselves from each other.

Rachel turned around and showed them which way they needed to move. She smiled as she waved her arms in the air. She looked over her shoulder to make sure they were following her. When she was happy with what they were doing, she turned to look at the rest of the room and froze. Her gaze connected with his and her smile disappeared.

Not a good start.

She said something to a teenage boy standing with the group of kids. He stepped forward and took over from her. The kids went back to waving their arms in the air and stepping sideways as Rachel walked toward him.

He didn't know if she realized just how pretty she was. She wasn't reed thin or ultra-curvy, she was somewhere in-between. Somewhere that looked great in jeans and a bright red sweater with snowflakes knitted into the design.

It had been so long since he'd been attracted to a woman, that he didn't know where to look. She was still staring at him with a worried frown on her face. So he took off his jacket and tried to look as though seeing her wasn't a big deal. But it was. Maybe even bigger than he thought it would be.

Rachel dodged two children who were crawling across the floor. She spoke to a group of girls with towels on their heads, then stopped in front of him. "Is Bella okay?"

Her blue eyes were worried. Something inside of him tightened, twisted, and left him spinning in mid-air.

"John?"

He cleared his throat, engaged his brain, and ignored his pounding heart. "Bella's fine. Tank has taken her to the mall."

"Who's Tank?"

"He works with me."

"Is that his actual name?"

John moved his jacket into his other hand. "We were in the military together. It's a name that stuck." Tank wouldn't appreciate him telling anyone the name he'd been born with. His new name was as much a part of his identity as the scars he wore.

In some convoluted way, Tank and John had both started over. They'd built lives that mixed the best of what they'd known with what they needed to do to survive.

Rachel winced when the Christmas choir screeched out a note that only angels should sing. "If Bella is all right, how can I help you?"

John thought about the list in his pocket, the reasons why asking Rachel to teach Bella was a good idea. She was waiting for him to say something, anything that would tell her why he was here.

He glanced across at the choir, then back at the stage. "I thought I'd check out the drama club. You said Bella might enjoy it."

Rachel's face relaxed into an easy smile. His heart sank.

"You've come at the right time. We're getting ready for our Christmas play." She pointed to the kids who were still crawling on the floor. "Over there are our nativity animals. Ruby, Clarissa, and Jason will be cows. Alexander and Oscar are the front and back end of a donkey, and Fleur is an owl."

John watched Fleur extend her pretend wings. "I didn't know they had owls in the barn where Jesus was born."

Rachel shrugged her shoulders. "I don't know either. But I don't think anyone would have minded if one snuck inside. Fleur has a thing for owls. She has the concentration span of a squirrel, so I needed something to keep her focused on what we're doing."

Fleur swooped low on the rear end of the donkey and John smiled. "How's that working out?"

"Pretty good. She's happy to stay in character for as long as we're practicing." Rachel glanced across at the choir. "We've divided everyone into groups for this rehearsal. It's easier to practice when we're only teaching a dozen children at a time. The songs are a work in progress."

A boy with bright red hair and neon freckles started to sing. The noise level in the room dropped to a whisper. John tried not to stare, but it wasn't easy when the notes coming from his mouth were so clear and pure. "He's really good. Who is he?"

Rachel sighed. "That's Franky. He has the most amazing voice I've ever heard."

"How old is he?"

"Ten. He comes to the library each day after school. His dad works long hours, so this has become his home away from home. It's the same with quite a few of the children who come to drama club."

John listened to the rest of Franky's song. After the last note dissolved into the room, the noise level increased. Everyone went back to what they were doing, quickly forgetting what they'd heard.

"What do the kids do at the library if they're not in drama club?"

Rachel glanced back at the children she'd been teaching. Everyone was moving in the same direction, spinning in time to a Christmas carol they'd started singing. "There are digital classes in the technology room most afternoons and art classes in another area. The children can only do each class once per week. They don't cost anything, so no one needs to miss out. For the other two days a week, they read books or volunteer as library helpers."

"Do you get paid to be here?"

Rachel shook her head. "No one does. We beg and borrow costumes for our plays and look for sponsorship for any props we need. Everything we do is on a no frills, shoestring budget."

She walked across to a bulletin board and showed him the program timetable. "If Bella is interested in other things, they're all listed here. Most of the time we have a good spread of ages, so there will be someone she can get to know."

"What classes do you take?"

Rachel's cheeks turned red. "I do one of each. It keeps me busy, but I wouldn't have it any other way. Once I'm working full time, I won't be able to do three classes a week, but I'll do what I can."

"How long is each class?"

"Two hours, but you could pick Bella up earlier if that works better. We give the kids something to eat at three-thirty, then go back to our activities until five o'clock." Rachel looked at him closely. "Why didn't you bring Bella with you?"

John shifted uncomfortably on his feet. "I didn't want her to get her hopes up."

Rachel nodded.

He glanced back at Fleur, the overactive owl. Bella would enjoy mixing with this crazy group of kids. She loved music and loved dancing. She'd fit in well alongside them, maybe even make a friend or two.

But that wasn't the main reason he'd come to the library. He glanced at his watch. "It's nearly five o'clock. Do you want to get a cup of coffee with me after you've finished here?"

Rachel's eyes widened.

A blush worked its way over his face. "It's not what you're thinking. I have something to ask you, a job I'd like you to consider."

"Is it the teaching position for Bella?"

John's gaze shot to her face. "How did you know?"

"Most of the town knows you're looking for a tutor. I can't do it. I'll be back to full time teaching in January. In the meantime, I'm enjoying my work here."

John didn't think his list of ideas would work. So instead of blinding her with logic, he named a salary that would make most people's eyes water.

Rachel blinked, then blinked again. "For six weeks' work? Are you mad?"

"It's eight weeks and I'm perfectly sane. There are a few things you need to be aware of, but we can sort those out later."

"Such as?"

John wouldn't discuss state-of-the-art surveillance systems or bodyguards in the middle of Rachel's drama club. "I'll tell you more over a cup of coffee. Are you interested?"

He held his breath while she thought about her answer.

Rachel looked down at her sneakers, then across at the barnyard animals. "If I tell you I'm interested, it doesn't mean I'll say yes."

John nodded.

"And it doesn't mean the money you're offering has changed my mind."

"Okay."

Rachel crossed her arms in front of her chest and glared at him. "I guess we're going out for coffee, then. I'll be ten minutes."

It wasn't the most positive response he'd ever heard, but he'd take it. Whether she knew it or not, Rachel McReedy would become Bella's tutor.

RACHEL PAID for her coffee and watched John hang his jacket over the back of a chair.

He glanced at her as he sat down.

She didn't know what he was thinking, but it didn't look good. His frown was out in force, and even the delicious smell of roasting coffee beans didn't seem to make a difference.

She was glad they were having coffee close to the library. With the snow falling outside, the Lindley Perk Coffee Shop wasn't a busy hive of activity. There was less chance of someone seeing them here than in town.

If Tess heard about this meeting, she'd assume Rachel had decided to teach Bella. She'd think she was happy to accept the crazy amount of money he was willing to pay to educate his daughter.

Rachel wasn't here because she wanted his money. She was here because she was curious. She sat opposite him and leaned forward, keeping her voice low. "Why do you want to pay Bella's tutor so much money?"

John's gaze moved from the front counter to Rachel's face. He kept his expression neutral, hiding what was going through his head. "You don't believe in small talk, do you?"

"I thought it was small talk," Rachel said quickly and without a smile. "If I was being blunt, I would have asked you what Bella's tutor has to do for that much money."

John's lips twitched. "I take it you're not impressed?"

"Do you know the hourly rate I'm paid at the school?"

John shrugged his shoulders.

She guessed a man who had more money than anyone she knew wouldn't be too interested in what she earned.

"It must be enough to get by, or you wouldn't do it."

Rachel snorted. Working part time barely gave her enough money to pay her bills. She was using her savings, and that wasn't something she wanted to keep doing.

"So apart from being allergic to my money, what is it about the job you don't like?"

She narrowed her eyes. "I didn't say I was allergic to your money. It's the person who's prepared to spend that much money that worries me."

John didn't say anything.

The waitress brought their drinks across to the table. "One grande latte and one half-strength hot chocolate. Can I get you anything else?"

Rachel shook her head. "Not for me, thanks."

John said the same thing, then went back to staring silently at her.

Rachel sipped her hot chocolate, savoring the heat of the mug between her hands. "You said there were other things potential teachers would need to be aware of. Do you want to tell me what they are?"

He looked down at his coffee. She could almost see the cogs of his brain churning through what he wanted to say. "Having a lot of money isn't always a good thing. People can take advantage of you, deceive you in ways you never thought they would. Or they can do worse. My company looks after wealthy clients and their property. We know things about people that would be dangerous in the wrong hands."

He looked at the empty tables around them. "I get emails from people who make me extremely cautious about Bella's safety."

"They send you threats?" Rachel left her hot chocolate on the table. "Why would they do that?"

"They want something to bargain with. I've kept a low profile in the media. No one knows much about me except I have a daughter. And no one, not even the most persuasive person, gets close to Bella."

"Is that why Tank goes with her to the mall?"

"If I'm not with Bella, Tank or Tanner go with her. Mrs. Daniels wouldn't be able to keep her safe if someone tried to kidnap her."

Her eyes widened. "You can't be serious?"

"I wish I wasn't."

"But she's only a child. Why would someone kidnap her because of what you know?"

John watched a woman push a stroller into the café. "I gave up trying to figure out people's motivation a long time ago. Until now, it's been relatively easy to look after Bella. She came with me whenever I needed to travel. Her tutor and a bodyguard came with us. But since we moved to Bozeman, things have been different. Bella needs a routine. She needs friends. I couldn't give her that when we were moving around the country."

"Is that why you moved to Bozeman?"

He picked up his drink. "Partly."

Rachel waited for him to tell her more. When he didn't, she leaned forward, keeping her voice low. "So the tutor you want to employ would need to know how to look after Bella?"

John shook his head. "I have staff who can do that. Bella's tutor would need to know how to take orders."

"You think I couldn't?"

"You care about Bella. If she was in danger, you'd need to act quickly and follow what Tank, Tanner, or I said."

"That's only if I applied for the job."

John sat back in his chair. "I already know the salary I'm offering is four times what you'd earn at the local school. I also know your full time teaching contract doesn't start until January. What's stopping you from saying yes?"

It was Rachel's turn to squirm under his gaze. "I've made a commitment to the school. They might not be able to find another substitute teacher."

"What if they could?"

"Then I might be interested," Rachel conceded. "But that's a big might. It's not easy finding part time staff, especially this close to Christmas."

"And you wouldn't have a problem with one of my security guards following you?"

She shook her head. "It would only be for two months. Once school starts in January, Bella will be joining her class and I'll be working full time."

John smiled for the first time since she'd sat down.

Her breath caught. This wasn't the reaction anyone should have for their potential boss. It was just as well he wouldn't be at home for most of the day. "What hours would you want me to work?"

"Nine to three." John tilted his head to the side. "Is that a problem?"

"No, that's fine. I want to keep volunteering at the library."

"Does that mean you'll accept the position?"

Rachel thought about the job John was offering her. She liked Bella, so teaching her would be fun. The money he was offering would make up for some of the saving she hadn't been able to do when she was teaching part time. As long as she spent as little time as possible around her boss, she'd be fine.

But before she could accept the position, there was one last thing she needed to sort out. "I have to talk to the principal at Bozeman Elementary. If they can't find someone to replace me, I won't be able to leave."

"I'd better hope they have someone else, then."

Rachel picked up her bag and coat. "I'll let you know what they say. When would you want me to start?"

"As soon as possible."

She stood and John did the same. "I still think you're paying too much, but I won't complain. Thank you for giving me the opportunity to work with Bella."

"I should be the one thanking you."

"Okay, well..." She looked around the café. "I guess I'll speak to you soon."

"I'll walk you to your car."

She shook her head. "I'll be okay. Bye." And before John could say anything, she walked out of the café. The cold air hit her face, cooled down her body, and made her worry about what she'd just done.

CHAPTER 7

A week later, Rachel stopped her car in front of the gates separating John's home from the road. She rolled down her window and pushed a button on a pole. The black iron gates slid open and she drove up the driveway, staring at the house hidden behind snow-covered pine and spruce trees.

The traditional two-story home wasn't what she would have imagined a billionaire would live in. She'd expected something grander, something big and overwhelming that looked like an art gallery instead of a family home.

She stopped beside the front porch and unbuckled her seatbelt. She tried to imagine what it must be like to have so much money you didn't have to worry about paying the next utility bill. If John's biggest worry was someone following him, then he could count himself lucky.

The front door opened and Bella stepped onto the porch. Her wide smile and laughing brown eyes calmed some of the nerves racing through Rachel's body.

A man followed her. He had wide shoulders, long legs, and an awareness about him that screamed bodyguard.

Rachel stepped out of her car and waved at Bella. "Hi. I'll just get my teaching things." She opened her passenger door and wiggled the first box of crayons, paints, paper, and stationery toward her. She didn't know what Bella did or didn't have in her home, so she'd brought everything with her.

"I can help you with that."

Rachel turned and smiled at Bella's bodyguard. "Thank you." She passed him the first box and looked at the second. "I might have brought too much."

He looked inside the box he was carrying. "Bella has most things she needs, but at least you came prepared. I'm Tank."

"It's nice to meet you, Tank. I'm Rachel."

Tank nodded. She supposed he knew exactly who she was.

He held the first box under one arm and waited for her to pass him the second. "I'll take these to Bella's classroom. If there's nothing else to bring inside, I'll move your car into the garage when I get back."

Rachel passed him the second box. "I'll leave the keys in the ignition." Before she could thank him again, he disappeared inside.

Picking up her tote bag, Rachel closed the passenger door and took a deep breath. She was about to start her first day of her new job.

It would be fine. The two months would go fast. Before she knew it, she would be back at Bozeman Elementary, teaching a class of students without a bodyguard in sight.

"Ms. McReedy, come and see our classroom."

Bella was practically hopping from foot to foot. Excitement shone from her face as Rachel made her way up the stairs. She gave Bella a quick hug before walking toward the front door. "Let's go inside. It's cold out here."

"Mr. Daniels said it's cold enough to freeze his whiskers."

"Mr. Daniels is a wise man."

A soft chuckle drifted across the room. "Don't tell him that. His head will get so big it will pop off his shoulders." A woman walked toward Rachel. "I'm Patty Daniels. It's nice to meet you, Rachel."

Rachel held her hand out. "It's nice to meet you, too, Mrs. Daniels."

Mrs. Daniels waved her hand in the air. "Call me Patty. When an adult calls me Mrs. Daniels it reminds me of my mother-in-law."

Patty looked nothing like the housekeeper Rachel had imagined. She'd expected to see someone in their mid-sixties with gray hair and a no-nonsense approach to life. Patty might have been in her mid-sixties, but she had short brown hair, a wide smile, and twinkly blue eyes that hinted at a streak of mischief.

"Tank has taken your teaching things into Bella's classroom. Can I get you a hot drink to warm you up?"

"Thank you. That would be great." Rachel needed to find out as much about Bella as she could. A hot drink sounded like a good way to begin.

When she'd called John to let him know she could take the job, he hadn't told her very much about what the last tutor had been doing. He'd sent her Bella's academic record and a study plan of what Mrs. Daniels had been teaching her. There were notes about what Bella enjoyed and didn't enjoy. It had filled in some blanks, but left others wide open.

Rachel held her hand out to Bella. "What if we all have a hot drink together? We can get to know each other a little better."

Bella nodded and took Rachel's hand. "Mrs. Daniels made some peanut butter cookies this morning. Do you like peanut butter?"

"I love peanut butter."

Patty led the way into the kitchen while Bella chatted the whole way. Their home was every bit as traditional on the inside as the outside. A wide staircase wound its way upstairs from the front entranceway. Painted in a soft shade of buttermilk, the area was warm and inviting.

They walked through a large set of double doors. The living room's paneled walls and marble fireplace gave the area a sense of grandeur, a feeling of permanence. The view from the windows was far prettier than she'd imagined a house in town could be. Snow-covered trees glistened in the large backyard, creating a picture-perfect winter scene.

There were no fences separating John's home from the other properties nearby, nothing to say they were in residential suburbia.

Patty must have known what she was thinking. "The backyard overlooks two vacant lots the owners of this property bought. I never get tired of the view from this room. It changes so much with each season."

Rachel was confused. "Doesn't John own this home?"

"No. He has a long-term lease."

Bella looked up at Rachel. "Dad's going to build a new house when the snow melts."

Patty nodded. "He bought a parcel of land at Emerald Lake. The new house will be even prettier than this one." She walked through another set of double doors and turned to Rachel. "Welcome to the heart of the home."

Rachel looked around the huge kitchen. She could have squeezed her entire apartment into the beautiful space. Everything sparkled—from the marble counter to the pendant lights hanging from the ceiling.

The smell of sweet cookies filled the air and made Rachel sigh. "This is wonderful. You must enjoy spending time in here?"

Patty looked around the kitchen. "It's a lovely space. Whoever designed it knew about cooking."

Bella disappeared behind a set of pantry doors and reappeared holding a plate of cookies. "Mrs. Daniels makes the best food ever. I helped her bake these cookies." Carefully, she carried them to a wooden table.

"They look delicious."

Bella nodded solemnly. "We measured out the ingredients. Mrs. Daniels is teaching me about fractions."

Patty took three mugs out of a set of drawers. "You're a natural at math. I've never seen anyone learn what three-quarters of a cup of sugar looks like so quickly. Would you like coffee or hot chocolate, Rachel?"

"Hot chocolate, please."

"Me, too, Mrs. Daniels." Bella sat at the kitchen table and waited for Rachel. "Hot chocolate is about my most favorite thing in the world."

Rachel sat beside Bella. "So you like math, hot chocolate, and baking. What else do you like?"

Bella thought hard. "I like the beach, ice cream sundaes, and pasta. My friend Poppy is nice, too. I met her at my ballet class."

"What about triple fudge cookies?" Patty added. "You ask me to make them at least once a week."

"I *love* your triple fudge cookies. I love them even more because Dad likes them, too." She turned to Rachel and lowered her voice. "He dunks them into his coffee, then eats them before they fall apart. Don't tell Mrs. Daniels. She keeps telling him off."

Rachel leaned toward Bella. "Your secret's safe with me."

Bella held out her hand. "Pinky promise?"

"Pinky promise." Rachel curled her little finger around Bella's and smiled. "Where's your dad?"

John was supposed to meet her nearly twenty minutes

ago. She'd written down the questions she needed to ask him, rehearsed how the conversation would go. She'd start their professional relationship with the minimum of fuss and high expectations of a successful ending.

She thought back over their conversation four days ago. He'd definitely said he'd be at home when she arrived. Maybe Bella's education wasn't high on his list of priorities? Maybe he had different expectations about how the teaching position would work?

Patty left a mug of hot chocolate in front of Bella, then put a second mug in front of Rachel. "Don't worry. John was called into work urgently. He's sorry he couldn't be here, but he wouldn't have gone unless it was important."

"Dad keeps people safe," Bella said matter-of-factly. "Sometimes he has to miss important things."

Patty pulled a chair away from the table and sat down. "He doesn't mean to," she told Bella. "Your dad tries his best."

It didn't look as though John's best coincided with his daughter's.

The back door opened and Tank strode into the kitchen. "You're having coffee already?" He glanced at the plate of cookies. The corner of his mouth tilted into an almost smile. "Is there enough room at the table for me?"

Patty patted the back of the chair beside her. "Of course, there is. Come and warm up. I was just telling Rachel that John had to go into work early this morning."

Tank's face fell into an indifferent mask. "He'll be back as soon as he can."

Rachel didn't ask what the problem was. Tank didn't seem inclined to share any information, and she needed to keep their working relationship professional.

"Did Dad remember we're going to the mall this afternoon?" Bella looked hopefully at Tank. "Poppy's birthday is on Wednesday. He said we could buy her a present."

Tank took the cup of coffee Patty handed him. "I'll remind him, Bella. But just in case he can't make it, I could go with you."

Bella looked heartbroken. "He said he'd take me, Tank."

"I know."

Rachel looked between Tank and Bella.

Tank was trying hard to make up for the disappointment written across Bella's face. "I'll call him at lunchtime and see if he can come."

Rachel glanced at Mrs. Daniels. She was watching Bella with a worried frown.

She knew what it was like to be put behind all the other things happening in a parent's life. "If your dad can't make it, I could go to the mall with you and Tank." She forced a smile and pretended she didn't know how Bella felt. "You could tell me what Poppy likes. It would be like a treasure hunt."

Bella looked down at her hot chocolate. "I guess that would be okay. But only if Dad can't make it."

She hugged Bella's shoulders. "It will be fun. After we've been shopping, you could come to drama club with me."

A smile lit Bella's face. "Really?"

Rachel didn't look at Tank. Drama club wasn't on his schedule today, but schedules were made to be broken. Surely he'd be able to fit it into his plans?

Tank slid her car keys across the table. "You'll need these if you're going to the mall and the library. I'll follow you in my truck."

Rachel didn't know how he knew drama club was at the library, but it didn't matter. What mattered was that Bella was now happily munching a cookie. If her dad couldn't come home early, she had something else to look forward to.

And that, Rachel knew, was as good as it got sometimes.

～

JOHN STUDIED the police report in front of him. One of his security teams had been transporting a wealthy client's collection of eighteenth-century jewelry across two states. They were heading toward New York when they'd been ambushed outside of Stamford. No one was seriously hurt, but it was close.

Even though the jewelry wasn't taken, the vehicle his team drove would be written off.

John's eyes traveled over the report, stopping at the third paragraph. Until they'd hit Port Chester, the journey had been uneventful. That changed when they'd driven over the Rippowam River.

All of John's teams followed strict pre-assignment protocols. Before they left, they checked all national and state websites, making sure they knew of all planned events that could affect their assignment. They checked weather conditions and accident reports. Traffic congestion data was analyzed and they planned their journey to avoid any unnecessary holdups.

They'd done everything they should have, but they'd still been caught in unscheduled roadworks.

The team quickly realized something wasn't right. As they'd overtaken the traffic to get away from the slow-zone, two black SUVs had blocked their path.

Tony Martinez, the driver of Fletcher Security's SUV, had swerved to the opposite side of the road, slammed into one of the vehicles, then kept driving.

They'd made it to their destination, delivered the jewelry, then sent through their report with the dashboard camera images.

Sam and Tanner, two of John's team based in Montana, had been studying the video for the last few hours. After pulling every piece of data they could find, they were no closer to locating the owner of the SUV.

A quick knock on John's door pulled his attention away from his computer.

Tanner stood in the doorway. "Sam and I are heading home. Are you coming?"

John glanced at his watch. It was eight o'clock—too late to do anything more for his team in New York. "How's Tony?"

"Better than your SUV. He'll contact the insurance company tomorrow."

John sent Tony a quick email. "We can do that from here. He has enough to worry about." He frowned at the printouts on his desk. He'd looked through each paper at least a dozen times. Nothing that had happened today made sense. Compared to some contracts they carried out, this was a routine operation. Nothing should have gone wrong.

He scooped all the papers into a pile and locked them away in his bottom drawer. "I'll leave with you and Sam. Bella will be upset I missed her bedtime."

Tanner stared solemnly at him. "Don't make work your entire life. Before you know it, Bella will be at college. Make the most of having her with you."

From anyone else, those words wouldn't have had the same impact. But John knew about Tanner's past, the heartache that had followed him to Montana. "I wish it was that simple."

"It is." Tanner waved John through the open door. "Sam's waiting for us at the main reception desk. Don't ask her how she's feeling."

John grabbed his jacket and left his office. "What happened?"

"She was supposed to go on a date tonight. The guy had a hard time believing she couldn't meet him for dinner."

"Sounds like she needs to date someone else."

Tanner grinned. "I told her the same thing. You don't want to know what she said."

John flicked the lights out in his office, locked the door, and headed toward the front of the building. "Sam wouldn't know how to be rude if she tried."

A woman in her late twenties walked down the hallway, frowning ferociously at Tanner. At five-foot-five, the top of Sam's head wouldn't have reached John or Tanner's shoulders. But size, in Sam's case, meant absolutely nothing.

"I heard that, John Fletcher. Just because I'm quiet, it doesn't mean I don't get annoyed." Her blue eyes were flashing fire. If he'd been a betting man, John would have put ten dollars on her trying to box his ears if she could have reached that far.

Tanner's grin became a whole lot wider. "It's just as well your boyfriend can't see you now. He'd run straight toward the Rockies and never come back."

Sam stuck her hands on her hips. "I don't care if I never see him again. And he wasn't my boyfriend. He was a friend of a friend." Her nose tilted in the air. "It was a pity he didn't have a few extra brain cells between his ears. I wouldn't have canceled our date unless it was important."

"That's my girl," Tanner said proudly. "Kick his sorry ass out the door and look for someone better."

Sam sent Tanner a withering glare. "I'm taking a vacation from dating. Being surrounded by men all day is damaging my ability to think rationally." She turned her back on them and strode along the corridor.

Tanner turned to John and gave him one of his 'I-told-you-so' looks.

John shrugged. He was too surprised by Sam's outburst to do more than follow her.

He might know about business plans, strategic warfare, and the latest surveillance techniques, but he was lost when it came to women.

Tanner lengthened his stride until he was walking beside John. "Was Bella looking forward to seeing Rachel today?"

"She was dressed before six o'clock. When I left home, she was sitting in the kitchen with Patty, counting the minutes until Rachel arrived."

Sam waited at the reception desk for John and Tanner. "I sent the images from Tony's dash-cam to a friend at the FBI. He'll have a look at them tomorrow."

John waved at a security guard as they left the building. "Thanks. You've both worked hard today. I appreciate what you've given up to stay here."

Sam glared at Tanner. "Don't say a word."

"I wasn't going to," he said with a smile in his voice. "I'm heading home to eat left-over pizza. Want to join me?"

Sam wrinkled her nose. "No, thanks. I need sleep more than cold pizza."

John shook his head, too. "I have to give a little girl a kiss goodnight. See you tomorrow." As he left the parking lot, he went through the day he'd planned before Tony and his team were ambushed. That's when he remembered his promise to go to the mall with Bella.

With a sinking heart, he knew he was heading toward the worst dad of the year status. Instead of choosing a birthday present for Bella's friend and eating hot dogs, he'd been buried in paperwork.

Tanner was right. Something had to change.

CHAPTER 8

*J*ohn tiptoed into Bella's room, trying not to wake her. The night-light shone with a soft pink glow. He stood where he was, watching his daughter as she dreamed what he hoped were sweet dreams.

As soon as he moved, his foot hit a squeaky floorboard and Bella's eyes opened.

"Daddy." She jumped out of bed and rushed toward him, wrapping her arms around his waist. "You were supposed to come to the mall with me."

John hugged her tight. "I know, sweet pea. Something happened at work and I couldn't make it. Mrs. Daniels said you went to the mall with Rachel and Tank. Did you have a good time?"

Bella let go of his waist and pulled him across to her bed. "It was awesome. We went there after we finished math. Guess what we found for Poppy?"

"A pogo stick with pink tassels?"

Bella shook her head. "No," she giggled.

"A purple people eater with yellow spots?"

Bella shook her head again. "I'll give you a clue. It makes a noise."

John hoped she hadn't bought Poppy a puppy or a kitten. They might be making a trip back to the pet store if that had happened. "A soft toy shaped like a sheep that goes, baa?"

Bella wiggled off her bed and took a box off the dresser. "Close your eyes, Dad."

He closed his eyes. She turned on the lights, then lifted something out of the box.

"You can open your eyes now," Bella said from beside him.

John looked at his daughter, then across at the toy poodle sitting on the floor.

Bella handed him a remote control. "It's a miniature Labradoodle. Once she gets used to your voice, she'll follow all of your commands. Watch this…"

She took a step away and said, "Jasmine, heel." The toy dog stood up and walked across to Bella, sitting in front of her with a little yip.

"Good dog," Bella crooned. She scratched behind the toy's ears, then said, "Jasmine, follow." Bella walked across the room and Jasmine followed. When Bella stopped, Jasmine stopped.

John stared at the toy dog. "That's pretty advanced technology for a nine-year-old's birthday present."

Bella grinned. "She poops, too."

He looked at the remote control. Sure enough, what he presumed was a poop button was strategically placed at the bottom of the console. "How much did Jasmine cost?"

Even though they had a lot of money, he wanted Bella to appreciate life and work hard for what she wanted. She received pocket money each week, but she had a list of chores she needed to do to earn it. He didn't want her thinking life came served on a silver plate. Or in this case, served to her friend with a battery-controlled remote.

"The lady in the store said it was the last one. It was the demo...demonstrating...the one they show people. Jasmine had a broken leg, but Tank knew a man who could fix it. I didn't think Poppy would mind if Jasmine has been to the robot doctor." Bella looked worried. "Rachel thought it would be okay to give Poppy a dog. Jasmine's not real and she doesn't even need to poop because she only pretends to eat food."

John looked into his daughter's big brown eyes.

"Please, Dad. It was only a few dollars over my limit. I told Rachel I would help Mrs. Daniels vacuum the house tomorrow and take the trash out twice. Tank said I could help him clean his truck."

John was finding it hard to believe the cost of the toy was only a few dollars more than Bella's budget. Broken paw or not, the technology behind it should have made it retail for hundreds of dollars.

He looked at the dog, then back at Bella. He felt guilty he hadn't gone to the mall with her. Guilty he couldn't spend more time with her each day.

He relaxed his face muscles and got rid of the frown Bella thought was for her. "I think Poppy will love her birthday present. It was a great choice." He hugged his daughter tight and thanked his lucky stars for Tank and Rachel. Bella had enjoyed her time with them and she didn't think he was a jerk for staying at work. "What do you say about going to bed now?"

She picked the toy dog off the floor and flicked a black switch on its stomach. "Can you read me another chapter of my book?"

"Where are we up to?" He put the dog in its box and closed the lid.

Bella passed him her copy of *Anne of Green Gables*. "The last chapter. Why do you think Marilla was angry with John Blythe when she was younger? She really liked him."

"I think she was trying to find her own happiness," John said carefully.

"Just like us." Bella climbed into bed and wiggled down until only her head appeared above her blanket. "I love you, Dad."

"I love you, too." He sat beside Bella and opened her book to the last chapter.

As he started reading, he thought about the characters L.M. Montgomery had created. More than one hundred years after *Anne of Green Gables* was first published, Bella could still connect with Anne and the ups and downs of her life.

He wondered what a modern-day Anne Shirley would have been like. He looked down at Bella and sighed.

She would have been just as brave and stubborn as Bella was. And just as willing to let people into her heart.

JOHN SAT on the couch at Poppy's birthday party, listening to a woman tell him about her vacation in Canada. Bella was sitting with a group of girls, painting her nails. He'd never been to a nine-year-old girl's birthday party before. It was a crazy combination of sugar-loaded food, beauty products, and pink presents.

So far, the ten girls at the party had braided their hair with tiny beads, decorated cupcakes, and made tattoos out of glitter. It definitely wasn't the traditional *Pin the Tail on the Donkey* and *Musical Chairs* party he'd been expecting.

"Do you enjoy living in Bozeman?"

John focused his attention on Donna, the woman sitting

opposite him. "It's a great place. It took a while to settle in, but having my brother here has helped."

"Is that why you moved to Montana?"

John nodded. "I'd been looking for a building to convert into my business' headquarters. When the old flour mill came on the market, Grant and I had a look and decided it was worth the investment."

He wouldn't tell Donna his brother had kept him sane after his wife died. He hadn't known how to raise a toddler, or even how to live a normal civilian life. It had taken him another four years to realize Bella needed to be close to family as much as he did.

He watched Bella blow on her nails. She compared her nail color with the girl beside her and they both giggled. She'd grown so much since Jacinta had died. Six years ago, she was running around in diapers, chasing the neighbor's cat and climbing anything she saw.

"If Bella wants to come to our home for a playdate, I'm sure Anna would love it. The two girls get along so well."

John watched Bella pass Anna another bottle of nail polish. "Thanks. I'll check with Bella."

He picked up his cup of coffee and checked the time. It was nearly five o'clock. Tanner was waiting outside for them, parked on the side of the road and trying to look as inconspicuous as possible.

"Coffee anyone?" Poppy's mom carried a tray of coffee across to the parents.

When she reached John, he shook his head. "Not for me. I have one already."

"Would you like a piece of birthday cake to go with your coffee?"

He looked at the bright pink frosting and frowned. "Sure. Just a small piece, though. Bella and I need to go home soon."

Donna, the woman sitting opposite him, pouted. "It's far too early for that. We were just getting to know each other."

John gulped back the last of his coffee. He might be a little rusty in the dating department, but he knew when someone was flirting with him. Anyone else would have said something witty, broken the silence that had descended around the table. But not John. He couldn't think of one thing to say that wouldn't hurt Donna's feelings.

It wasn't that she was unattractive. In fact, she was probably one of the most attractive women he'd ever met. And it wasn't that she didn't interest him. She did. But not in the 'let's date' kind of way she was hinting at.

He'd married the only woman he'd ever love. He couldn't imagine spending time with many women, especially the romantic kind of time he'd never been very good at.

An image of Rachel popped into his head and he sighed. She was off limits and, even if she wasn't, nothing would happen.

He left his mug on the table. "It was great spending time with you, but I really need to go." He looked at Poppy's mom and tried to smile. "Thank you for inviting us to your home. I have a feeling Bella will be talking about this birthday for a long time."

Poppy's mom smiled. "I'm glad you had a good time. I know another little girl who's incredibly happy. Poppy loved the robotic dog you bought her."

"It was all Bella's idea."

"Well, it was very sweet. While you're getting Bella ready, I'll get each of you a slice of cake to take home."

Before John could tell her not to worry, she disappeared into the kitchen. He glanced at Donna and tried not to worry about the glare she sent back to him.

It was just like college all over again. Except, this time, there wouldn't be a happy-ever-after ending for anyone.

Cupid had left the building, now all John had to do was get Bella into their truck.

He looked at where he'd last seen her. She'd moved across the room to another group of girls. She was sitting on the floor, laughing and talking, and waiting to have her hair curled. Where had the last eight years gone? His little girl was growing up, and he wasn't sure how he felt about it.

He walked over to her and knelt on the floor. "We need to go home."

"But I haven't curled my hair," Bella said with a disappointed sigh. "Could we stay for five more minutes?"

John shook his head. "We need to leave. Do you want to thank Poppy for inviting us?"

"I already have, but I'll go and say goodbye."

"I'll get our jackets."

She nodded and John went into the hallway. He looked through the windows on either side of the front door. The snow was falling thick and fast, covering everything in its path with a white, icy blanket of snow.

Quickly, he texted Tanner to let him know they were leaving. All he had to do now was get himself and his daughter home safely.

RACHEL SLAMMED the tailgate closed on her truck and hauled the last box of bridesmaids' dresses into Tess' loft.

Since taking the job as Bella's tutor three weeks ago, she'd had less time to help at The Bridesmaids Club. With Christmas fast approaching, all her friends were finding it more difficult to balance their own lives with the brides and bridesmaids who were desperate for dresses.

Tess and Rachel had decided to put a few hours aside on Saturday morning to go through the boxes and letters that had arrived during week. Bella had been at home, waiting for her dad to come back from a meeting in Washington, D.C. Rachel had invited her and Tank to The Bridesmaids Club, hoping to fill Bella's day with something interesting before John returned.

"I'm bringing the last box in now," Rachel yelled from the top of the stairs. The loft door opened and she stumbled inside. "Thanks, Bella."

"That's okay. Tess said to leave the box on the kitchen counter. If we wipe the snow off the box, the floor won't get wet."

"Good idea." Rachel slid the box onto the counter and flicked the fresh snow into the sink.

Tess walked out of the spare bedroom carrying a handful of clothes hangers. "These should be enough for this week's dresses. Hopefully, no one sends any over Christmas."

Rachel looked at the three boxes on the counter. "If they do, we'll be seriously out of room."

Tess grinned. "Do you remember how much space there was in my apartment above Angel Wings Café?"

"You were surrounded by dresses. I'm surprised you could move."

"It was worse when new boxes arrived. I used to stack them in the kitchen until I could find room for them."

"I'd like to live in a house filled with these dresses," Bella said wistfully. "It would be like living in a Disney movie."

Tess laughed. "Or an out-of-control train filled with satin and lace. If you hear of anyone who wants to rent my old apartment, Rachel, let me know. Or better yet, take them there to have a look. With Christmas getting close, I don't have a lot of spare time."

"Have you moved your spare back door key, yet? That little magnetic box above the doorframe was so obvious."

"It's still there. Who's going to break into my apartment?"

Rachel sighed. "No one if they find the key. You might as well leave the door wide open."

Bella moved around the counter. "What's a magnetic box?"

Tess held her hands out to show Bella how long the box was. "It's a little box, about this big, that sticks to the metal above my door. It's for emergencies."

Bella frowned. "Dad told me what to do in an emergency. I call 9-1-1. He's coming home tonight."

Rachel gave her a hug. It had been a tough few days. John called each morning, but it didn't make up for her dad not being at home. The more time Rachel spent with Bella, the more she realized just how much John's absence was affecting his daughter.

When he was gone, Bella became quiet, withdrawn, and easily distracted. At first, she thought it was because Bella was waiting for the sound of her dad's car in the driveway, or his voice in the entranceway. But his meeting this week had left Rachel even more worried.

"Do you want to help me open a box of dresses, Bella?"

A big smile filled her face. "Yes, please."

Rachel used a pair of scissors to cut the tape and Bella opened the flaps.

The owner of the dresses had left a photo of her brides-maids inside the box. Standing in front of the bridesmaids, looking as happy as a polar bear in winter, was a little white dog. "Look at this, Bella. The doggie in the photo looks like the little toy dog you gave your friend."

Bella stood on the edge of a stool and looked at the photo in Rachel's hand. "It does. It looks just like Jasmine. Could I show my friend Poppy the photo?"

"Of course, you can," Rachel said. "I'll leave it in my bag so we don't forget to take it home."

Tess opened another box and pulled out a dress with a bright floral pattern on the fabric. "Wow. This one's different." She peeked inside the box and pulled another matching dress out. "Do you think our spring bridesmaids will like these dresses?"

Bella sighed. "I think they're really pretty."

Rachel grinned at Bella. "I'm sure someone else will feel the same. They'll look stunning when Molly photographs them for our catalog." She handed Bella a dress. "Take this to Tess. She'll help you put it on a hanger."

Bella carefully took the dress across to Tess. "I've seen your catalog. I like the Cinderella Collection the best."

Tess smiled. "Why do you like that collection?"

"Because the dresses are beautiful and sparkly."

Rachel found a hanger and put the second floral brides-maid's dress beside Tess. "Would you like to see the Cinderella dresses we have at the moment?"

Bella nodded her head so hard it was a wonder it didn't pop off her shoulders.

Tess looked through the living room's large picture window. "While you're doing that, I'll ask your friend if he wants to come inside. The snow is getting heavier."

Rachel glanced at the flurry of snowflakes falling outside. "I didn't realize how bad it was. I'll call Tank on his cell phone."

Tank had met Tess when they'd first arrived at her home. For some reason, he'd insisted on staying in his truck and not coming inside.

A loud banging on the door made them all jump. "I guess Tank is tired of waiting in the cold," Tess said. "You'd better invite him in before he turns into Frosty the Snowman."

Tank nodded at Tess when he walked into the loft. "It's cold out there." Bella handed him a towel as he stood in the kitchen, shaking the snow off his jacket. "Thanks, Bella."

"You're welcome," Bella said seriously. "Rachel told me to

dry my hair in case I got a cold. You're a lot wetter than I was."

He smiled at his little helper. "It's snowing a lot harder than when you came inside. We'll have to leave in the next few minutes if we want to get home safely."

"Will Dad be all right?" Bella asked.

Tank folded the towel and left it on the edge of the counter. "He'll be fine. If his flight is canceled, he'll stay in Washington, D.C. for longer."

"Are you sure?"

Rachel looked between Bella and Tank. Bella was so worried about her dad it nearly broke her heart. "Your dad will be extra careful because he knows you're waiting for him. Let's get our jackets so we stay warm when we go outside."

Bella walked across to the coat stand with Rachel. "Are you sure Dad will be okay?"

"Positive. Do you want to call him when we get back to your house?"

Bella pushed her arms into her jacket. "Can we call him now?"

Tank shook his head. "We'll call him from home."

Rachel knelt in front of Bella and zipped her jacket closed. "While you're talking to your dad, I'll make us some hot chocolate. Does that sound like a good plan?"

Bella nodded, then turned to Tess. "Thank you for letting me see your dresses."

"That's okay. Rachel has a key to the loft. If you want to come back and look at the Cinderella dresses, you're more than welcome."

Bella looked up at Rachel. "Can we come back tomorrow?"

"We'll see what your dad has planned." She might as well

have said yes. The grin on Bella's face was worth every minute it would take to drive through the snow.

Rachel zipped her jacket to her chin and held Bella's hand. "I'm sorry we have to leave early, Tess. I'll try to get back soon to tidy up the rest of the dresses."

"Don't worry about it. The dresses are all here now. I'll sort them into styles and get them ready for Molly to photograph. We don't need to add them to our website straight away."

Rachel picked up the folder of letters she needed to reply to. "I'll do these from home tonight." She looked around the room, checking to make sure they'd left nothing behind. "It looks as though we're ready to leave, Tank."

He glanced through the window. "Let's get going. It was nice meeting you, Tess."

"It was good seeing you, too. Drive safely."

As they walked carefully down the stairs to their vehicles, the icy blast of air hitting Rachel's face made her shiver. Tank was right. If they'd stayed at Tess and Logan's home for another hour, they might not have made it home.

"I don't like this weather," Tank said from in front of them. "You're both coming with me."

Rachel grabbed Bella around the waist as she slid on a slippery patch of ice. "I can drive myself home. You take Bella."

"It wasn't up for discussion. You're both coming with me." He unlocked his truck and lifted Bella into the back seat. "Make sure your seatbelt is tight."

Rachel wiped the snow out of her face and glared at Tank. "I know how to drive when it's snowing. I'll be okay."

Tank opened the front passenger door. He didn't say a word. He didn't need to. His face was as hard and uncompromising as the patch of ice Bella had slipped on.

"You don't need to get mean and grouchy," she muttered. "I'll go with you."

Tank's lips twitched. Rachel stepped into the truck and Tank closed the door.

He hurried around the vehicle. As soon as the engine was running, Tank turned on the heater, sending a stream of warm air into the cab.

Rachel patted her cheeks. "It feels like icicles are pricking my skin."

"Me, too," Bella said from behind her. "Dad doesn't like driving in the snow."

Rachel frowned. Tess had told her John had served in the military. It didn't make sense that he wouldn't be used to driving in all kinds of weather. "Why doesn't he like driving in the snow, Bella?"

"Mommy died in a car accident when it was snowing. It makes him feel sad."

Rachel's gaze shot to Tank. He looked at her before reversing out of the driveway. "How do you feel about being in a truck when it's snowing?"

"I don't mind," Bella said matter-of-factly. "I was only little when Mom died. I don't remember what happened."

Rachel had never been more pleased Tank was driving. If they'd been having this conversation when she was driving them home, she would have needed to pull over. And with the amount of snow coming down outside, that would have only gotten them into trouble.

"Tank's a good driver, Bella. He'll keep us safe."

"I know. Dad says Tank's his guardian angel."

Tank's gaze shot to his rearview mirror, then across to Rachel. "Don't ask."

Rachel sighed. Bella and John's life was more complicated than anyone's she knew. She could feel herself getting pulled into their lives, becoming part of something she didn't understand. She cared about Bella and wanted her to be happy.

She still wasn't sure what she felt about John. He was a mystery she wasn't prepared to solve, not when it would jeopardize her relationship with his daughter. She didn't doubt he loved Bella, but there were things about his life that made his daughter unhappy. Some of them he couldn't change. Others he could.

Rachel didn't know why Tank was John's guardian angel, or why he needed to look after Bella. What she did know was Bella missed her dad, and that was something she could help change.

CHAPTER 9

*J*ohn woke to the sound of sleigh bells ringing through his home. He rolled onto his back and rubbed his eyes. It was still dark outside. No one in their right mind would stand on the sidewalk singing Christmas carols at this time of the morning.

He listened again, then lifted his arm to his face, squinting at his watch. Seven o'clock was a strange time to be hearing bells, but Christmas music was definitely coming from somewhere close by.

After the time it had taken to get home from Washington, D.C, he should still be sound asleep. His flight had left five hours late. Landing in Bozeman at two o'clock in the morning had been a nightmare. The plane had dipped and dived so often he'd given up thinking they would land safely.

At one point an overhead locker had sprung open, dropping its contents on the passengers below. The coats and scarves weren't a problem, but the heavy bags were. After more than one startled howl of pain, the cabin crew locked everything away and found ice packs for the passengers' heads.

In the ten minutes it had taken to land, he'd heard more Hail Marys being recited than he ever had at church. The spike of adrenaline reminded him of his time in the military, the days when he never thought he'd wake up again. But here he was, lying in bed and wondering if he'd fallen into the twilight zone.

Apart from finally leaving the plane, the second-best thing he'd done was driving home with Tank. He'd kept a careful eye on the weather reports while he was in Washington, D.C. As soon as he'd seen the cold front settling over Montana, he'd called Tank and asked him to pick him up. He hated driving in snowstorms almost as much as he hated being in planes that felt like roller coasters.

Tank had met him in the baggage claim area. The drive into town was slow, silent, and uneventful.

As soon as he'd arrived home, he'd kissed the top of Bella's sleeping head and collapsed in a heap under his blankets.

He lifted his head again, then sat up in bed. Christmas music was definitely coming from somewhere inside his home.

John pulled on an old pair of sweatpants and a T-shirt and walked barefoot down the wooden staircase. He followed the music and stopped at the kitchen door.

Bella was standing on a chair beside Rachel. She was adding brown sugar and butter to the big electric mixer on the counter, watching the ingredients spin inside the bowl.

Rachel passed her an egg. "Has Mrs. Daniels shown you how to break the shell?"

Bella nodded and turned off the mixer. "Tap the side and pull it apart. What if some shell drops into the butter and sugar?"

"We can easily get it out. Are you ready?"

Bella nodded. The first time she hit the side of the bowl

with the egg, nothing happened. She tried again, hitting the bowl a little harder. The shell splintered and she quickly tipped the egg into the bowl. With a grin that caught at John's heart, she turned to Rachel. "No shell."

Rachel held up her hand and high-fived his excited daughter. "Good job. Now we add the molasses and vanilla, then turn the mixer on again."

Bella looked at the glass bowl Rachel passed her. "All of it?"

Rachel nodded. "I'll get the flour and the spices ready." She opened one small packet after another, carefully adding teaspoons of spice to another bowl.

Bella watched Rachel, then looked across the room. *"Daddy. You're home."* She jumped off the chair and raced across the room. "I've missed you."

He hugged her tight. "I missed you, too."

"How was your meeting?"

"It was okay. I'm glad I'm home. What are you baking?"

Bella held his hand and led him to the kitchen counter. "We're making gingerbread cookies for the drama club's Christmas play. Do you want to help?"

"If you show me what to do, I'll give it my best shot."

Bella jumped onto the chair and held a small container toward him. "Put this in the mixing bowl, Dad."

He sniffed the spices. "Is this cinnamon?"

"Cinnamon, nutmeg, and ginger," Rachel said softly. "I hope we didn't wake you? When we heard your flight was delayed, we thought you might have stayed in Washington."

John looked away from Rachel's big blue eyes. A man could get lost in those eyes if he let himself. But he wasn't the type of person to let himself fall that easily for a woman, especially after what he'd learned this week. "It's not so bad waking up to the sound of Christmas bells. It was better than waking up in a crowded airport. Hundreds of people waiting for rescheduled flights. I might have ended up at the airport for another two days if my flight was canceled."

Rachel passed Bella a bowl of flour. She watched her add it to the gingerbread ingredients, then glanced at him. "You're probably wondering what I'm doing here this early?"

The thought had crossed his mind. "You don't need to look after Bella on the weekends."

"I promised Bella I'd take her to The Bridesmaids Club and yesterday was as good a day as any. While we were there, the weather became so bad Tank drove us home. Mrs. Daniels thought it was safer for me to stay here last night."

"Patty was right." He watched Rachel's hands relax against the edge of the counter. "Do you need a ride back to Tess' home to get your truck?"

Rachel's mouth dropped open as if she was going to say something, then changed her mind.

He thought about what he'd said and felt like an idiot. "I didn't mean I wanted you to leave now. I meant later, when you're ready to go home. You can stay for as long as you like."

Rachel slowly nodded. She took the empty flour bowl out of Bella's hands, then looked at him. "Tank said he'd take me to Tess' at nine o'clock."

"You'll need a shovel to get rid of the snow on your truck. It was nearly blizzard conditions when we drove in from the airport."

Bella looked at her dad. "I saw lots of pretty dresses at The Bridesmaids Club. I helped hang them on a special rack. Tess made cake and Rachel took the Christmas CD with us."

"Sounds like you had a great time."

"Mrs. Daniels and I made cookies before I went with Rachel. I took some for Tess. Can I go again, Dad? Tank wanted to come home early because it was snowing. Tess said it was okay if I go back to look at the dresses."

John looked at Rachel. "If it's okay with Rachel, it's okay

with me."

"Of course, it's all right. It will be good to have another pair of hands to help unpack the boxes." She looked at the mixing bowl in front of them. "We've nearly finished the dough. Just two more ingredients to add."

"Then we can roll it out and make the gingerbread cookies?"

"We need to leave the dough in the refrigerator for a little while. We could have breakfast and get ready for the day while it chills?"

"And then can we roll it out?"

"You bet. Mrs. Daniels has lots of cookie cutters. Your dad could make some, too."

The last time John had made Christmas cookies was when he was a boy. Grandma Fletcher spent most of December baking. Some cookies and cakes were given to family and friends. But most of the baking went to the local shelter, helping other people enjoy the Christmas spirit.

He picked up one of the cookie cutters. "Does the cookie cutter person get to sample the cookies after they're baked?"

Bella giggled. "You can have two, but you have to wait until after we've frosted them." She leaned across to John and whispered, "They need to be decorated. Otherwise, they're not really Christmas cookies."

He smiled at his daughter. "Thank you for telling me," he whispered back.

Bella added the last two ingredients to the bowl and turned the mixer back on. Christmas music filled the kitchen while Bella and Rachel got the dough ready.

"You've done this before," John said to Rachel.

"Just a few times. Christmas wouldn't be the same without special cookies."

Bella patted the top of the dough in its plastic wrap and smiled. "All done."

Rachel carried it across to the refrigerator, then washed her hands under the faucet. "Now comes the exciting part. The clean-up."

Bella groaned. "Do we have to?"

He studied the kitchen and smiled. Flour was sprinkled across most of the counter and a collection of dirty spoons and bowls surrounded Bella. "It's not as bad as it looks. Rachel's already put most of the ingredients away."

Rachel passed Bella a warm dishcloth. "I'll get the bowls ready to be washed while you wipe down the counter. Your dad can sweep the floor."

Bella sighed. "Okay."

As they moved around the kitchen, the Christmas music changed and a children's choir started singing.

John took the broom out of the mudroom. "Nice music."

Rachel's eyes danced with laughter. "It's the same songs Bella will be singing in the drama club's Christmas play."

"And I know all the words," Bella said quickly. She put down the dishcloth and wiped her hands on the pink apron Rachel must have wrapped around her waist. When the choir started singing the second verse of, *Silent Night,* Bella took a deep breath and started singing with them.

Tears clouded John's eyes. He remembered another Christmas many years ago when another young girl had sung the same song.

Jacinta was about sixteen years old when he'd first heard her sing. She'd loved music and had the kind of voice that made people stop and listen. Even then, he'd known she would be an important part of his life.

The song ended and Bella looked worried. "Are you okay, Dad?"

He wiped his eyes and gave her a hug. "You remind me of your mom. She was singing the same song on the night I met her."

"Did she like singing?"

"She did, but I think it was being part of a choir that really made her happy. Our high school choir used to visit the local retirement villages and the hospital. Your mom enjoyed making people feel better."

Bella thought about what he'd said, then smiled. "Do you think gingerbread cookies will make people feel better, too? We could take some to Mrs. Daniels' mom. She lives in a retirement village in town."

He gave Bella another quick hug. "That would make Mrs. Daniels' mom very happy."

Bella jumped off the chair. She took the recipe book they'd been using out of a drawer and flicked through the pages. "Is it okay if we make more gingerbread cookies, Rachel?"

Rachel leaned against the kitchen counter, watching Bella and John closely. "As long as our cookie cutter stays, it's a great idea."

"Can you stay, Dad?"

"The only thing I want to do is visit Emerald Lake. If we make the gingerbread now, I can book the helicopter for later this morning."

Bella clapped her hands together. "Rachel could come with us. We haven't shown her where our new home will be built."

John tried not to frown when he looked at Rachel. With a red and green apron covering her clothes and a dusting of flour across her cheeks, she was ready for anything Christmas could throw at her. But that didn't mean she wanted to spend more time with them.

She probably had lots of other things she'd sooner do on a Sunday morning. Things that didn't include an eight-year-old, a team of bodyguards, and an overprotective father. And then there was the billionaire issue.

Rachel opened a bag of flour. "I didn't know you'd bought one of Jacob Green's properties. I've seen the photos Molly took of the lake. It's lovely."

"So you'll come with us on the helicopter?" Bella asked. "You could sit beside me. It's not too scary."

Rachel picked up a measuring cup and dipped it into the bag of flour. "A helicopter ride sounds exciting. I'd love to go with you."

He nearly dropped the broom.

Bella's face broke into a wide grin. "This is the best day ever. Wait until I tell Mrs. Daniels where we're going."

John had no idea what Patty would say. He hadn't invited a woman anywhere with him and Bella for years. Even though Rachel was his daughter's tutor, it felt strange to have her join them.

Strange and new, and maybe a little like the beginning of something that could be amazing.

RACHEL GAZED through the helicopter's window, staring at the beautiful landscape. Snow covered everything, from the top of the tallest mountains, to the pine trees huddled together on the valley floor. Last night's snowstorm had left its mark on the world—a mark that was far more beautiful and majestic from the air than it was from the ground.

Bella pointed to a herd of buffalo.

Rachel watched them lumber across the frozen field, looking for food buried beneath the snow.

For as long as she lived, she'd never tire of the simple beauty that surrounded her. Montana was the most magical place she knew, and the one place she would always call home.

"Look to your right," John said through her headset. "Emerald Lake is over the next ridge."

She kept her eyes on the scene unfolding below her. Big Sky Resort, one of the most famous ski destinations in America, was nestled in the mountains on the left-hand side of the helicopter. John had told her Emerald Lake wasn't far from the winter playground that attracted thousands of tourists to Montana each winter.

She wondered why he'd bought a parcel of land in the middle of nowhere. He didn't seem like the type of person who'd enjoy the solitude or peace that came from being miles away from the nearest store.

The helicopter drifted over the ridge and Rachel's mouth dropped open. "It's beautiful," she whispered into her microphone. The circular lake was frozen solid, but it still looked incredible in the mid-morning sunshine.

John didn't reply, but that didn't surprise her. A person could lose themselves in the pure energy surrounding them or, if they were lucky, find something that was missing.

The helicopter carried them across the center of the lake toward an area covered with tall trees.

"Jacob and Molly's property is over there," John pointed to their left. "One of the other parcels of land has sold and the last one is still on the market."

She held onto her armrest as the pilot landed on a snow-covered plateau. "When are you moving out here?"

John took off his headset. "We start building in early April. If everything goes to plan, we should move in around the end of September."

Rachel opened her door and breathed in the cold mountain air. She looked around and smiled at a hawk circling in the clear blue sky. It was almost as if the rest of the world had disappeared and left them to enjoy the morning.

"Welcome to Emerald Lake," John said from behind her. "What do you think?"

"I couldn't work out why you'd want to live here, but now I know why. It's absolutely stunning. If I had enough money, I'd buy the last parcel of land and live here myself."

"If you keep working for me, you could put a deposit on the land by next Christmas."

Rachel laughed. "I told you I was being paid too much. Just be thankful Bella's going to school soon. You'll be able to save thousands of dollars each week when you aren't paying my salary."

"I'm not paying you that much," John growled.

"Are you sure?" She bit her bottom lip. She needed to keep their relationship professional. No flirty talk allowed. John's gaze traveled to her mouth, then back to her eyes.

Bella clambered out of the helicopter and stood beside her dad. Her laughter echoed around the mountains and helped ease the tension between Rachel and John. "Isn't this the most amazing place you've ever seen? In the summer, I'll swim in the lake with Dad. I'm not allowed to go on my own, but that doesn't matter. Tank and Tanner could go with me if Dad's at work. Mrs. Daniels doesn't like swimming, so I guess she won't want to come. I wonder if she'd be okay watching me?"

"I'm sure Mrs. Daniels would watch you while you were swimming," Rachel said. "Do you want to show me where your home will be built?"

Bella walked across to Rachel and held her hand. "I think it's over this way."

John put the house plans he'd brought with him under his arm. Rachel could feel his gaze on her, watching where Bella was taking her.

"How do you know where you're going?" she asked Bella.

"I'm kind of guessing. Last time we came here, it wasn't

snowing as much. There were big orange pegs in the ground. Dad showed me where each room was." Bella stopped in the middle of the plateau and looked around. "I think this is it, but I'm not sure." She looked at her dad. "Is this the right spot?"

John walked toward them. "You're standing on the front porch," he said with a smile. "If you're not careful, you'll be walking in the front door with your wet shoes on."

Bella took a step forward and smiled. "Will you tell Mrs. Daniels I nearly tracked snow and mud inside?"

John bent down and kissed the end of Bella's nose. "Your secret's safe with me."

Bella looked at the papers under his arm. "Show Rachel the drawings, Dad."

Rachel watched Bella's face as John unwound their house plans. She was so excited she was practically hopping on the spot.

"This isn't an exact measurement," he said. "But, if you walk forty feet that way, you should see the view from the living room."

Rachel counted out forty feet as she moved away from him. "Tell me about the living room. What will it look like?"

John glanced at the architect's plans. "There's a big stone fireplace down one end of the room. There'll be enough seating for at least ten people. The inbuilt sound system will make everything you've seen look like it was around when Noah first thought about building an ark."

Rachel smiled. "You seem overly sure about that."

John shrugged. "I'm a gadget man."

He didn't need to add that he also had enough money to buy what he wanted. "Can you walk outside from the living room?"

"There'll be two sets of oversized French doors." John followed Rachel's footprints. He looked down at his plans, then held his arms out toward the lake. "The first set is here. The second set is six-feet farther along."

Bella waved her arms in the air. "And over here is Dad's office. It's at the front of our house so he can see who's coming and going."

Rachel looked at John. "A regular Sherlock Holmes. Who do you think will come out here without calling you first?"

"Oh, I don't know. Maybe a teacher who's looking for somewhere her drama club can practice singing?"

Rachel tapped her finger to her chin. "The only problem I can see is making sure all the children leave. They'll like it so much they'll want to stay."

"We'll have lots and lots of bedrooms," Bella said excitedly. "Do you think the drama club would really come out here to practice?"

Rachel looked at the lake. "As long as we could get enough parents to drive the children to Emerald Lake, I think they would."

"That would be so great," Bella sighed.

"Show me the rest of your home," Rachel said quickly before Bella planned the first visit. "Where's the kitchen and dining room?"

Bella stomped across to her dad, knees bent, wading through the ankle-deep snow. "They're over here." She took a few more steps, then spun in a circle with her arms wide. "Mrs. Daniels helped plan out where everything will go. We'll be able to see the lake when we eat breakfast."

Rachel walked across to Bella and imagined sitting at a table, soaking in the beauty around them.

"When we came out here in the fall, a flock of geese were living on the lake. Mrs. Daniels said they might have babies one day and I'll be able to see them."

"You could take a photograph of them and show the children in your class."

Bella nodded. "I'm going to have a kitten, too. Come and see where my room will be." She held Rachel's hand and walked no more than a dozen steps away from where they'd been standing.

John watched his daughter with a tender smile. He caught Rachel staring at him, and she could have sworn a blush skimmed his cheeks.

"This is my room," Bella said proudly. "Except it's in the air at the moment. You have to pretend you're upstairs."

"It's a lovely room."

Bella looked around what would be her bedroom. "It will be pink," she whispered. "But I'm not telling Dad because I want it to be a surprise."

Rachel smiled. Bella's favorite color in the whole world was pink. She had pink stockings, pink sweaters, and even a pink lunch box. John would have to pull out his best acting face to look surprised when Bella told him.

"Dad's bedroom is over there..." Bella waved to her left, "and there are four other bedrooms along the landing."

"Four?" Rachel pretended to be surprised. It made sense to build a house with more rooms than John and Bella needed. With Big Sky resort so close, and another amazing ski season underway, John's family and friends could easily make his home their vacation base.

Bella pulled Rachel closer. "I'm getting lots of brothers and sisters one day."

The plans in John's hands fell to the ground. He picked them up and quickly glanced at Rachel. He cleared his throat and looked at his daughter. "I don't know if that will ever happen, Bella."

"I overheard Poppy's mom say you're a catch. What does that mean?"

John's eyes widened. He looked so flustered that Rachel smiled.

"It means your dad's handsome and nice." John's gaze stayed on her. Rachel's heart raced. She tried to think of something else to say, but the look on John's face was turning her brain to mush.

"Like Franky," Bella sighed. "He's handsome and nice, too."

John's gaze dropped to his daughter. "Franky?"

"From drama club," Bella said with a smile. "He has the most beautiful voice ever."

Bella had been to drama club three times, and she'd loved every minute. She enjoyed the company of the other children, including Franky.

Rachel wanted to tell John it was okay, that he didn't need the frown that was on his face. Franky was a nice boy. If John made a big deal out of what Bella had said, it could spoil the friendship that his daughter was making.

Rachel walked across to John and stood in front of him. "Tell me about the rest of the house. What room is your favorite?"

His eyes narrowed.

"Remember that you're handsome and nice," she whispered. "We can talk about Franky later."

John's blue eyes held hers, softened, then left her spellbound. All the talk about children and boyfriends was making Rachel's thoughts go to places they shouldn't. It was bad enough she was attracted to her student's dad. Worse that she was attracted to a workaholic.

John sent her a questioning glance before opening the house plans. "My favorite room is the living room."

He showed her the last page of the plans and she sighed. "It's lovely." The architect had made a three-dimensional image of what the living room would look like. With its exposed timber ceiling, stone fireplace, and slate floors, it was the kind of rustic hideaway anyone would enjoy coming home to.

"The floors are heated. You'll be able to walk around in bare feet in the middle of winter."

Rachel moved closer, studying the colors the architect had chosen, the way he'd placed the furniture and fittings. "I like the shape of the sofas and chairs."

"The furniture and paint colors haven't been finalized. I have to let our interior designer know what we want."

"It will be a beautiful home no matter what you choose." She looked at the plans, then across at the lake. "You'll see the entire lake from the living room."

John nodded. "The building sites for the other properties are closer to the water. By being back from the lake, we get more of a panoramic view and it keeps Bella away from the water."

"You're worried about her?"

John's gaze caught hers. They were standing close, closer than Rachel realized. If she stood on tiptoes, she could have kissed the frown off his face, taken away the worry clouding his eyes.

John's gaze lingered on her mouth. "I'm always worried about Bella," he said gently. "She means everything to me."

Rachel jammed her hands into her pockets in case she was tempted to pull him close. Taking a step backward, she focused on the house plans. "The architect has done a wonderful job. Bella will love living here."

John opened his mouth to say something, but Bella rushed across to them. "Look at the lake."

Rachel turned to see what Bella was so excited about. Close to shore, farther around the lake, someone was ice skating. Her blades sent a fine spray of snow into the air as she twisted and turned, dancing to the music filling her head. "Do you know who it is?"

John shook his head. "Maybe she's a friend of Jacob and Molly's. She's closer to their property than ours."

Rachel held her breath as the woman jumped into the air. Twisting into a spin, she landed safely with one leg extended and her arms open wide.

Bella looked up at her dad. "Can we go and see her?"

"She's too far away. By the time we get down there, she'll probably be gone." John looked back at the skater. She was turning slowly in a figure eight, cutting the ice like someone who was born on skates. "Next time I'm talking to Jacob I'll ask him if he knows who she is."

"Do you think I could learn how to skate?" Bella asked her dad.

"After you start swimming lessons," John promised.

Bella looked at the lake. "I bet she's been in the Olympics."

The wistful note in Bella's voice made Rachel smile. "You could write a story about an ice skater tomorrow. She could have all sorts of adventures."

"She could be an ice skater who's a princess." Bella held her dad's hand. "A handsome prince could rescue her from something terrible."

John put the house plans in his pocket and lifted Bella into his arms. "Before any rescuing takes place, do you want lunch? Mrs. Daniels made us a picnic."

Bella wiggled free of her dad's hug. As soon as her feet hit the snow she ran toward the helicopter. "First one to the helicopter gets to choose a cookie."

John looked at Rachel and grinned. "What do you think?"

Rachel didn't wait to find out whether he was talking about a picnic or something else. She started running after Bella, determined to put more than distance between John and her feelings for him.

Some things were better left undone, and this was one of them.

CHAPTER 10

*J*ohn closed his eyes and rested his head on the back of his brother's sofa. This last week had gone from bad to worse. The only good thing to come out of everything was the trip with Bella and Rachel to Emerald Lake.

Grant nudged his feet on his way past. "You can't fool me. You're not asleep, you're avoiding my questions."

"Which one?" John opened one eye. "And if it's the one about my non-existent love life, then you won't get an answer."

Grant grunted. "Fine. Start with the teacher. Does Rachel enjoy working with Bella?"

"Of course, she does. What's not to like?"

"Oh, I don't know. The gorilla beside me could have an influence on her happiness. I heard you went to Emerald Lake the other day."

That got John's attention. "How did you find out?"

"Mrs. Daniels," Grant said smugly. "I called her to see where you were. She told me you'd taken a helicopter out to the lake. Did you see much apart from the snow and ice?"

"Scoff all you like. I wanted to see what the view from the house would be like in winter."

"You took a helicopter out for that? You have more money than common sense."

"Probably," John muttered. "So, how's the world of mountain rescue?"

John's brother had been a volunteer with the Gallatin County Search and Rescue Team for the last eight years. He'd seen some horrific accidents but, he kept going back, year after year, to help the people who needed it.

Grant left his mug of coffee on the table in front of him. "Avalanche season is well and truly here. We had a fatality on Sunday. A family was out on their snowmobiles and triggered an avalanche. Their teenage son was killed." He shook his head. "You'd think they'd learn by now. We've been issuing warnings all week. They had all the safety gear you can buy, but it didn't help their son."

"How was the team after you returned?"

"Not great, but they pulled two of the family out, so that was something. You changed the subject."

"It didn't work for long."

Grant pointed at the newspaper. "The fighting in the Middle East looks as though it's getting worse. Another five soldiers were killed in separate suicide bombings last week. Do you think your drone can help?"

John hadn't told Grant much about the prototype drone he'd been working on. It was more than commercially sensitive information. If what he'd learned last week was true, it could be deadly.

"It has the potential to help. But that's up to the Department of Defense. They own the technology." John wished it was that simple. It could have been, but people with more money than he'd ever see were spinning the militia wheels in Europe.

"Are you sure everything's okay? You've been looking more stressed than usual over the last few weeks." Grant looked closely at him. "You can't tell me, can you?"

John nodded. "I wish I could, but it would put you in danger."

"What have you gotten yourself into?"

"More than I thought."

"You could always go to Dad's hideout. He might have been extreme, but he was prepared."

John and Grant had the same mom, but different fathers. Grant's dad had been a survivalist. He'd created a world within a world, preparing for the worst that could hit mankind. Unfortunately, it wasn't a post-apocalyptic America that had killed him. It was a car accident fifty miles southwest of Chinook.

A year after he'd died, Grant's mom met and married John's dad, a rancher from Bozeman. John arrived a year later and he'd never thought of Grant as anything other than his brother.

John closed his eyes and tried to sort through the words he wanted to say. "I don't need to use the hideout. Not yet."

"You'll tell me if it gets worse?"

John nodded. "I'll tell you as much as I can."

Grant looked at him over the rim of his mug. "Just so you know, I restocked the house with fresh water and food last month."

"You don't believe in conspiracy theories or end of the world predictions."

Grant smiled. "I guess I'm more like my dad than I think. I like to be prepared, and his bunker makes more sense than most things in life."

The bunker Grant was referring to wasn't your standard subterranean hole in the ground. It was an elaborate network of rooms that were linked together in Hill County, Montana.

Grant scowled at John. "Is the money you've made worth what you've been through?"

"It's not as simple as that."

"Sure it is."

John's life hadn't been simple for the last six years. He'd pushed himself hard and told himself it was because he wanted to provide a good home for Bella. But it went deeper than that. Making money was his way of proving he was more than the grieving single parent who'd returned from the Middle East.

He was a former Navy SEAL and no one would threaten his family.

"You're not thinking of doing anything stupid, are you?"

He glanced at his brother. "You know me, cautious to the core."

"Yeah, right. You're the least cautious person I know. If you get into trouble, head to Dad's bunker."

John's cell phone beeped in his pocket. He pulled it out and looked at the caller display. "I have to take this." He pushed a button and held the phone to his ear. "What is it, Tanner?"

"Simon called. The New Orleans contract is in trouble."

"I'm on my way."

Grant didn't bother asking what had happened. He handed John his jacket and pulled him into a hug. "Don't do anything stupid. You have a daughter and a brother who love you."

"I'll never forget." He opened the front door and walked down the icy porch steps.

Something beyond the normal issues his company dealt with was going on, and he knew who was behind it.

RACHEL ADJUSTED a little girl's angel wings, then moved to the next child in front of her. The drama club's Christmas play would start in fifteen minutes. It was a sell-out audience and all the children's parents, except two, were sitting in the library auditorium, waiting for the opening song.

Bella raced across the stage and stood beside Rachel. Her usually sunny smile was nowhere in sight. "He's not here, yet. Mrs. Daniels is sitting beside Tanner, but I can't see Dad."

Rachel gave Bella a quick hug. "He said he'd try to be here. Tanner's recording the play, so even if your dad isn't here, he'll still get to see it."

"But it's not the same." Bella's hands were fluttering at her side and her eyes were full of tears. "He said he'd be here. Everyone else's parents are here except my dad."

Franky was next in line, waiting for his final inspection before taking his place on stage. "My dad's not here either," he said quietly. "He had to work at the gas station."

Bella's big brown eyes settled on her friend. "Did he try his hardest to be here?"

Franky nodded. "He doesn't get much time off. He said he's here in spirit, whatever that means."

Rachel straightened Franky's halo. "It means he wishes he was here. When you're singing on stage, your dad will be sending lots of love your way."

"But it's not the same as being here." Bella blinked back the tears from her eyes and looked at Franky. "Is someone else here from your family?"

Franky shook his head.

"You could borrow Tanner's video. He's pretty good and won't miss much."

Franky looked down at the ground, studying his worn sneakers as if they were covered in gold. "We don't have anything to play it on."

Bella's hands stopped twisting together. "You could come

to my house with your dad. We could watch the play together and tell them about the parts Tanner missed."

Franky's gaze never left Bella. He was such a serious little boy that Rachel had no idea what he was thinking. The librarian who helped at drama club told her Franky's dad worked at a gas station, earning what little he could to support his family. He didn't have a lot, but he did love his children.

"I don't know if coming to your house is a good idea." Franky lowered his voice. "Dad's not home very much. It might not suit your dad to have us there."

"My dad won't mind," Bella said slowly. "He's not home very often, either." She glanced back at the curtain spread across the stage. "At least Mrs. Daniels and Tanner are here."

Franky nodded. "Your dad could be here in spirit, the same as mine."

Bella took a deep breath and straightened her dress. "I guess he could. I'd better stand in my place. Thanks, Franky."

He nodded solemnly and watched Bella run across the stage. "Do you think Mr. Fletcher will make it, Ms. McReedy?"

Rachel gave his halo one last tweak. "I don't know, Franky. But what you said to Bella made her feel better. Your dad would be proud of you."

"Dad says sometimes life doesn't turn out the way you want it to. You gotta make lemonade out of lemons."

"That you do, Franky." Rachel blinked back the tears in her eyes and plastered a smile on her face. "You look very handsome in your angel costume. Are you ready for your song?"

"Yes, ma'am. I've been practicing real hard."

"Enjoy every minute. Go and stand in your place. We only have ten minutes before the curtain opens."

Franky ran to his place in the choir and Rachel moved to

the next child in line. John had left for New Orleans two days ago. She didn't know what was going on, but it must have been serious.

Tanner and Tank were sticking to Bella and her like glue. Bella almost hadn't been able to come tonight. After nothing short of pleading, John reluctantly agreed with Rachel and let his daughter perform with the drama club.

Now all she needed to do was make sure everyone remembered their lines, cue the choir to sing at the right times, and keep Bella safe.

Not your typical Friday night in downtown Bozeman.

JOHN WALKED into the main entrance of the library, checking his watch for the hundredth time. He'd called Tanner on his way out of the airport, checking to see where Bella was. His flight had been so late leaving that he'd half expected her to already be at home. But she was still at the library, enjoying the after-play party with the other children.

He turned left toward the auditorium, making room for a group of children dressed as shepherds and angels. They passed him in the hallway, talking ten to the dozen, laughing with their parents about tonight's performance.

John wasn't looking forward to hearing what his daughter had to say. He might have found some of the people responsible for sabotaging his business, but he'd let Bella down. It was bad enough she didn't have her mom with her. All she had was a delinquent Dad who disappeared for days on end.

He opened the auditorium doors and stepped inside. Down one end of the room was the stage. A painted stable took pride of place in the center, with a bright star hanging above it. In another corner of the auditorium, tables filled with food were clustered together. John looked at the speakers mounted on the walls. Christmas music competed with excited voices, filling the room with a barrage of noise.

He looked for Tanner. His cell phone vibrated and he took it out of his pocket. *Under the mistletoe on your right.*

John knew Tanner had a sick sense of humor, but his text was a fitting end to the worst few days of his life. If Tanner thought he would kiss someone under a plastic piece of mistletoe, he was wrong.

His gaze traveled across the room, stopping when he saw his bodyguard standing beside Bella. Tanner knelt down, smiled up at the camera, and hardly blinked when the flash shone in his eyes. The mistletoe dangled above their heads like a giant spider, waiting for the next person in line to succumb to some Christmas madness.

"I didn't think you'd make it," Rachel said from beside him.

John stuck his hands in his pockets and kept his gaze locked on his daughter. "It took longer to sort the problem out than I thought."

"You're lucky Bella is so forgiving. She was disappointed you weren't here."

He bit back the words that rushed to his mouth. "You think I don't know that?"

Rachel crossed her arms in front of her chest and glared at him. "I know I'm only Bella's tutor, and I probably don't have the right to say what I'm going to say—"

"But you're going to say it anyway?"

Rachel took a deep breath. "Forgiveness only lasts so long. One day you'll wake up and Bella will be eighteen years old and ready to leave home. You'll regret the times you missed something important in her life. What happened to your face?"

He touched the edge of his bruised jaw. "I ran into a door."

"Last time I checked, doors didn't come with knuckles. Have you seen a doctor?"

"I can talk and eat. I don't need a doctor."

Rachel rolled her eyes. "It's not bad enough you're a workaholic, now you're being plain stupid. You could have broken a bone or something worse."

"There isn't much that can go wrong with a jaw."

Rachel's low growl sent goose bumps along his skin. "It's not your jaw the doctor needs to check—it's your brain."

A group of children and their parents stood in front of them, taking photos of each other.

Rachel pulled him to the side of the room and stood toe to toe with him. "Only someone with nothing between their ears would drop everything and get into a fight. Especially if they were in some out of the way place."

"New Orleans isn't some out of the way place, and I didn't choose to get into a fight. We were ambushed by six men in full body armor. You try getting out of that without a few scrapes and bruises."

"What were you doing in a fight? You're supposed to be a pen-pushing businessman, not Rambo on steroids. You were lucky you didn't get shot."

He clamped his jaw tight, groaned, then stepped away from Rachel's laser beam stare.

"You were shot?" Her mouth dropped open. "Where?"

"It's only a graze."

Her eyes narrowed. "Where?"

"My arm. What's gotten into you, anyway? You haven't strung so many words together since I met you."

"I haven't said anything because I didn't know whether you were deliberately keeping away from Bella, or you couldn't help it. I'm worried about her. She misses you."

"And which one is it?"

Rachel frowned.

"Am I deliberately keeping away from her or can't I help it?"

"I don't think you're doing it on purpose. But maybe you could ask someone else to sort out the problems at your work?"

John looked back at the mistletoe. He'd been thinking the same thing, but he wouldn't talk about that in the middle of the auditorium.

Bella was still standing under the mistletoe, but this time she was standing beside a tall, skinny boy with red hair. The angel halo attached to his head shone in the overhead lights. "Isn't that the boy with the amazing voice?"

Rachel glared at him before turning her attention to Bella and her friend. "That's Franky. And yes, he has an amazing voice. I'm surprised you remembered."

John wasn't going to answer her. He was going to see his daughter.

"Your brother called Bella to wish her all the best. He seems like a nice person."

John grunted. He walked around another group of people and Rachel followed him.

"He said he'd come to the play to watch Bella, but she wanted to keep the seat for you."

"If you're trying to make me feel worse, you're doing a good job."

Rachel walked ahead of him and stopped him in his tracks. "I don't want you to feel worse. I want you to spend more time with your daughter."

"Dad?" Bella side-stepped around Rachel and headed straight into his arms. "I missed you. Is everything okay?"

He held her close. "Everything's fine. How was the play?"

Bella's face glowed as bright as the lights on the

Christmas tree behind her. "It was wonderful. I remembered all the words to the songs."

"That's great, Bella."

"Why couldn't you be here?"

John looked into her brown eyes and felt like the worst father in the world. "Some people were trying to hurt a person who asked for our help. I needed to make sure the person arrived home for Christmas."

"And did they?"

John nodded.

"That's okay, then. Franky's dad couldn't make it either. Can we invite him to our place to watch the play? Tanner recorded it on his phone. He said he didn't miss anything this time."

He pulled Bella into his arms. "Franky and his dad can come over for dinner, if they want to. If Franky gives us his phone number, I'll give his dad a call."

"Okay. I'll find Franky now." Bella darted between the people behind her. Tanner moved fast to keep up with her.

"Does she need a bodyguard all the time?" Rachel whispered.

John wiped his hand over his eyes. He was so tired he could have fallen asleep standing up. "I need to talk to you about what happened today, but I can't do it here. We need to go home."

Rachel put a hand on his forehead. "You have a temperature." She looked across the room and waved at Patty Daniels. Within seconds, John's housekeeper was standing beside them.

"John isn't well, Patty. Can you take him out to his truck while I find Tanner and Bella?"

"I'll be all right. No one died from a temperature."

Rachel stuck her hands on her hips and glared at him.

"You're as stubborn as a mule, too. I'm not taking no for an answer. Where's Tank?"

"In my truck," he muttered.

"Thank goodness. Patty, tell Tank to take John to the hospital. We'll meet you there."

He wondered where Rachel's bossy streak had suddenly come from. He turned to say something to her, but she'd disappeared into the crowd of people around them.

Patty linked her hand under his elbow. "You'd better come with me. Why are we going to the hospital?"

"We aren't. We're going home."

"Are you sure?"

"As sure as I've been about anything in the last few weeks." John glanced around the room one last time. Tanner was walking toward him, talking to someone on his cell phone. Bella and Rachel were beside him.

At least they were together tonight. What happened tomorrow would be a whole different problem.

CHAPTER 11

"I'm not staying here," Rachel said. She was sitting in John's kitchen, enjoying a hot cup of tea with Patty, when John walked into the room. He'd had a shower, changed his clothes, and come up with his silliest idea yet.

At exactly ten o'clock at night, he'd told her she was staying at his house. Not for the night, not even for the week. But for the next month, or until whatever mess he'd made was sorted out. And what annoyed her the most was that he hadn't even asked if it was okay. He'd told her.

He didn't want to know what she thought about staying in his house or if there were other things she needed to do. His decision wasn't open for discussion.

Patty had wisely left them to their conversation. After John's first earth shattering announcement, Rachel wished she'd gone straight home from the Christmas play instead of waiting to see if he was all right.

"You don't have a choice." John sat at the table opposite her, frowning something fierce.

If he thought he could intimidate her with his macho-man tactics, he was wrong. "Of course, I have a choice. I have a life that involves more than these four walls. I will not hide inside while the rest of the world celebrates Christmas."

"You don't have to hide. You can do whatever you want, but I can't risk letting you go home each afternoon on your own."

"Fine. Ask one of your bodyguards to stay with me. My apartment isn't big, but I have a spare bed. They could drive with me to work each morning."

"You're safer here."

Rachel felt like stamping her foot. "I don't want to stay here."

John's mouth set into a grim line. "It's better than being kidnapped."

"What are you talking about? No one wants to kidnap me." She thought about the bullet graze on his arm, the antibiotics the doctor had given him. "You're delusional. You need to go to bed."

"I am not delusional."

"Don't tell me this is payback for making you see a doctor? It's just as well Tank and Tanner have some common sense between their ears. If you hadn't gone to the hospital, you could have been a lot worse than you are now."

John dropped his head into his hands. "What did I do to deserve you in my life?"

Rachel snorted. "Nowhere in my contract does it state I have to live here. And if someone's trying to kidnap me, then they'd better be worried. I've done self-defense classes and I know how to use a frying pan."

"A what?"

"A frying pan," Rachel said slowly in case his brain was having a hard time keeping up with their conversation. "You know. A metal pan with a handle that you use for frying food."

"I know what a frying pan is. What does it have to do

with being kidnapped?"

Rachel sighed. "You'd know if you were hit over the head with one."

John tilted his head to the side. "You're crazy."

"If you think that intelligent observation will change my mind about staying here, you're wrong." She picked up her mug and took it across to the kitchen counter. "In case I don't see you before Christmas, enjoy your vacation."

She opened the dishwasher and stacked her mug inside. "If you haven't already bought Bella a Christmas present, she was hoping Santa might bring her a puppy. But with what's happening in your life, I'd say it was the last thing you need."

Rachel turned toward the kitchen door and stopped. John stood in the doorway with his arms planted either side of the frame.

"What are you doing?" she asked.

"There's no point squinting your eyes at me like a ninja turtle. And don't get any ideas about using your karate moves on me. I was a Navy SEAL. I know how to protect myself."

Rachel walked up to him and poked him in the stomach with her finger. Okay, so he had tight abs, but that didn't mean she believed him. "You were punched in the face and shot in the arm. I'd say your defensive moves are a bit rusty."

"Really?"

Rachel didn't like the way he was looking at her. She squared her shoulders and waited to see what he'd do next.

When he didn't move, she went through her list of vulnerable parts on the human body. She could poke him in the eyes, nose and throat, but she didn't want to hurt him too much. That took out the groin and knees as well. She could always karate chop his arm where the bullet had scraped his skin, but that would be mean. That only left his stomach, and she knew how hard those muscles were.

His smile was enough to make her wish she'd been born bad.

"It's not as easy as it looks, is it?"

John had no idea what he'd just unleashed. There were lots of ways to be bad, and some of them didn't involve a whole lot of physical violence. In fact, some of them just required a steady hand and a devious mind. Rachel pulled her bad girl out and decided to work with what she had.

She stepped closer and John's smile disappeared.

Instead of a short, sharp jab to his abdomen, she ran her hands across his shoulders and down his chest. She stopped at the buttons in front of her nose. "Some people find these types of situations really easy to deal with."

John swallowed. "They do?"

Rachel nodded and took half a step forward. It was amazing what that small step did for her confidence. She could see John's pulse jump in the base of his throat, hear his breathing speed up and match her own.

Before she lost track of why she was standing hip-to-hip with her boss, her hands moved again, stroking John's chest through his shirt, creating havoc with both their heartbeats.

Maybe this wasn't such a good idea.

"Rachel?"

She lifted her face to his, focused on what she was about to do.

"Unless you want me to kiss you, I'd suggest we stop this now." When she didn't move, he dipped his head close.

Just before their lips touched, she moved her hands to his ribs and started tickling him. He jumped back, banged his arm on the doorframe, and said a word Mrs. Daniels wouldn't like.

"You really are crazy," he said as she slipped past him and ran for the front door.

"Takes one to know one," Rachel said over her shoulder as

she threw open the door. "Tell Bella I'll see her on Monday." She turned to run outside and ended up plastered against a hard male chest.

A pair of vice-like hands lifted her back inside. "Everything okay in here, boss?"

Rachel blinked a few times before she figured out what had happened. "Tank?"

"Yes, ma'am."

"What are you doing here?"

"Making sure you don't go home."

She stepped away from him and threw her arms in the air. "I don't believe this. You can't make me stay in this house."

John kept his gaze focused on her. "I've already spoken with the local police, the FBI, and the CIA. They want you to stay here."

Tank put his hand on the door handle. "I'll leave you alone. If you need me, I'll be outside." He shut the front door and left Rachel with one less escape route.

She looked at John. His half-amused smile reminded her of a cat who knew a bowl of cream wasn't far away. "You can get that smile off your face, John Fletcher. There'll be no repeat of our up close and snuggly moment. I was trying to get away from you, not kiss you senseless."

He sighed. "I'm getting too old for this."

"For the first time tonight you're actually making sense."

"You think so?"

Rachel tilted her nose in the air. "I know so."

He took a step forward. "Really? So how do you account for the blush on your face?"

Rachel put her hands to her cheeks and felt the heat of her bad girl actions. "It's warm inside, that's all. Now, if you've finished annoying me, I'm going to bed."

John's eyebrows rose.

"Alone, so don't get any funny ideas."

"I wouldn't dream of it. If we were sleeping together, I'd have to tie you to the bedposts to make sure you didn't strangle me during the night."

Rachel always knew she had an over-active imagination, but the pictures inside her head were way too x-rated for even a bad girl. She ignored the wave of heat hitting her face and turned toward the stairs. "I'll sleep in the same room I did last time."

John didn't move or say anything.

She looked over her shoulder as she walked up the stairs. John's heated gaze followed each step she took. Rachel smiled. She wasn't much of a bad girl, but it looked as though John appreciated her efforts.

RACHEL PUSHED the shopping cart down aisle three, then stopped to consult her list. "How many sets of Christmas lights do you think we need, Bella?"

Bella looked along the shelves. "Ten."

Tank groaned from behind them. "No one needs ten sets of lights."

Rachel held her hand to her ear. "My goodness, Bella. I think I heard the Christmas Grinch speaking." She waved her hand at the shelves. "Hand me what you want and I'll put them in the cart."

Bella quickly chose an assortment of lights. "What's next?"

"Tinsel." Rachel pushed the cart down the aisle, turned right and sighed at the rainbow of sparkly tinsel lining the shelves.

"It looks cheap," Tank said from behind her.

Rachel raised her eyebrows. "Is this pearl of wisdom

coming from a man who wanted to buy a blow-up Santa for the front porch?"

Tank crossed his muscly arms in front of his chest. "He was six-foot tall and had glowing lights inside him. I know quality when I see it."

"And we could have bought a matching reindeer," Bella said with more than a tinge of disappointment in her voice. "He would have looked good beside Santa."

Rachel tapped her list. "Focus people. We're here for interior decorations—and for junior ears, that means decorations for inside the house. I don't want to scare your dad before he walks in the front door."

Tank picked up a bright red packet of tinsel. "I don't like to burst your bubble, but he'll be mad whichever way you do it."

Rachel plucked the tinsel out of his hand and threw it in the cart. "Thank you for your vote of confidence. We'll have six more of those."

"There's ten-feet of tinsel in each packet," he said.

"You're right. You'd better make it ten packets."

Bella giggled as Tank started stacking tinsel. "This is fun. Why doesn't Dad like Christmas decorations, Tank?"

"You'll have to ask your dad." He looked around the store. "We'd better hurry if you want to put these decorations up tonight. It will take me a couple of hours to hang everything."

"Don't forget the tree. I saw a ranch selling Christmas trees on the way into town." Rachel walked along the aisle and pointed to the Christmas tree decorations. "What color do you want, Bella?"

"I want lots of colors. Can we have two of each?"

Rachel calculated how many decorations were hanging on each row and multiplied it by the number of columns. Two of each would be perfect. "You start down one end, and I'll go down the other. Tank can be our stacker."

Tank leaned forward. "You know I'm a bodyguard, don't you? I'm not your personal shopper."

Rachel patted his cheek. "Think of it as multi-tasking. If I have to stay in John's home, then I'm going to make it look as though it's Christmas. There isn't one decoration anywhere."

"Now we've got lots," Bella said proudly. "The decorations are so pretty. Dad won't know what to say."

Rachel had a feeling that would be the case regardless of what they bought. So rather than buy one or two token decorations, she was going the whole way. The house would be so bright and shiny that John wouldn't be able to find fault with anything.

"This will cost you a fortune," Tank said as he took another two decorations out of Bella's hands.

"Walmart never breaks the bank, and everything's half price. You can't go wrong."

Tank muttered something under his breath as Rachel loaded her decorations into the cart. She looked at the number of decorations, then back at the cart. "We need more room. I'll get another cart while you fill this one."

"You aren't going anywhere on your own. If you're heading to the front of the store, we're all going."

"Isn't that a little extreme? John's not here now. I won't tell him if you don't."

"I need to go with you."

"But it's such a short distance away. The longer it takes for us to talk about it, the sooner I could have been back here."

Tank turned the cart around and waited for Bella and Rachel to walk with him. "Like I said. All for one and one for all."

Bella danced beside Tank. "I know who said that. The Three Musketeers."

He looked down at her and smiled. "You know your stories."

"I love books. Dad says I'll turn into a bookworm one day."

A loud noise erupted from somewhere in front of them. Before Rachel could look over the aisles to see what was going on, Tank grabbed their hands and started running toward the back of the store.

"Keep your heads down and follow me."

"What about our decorations?" Bella wailed. "Someone might take them."

"Wait here." Tank crouched behind an aisle and scanned the store. Twenty feet away, an exit sign glowed on the wall.

Rachel glanced over her shoulder and tried to see what was going on. There was a lot of raised voices and banging still coming from the front of the store.

Tank pulled her and Bella down beside him. "Keep low and stay here."

"Wait. I think I heard someone laugh," Rachel whispered to Tank. "People don't laugh when it's something serious."

"When I hear gunfire, everything is serious."

"Shouldn't we at least see what's going on?" Rachel slid farther down the aisle, trying to see if anyone else was hiding.

Tank growled low in his throat. "We leave now and ask questions later."

"Excuse me? Can I help you?"

Rachel spun on her knees and saw a pair of black sneakers behind Tank. Above the sneakers was a pair of khaki-colored trousers and a Walmart shirt. "Caitlin? What are you doing here?"

"Hi, Rachel. I still work here when Tess doesn't need me at the café. It helps pay for college. What are you doing on the floor?"

Tank pulled Caitlin's hand until she was sitting beside them. "I heard a gun. We're getting out of here."

"It wasn't a gun," Caitlin explained. "The store had a competition to see who could pop the most balloons in two minutes. They held the final round outside the main entrance."

"They were balloons?" Tank looked almost as surprised as Rachel.

Caitlin nodded. "Walmart is the main sponsor of the competition."

Tank frowned at Rachel as if this was her fault.

She pushed her hair out of her eyes and stood up. "I guess we can keep shopping."

Caitlin looked between Tank and Rachel. "What's going on? Do I need to tell the store manager something?"

Bella jumped in the air like a jack-in-a-box. "Tank's making sure we're safe. Do you have any angels for the top of our Christmas tree?"

"Sure. Follow me."

Tank rolled to his feet. He grabbed hold of Rachel's hand and pulled her along the aisle behind Caitlin and Bella.

Rachel looked down the aisles they passed. "What about our cart?"

"I'm more interested in where Bella's going," Tank growled.

Rachel tried tugging her fingers out of his hand. "In case you haven't noticed, there's a big sale. If we leave our cart in the aisle, someone will take what's in it."

"It's not like you've chosen one-off decorations. They're made in China, for Pete's sake. There are thousands of the same decorations everywhere."

Caitlin stopped at a display of Christmas angels. "Here you go. These are half price as well."

Tank looked unimpressed with the display.

Caitlin put on her most professional face and smiled at Tank. "It's true that most of our decorations are made in China. But Walmart guarantees the quality of all its products. There's something for everyone in our stores."

"Like glow-in-the-dark Santas," Rachel said with a grin aimed straight at Tank.

Tank kept quiet.

Rachel studied the angel display. Some were made from glass, others from plastic with lights flickering in their bases.

Bella pointed to an angel with big, glittery wings and a red dress. "That's the one." She looked up at Tank and smiled. "It will look pretty on our tree."

Tank took the angel off the display. "Are you sure?"

"I'm sure," Bella said with a firm nod of her head. "Thank you for coming with us, Tank. This is the best Christmas ever."

Tank, the man most unlikely to be swayed by feminine attention, practically melted on the spot. He cleared his throat and patted Bella on the head. "I'm glad you're happy. Now let's find our cart and get out of here."

Rachel didn't need to be told twice. She hurried across the store and found their cart sitting forlornly in the middle of an aisle. "We're lucky it's so close to Christmas. Most people have bought their decorations by now."

"We're late bloomers," Bella said proudly.

Tank froze. "Who told you about late bloomers?"

"Mrs. Daniels. Poppy's getting a training bra for Christmas. When I asked Mrs. Daniels when I'd be getting a bra, she said I'm a late bloomer. We all get there in the end but, sometimes, it takes a little longer."

"That's too much information," Tank muttered as he pushed their cart toward a checkout counter.

Rachel took hold of Bella's hand and smiled at the blush on Tank's face. "Mrs. Daniels is a wise woman."

CHAPTER 12

*J*ohn opened the front door and stared at the entranceway.

"Surprise!" Bella shouted from the staircase. "Do you like what we've done?"

John's mouth dropped open and his mind went blank. He hadn't seen so much tinsel in one place in years. Six years.

"Your dad's blown away by how beautiful it is, aren't you, John?" Rachel looked down from the top of the ladder.

"What do you think you're doing?"

Rachel stuck another piece of tape on the ornament that was hanging below his chandelier. "We're bringing the Christmas spirit indoors."

Bella ran down the stairs and hugged her dad. "Isn't it great? We went shopping and bought a whole cart of decorations. Tank thought someone was shooting at us and we found a blow-up Santa. We weren't going to bring it home, but Tank thought it was too good a bargain not to buy it."

Bella was looking at him expectantly, waiting for him to say something that made sense. "Someone shot at you?" He was struggling to keep his voice level.

"No." Rachel wobbled on the ladder and he reached out to steady it. "Thanks. There were no guns. It was a balloon popping competition."

"And you thought it was a gun?"

Bella took a decoration out of the box on the hall table. "Tank thought it was a gun. We crouched on the ground and looked for a safe way out of the store. Do you want to see our Christmas tree?"

John wiped his hand across his eyes. "You bought a tree?"

Tank stuck his head around the edge of the doorframe. "Sorry, boss. There was no stopping them."

Rachel sent Tank a withering glare. "Did you, or did you not, have a good time buying the Christmas decorations?"

"I did once Santa was in my truck."

Bella grabbed hold of her dad's hand and pulled him into the living room. "We haven't put the Christmas angel on the top. We were waiting for you."

John stood in the middle of the room and looked at the Christmas tree. It was loaded with decorations in all sorts of colors, shapes, and sizes. Tinsel glittered from the branches and sparkling fairy lights flashed slowly through the tree.

Once he was used to the tree, he let his gaze wander around the rest of the room. A huge blow-up Santa and a reindeer sat in one corner, glowing from some kind of light inside them. The coffee table was decorated with a red table-cloth, pinecones, and candles. And to bring the whole night-mare together was Christmas music, wafting through the room on the sound system.

He didn't know what to say.

Rachel was looking at him, prompting his sluggish brain into saying something that was so far from the truth it wasn't funny. Until now, he'd kept their Christmas celebrations to a minimum. They'd unpack a small artificial tree, drive into town to see the Christmas parade, and go to church with Patty and her husband.

This year he'd been thrown head-first into the festive season, whether he wanted to be there or not.

Bella handed him a red and gold Christmas angel. "She's really pretty. Can you reach the top of the tree?"

"Wait there." Rachel darted out of the room and came back carrying the ladder. "This should work."

Her smile was supposed to be encouraging, only he couldn't see any reason to be part of what they'd created. Until he looked at Bella. Her eyes were full of excitement and wonder and so many other things he'd forgotten. He felt like a cold-hearted fool.

Tank opened the ladder. "You okay?"

John nodded. He had to be. Bella was looking at him as if this was the most natural thing in the world for him to do. But it wasn't, not by a long shot.

The smile on Rachel's face disappeared. She watched him closely, wisely choosing not to say anything.

Bella followed every step he took on the ladder. "Higher, Dad. The angel needs to be at the top of the tree."

He took another step, slipping the tie at the back of the angel around the tallest branch. "Is that all right?"

"Perfect." Bella sighed. "I'll get some Christmas cookies. We could have them with a big glass of milk."

John was grateful Tank went with Bella. He needed a few minutes to pull himself together and get over the shock of seeing so much tinsel.

"What's wrong?" Rachel asked as soon as Bella was out of the room.

"I don't do Christmas, not like this." He climbed down the ladder and sat on the sofa. Everything looked so shiny and new.

"I thought Tank was exaggerating."

"Tank never exaggerates." He listened to Bella chatting to Tank, the sound of her laughter as she got her cookies ready for them.

Rachel sat beside him. "Why don't you like Christmas?"

He kept his gaze focused on the fireplace. Red and orange flames leaped in the air. "My wife, Jacinta, died a week before Christmas. We buried her on Christmas Eve. Bella was hurt in the car accident and missed her mom's funeral."

"I'm sorry."

"You didn't know. I try to make it a good day for Bella, but something inside of me refuses to forget what happened. It took me three days to get back from Afghanistan after the accident. Jacinta's parents looked after Bella in the hospital. They wanted me to leave her with them."

"For how long?"

"Permanently." He could still hear Jacinta's parents arguing with him, trying to convince him Bella was better off with them. The cold logic of why they would make better parents made sense. He'd been overseas for most of the first two years of Bella's life. He knew nothing about looking after a toddler, and even less about being a dad.

When he left the military he had no job, a home he was a stranger in, and a daughter who kept asking for her mommy. He'd barely survived the first six months without Jacinta. But life had gone on. Jacinta's parents had given up waiting for him to fail and he'd realized being a dad wasn't as hard as he thought it would be.

John looked across the room at the blow-up Santa. "I think the reindeer and Santa are supposed to be outside."

"We didn't want to scare you."

The smile in Rachel's voice cut through the memories inside his head. "It must have cost you a fortune for the decorations. I'll give you the money for them."

"No, you won't. Everything was half price."

Tank walked into the room carrying a tray with four mugs on it. "Remind me to swap with Tanner next time Rachel wants to go shopping."

"You don't want to admit that you had fun." Rachel took the mug Tank held out to her and looked inside. "You made me hot chocolate?"

"I thought you'd like it better than milk."

The smile Rachel sent Tank made John frown. "Is there anything else you've planned and haven't told me about?"

Bella left a plate of cookies on the table. She sat on the other side of John, leaning in close. "We bought you some presents," she whispered, "but Rachel said I can't tell you what they are. They're a surprise."

He glanced at Rachel. She was sipping her drink, watching Bella. She hadn't learned that his daughter was hopeless at keeping secrets. After a few hours, the excitement of keeping information inside her was too much, and she'd tell everyone what she knew. "Have you gone decoration crazy in the rest of the house?"

Bella shook her head. "Mrs. Daniels had already unpacked the fairy lights for the kitchen. We decided to hang our decorations in the entranceway and living room." She walked across to the blow-up reindeer and hugged him tight. "Isn't Rudolph amazing? He's as tall as me. Do you think we could buy a snowman? He'd look wonderful beside Rudolph."

John focused on his daughter's face. Bella always looked forward to Christmas, but she'd never been this animated or excited. Each December, he tried to make up for what she'd lost—what they'd both lost—by not turning Christmas into a big deal. But Bella was happier than he'd ever seen her. After all the issues he was having at work, maybe this Christmas would be different.

"I have another idea," John said. "Instead of going shopping, why don't we make our own snowman in the backyard?"

Bella's mouth dropped open. "Out of real snow?"

John nodded. "You could ask Mrs. Daniels if she has any carrots we could use for his nose."

Bella's arms dropped from around the reindeer. She ran toward the kitchen, yelling over the Christmas carols for Mrs. Daniels.

Tank bit into one of Bella's cookies and stood up. "You've made one little girl happy. I'll let the rest of the team know we're heading outside."

Tank left the room and Rachel's worried gaze met John's. "You have more bodyguards outside? Why?"

This was one of the few times in his life when he didn't know what to say. Too much information could scare her, too little could be deadly. "There's something I need to tell you, but you have to promise you won't repeat it to anyone."

Rachel put down her mug of chocolate. "It sounds serious."

"It is. I received a death threat this morning."

RACHEL WATCHED Bella pat a lump of snow into a ball with John. Their faces were inches apart as they worked together to make the snowman's head.

She didn't know what was happening, but the more time she spent with them, the faster something seemed to unravel inside her.

"They're having a good time." Tank stood beside her, watching the fun taking place in the snow.

"They always have a good time together. I just wish John was home more often. Then he'd really see how much Bella loves spending time with him."

Tank's gaze traveled along the trees surrounding the property. "He knows."

"Why doesn't he do something about it?"

He glanced quickly at her before transferring his gaze back to John. "He tries. You need to cut him some slack. A lot is happening at the moment."

Rachel didn't need to be reminded. John had explained about the threat to his life, the steps they'd put in place to make sure everyone was safe.

Tank nodded at Bella. "She's a great kid, but it hasn't been easy. After his wife died, John took Bella to physical therapy classes for a long time. She had trouble walking for about a year. While he was looking after Bella, he was trying to figure out what he wanted from life."

"He figured it out pretty well." She watched John lift the snowman's head onto its body. "Starting Fletcher Security was either the smartest business move he made, or there's more to his business than I know."

Tank crossed his arms in front of his chest. "You'll need to talk to John about that."

John glanced at Rachel and his smile dimmed.

"You confuse him," Tank muttered. "He's used to planning everything down to the last detail. He doesn't know what you're going to do from one minute to the next."

"That's unfair. You and Tanner have been following Bella and me around ever since I started working here. You know exactly where I am at any given time because you're right behind me."

"We weren't supposed to go shopping."

Rachel scuffed the snow in front of her with the toe of her boot. "I needed to get my clothes from my apartment. Walmart isn't far from where I live."

"It was too dangerous."

She bent down and picked up a handful of snow. "I

couldn't stay here over Christmas with no decorations. It's not Christmas without lights, tinsel, and a tree."

She rolled the snow into a ball and aimed for John. "Maybe your boss needs to unwind and let you and the police worry about the baddies." The snowball flew through the air and landed with a thud on the back of John's jacket.

He turned around and looked at Rachel. She shook her head and pointed at Tank.

John didn't look convinced. He knelt beside Bella and whispered something in her ear. She looked at Rachel and smiled.

Tank stuck his hands in his jacket pockets. "John's my friend. Make sure you don't break his heart. He couldn't go through that again."

He started to turn away, but Rachel held onto his arm. "Wait, Tank. I don't plan on getting anywhere near his heart. John is my—" Rachel's words were cut short by a snowball exploding against the side of her face. She turned just in time to see another one hurtling toward her. She ducked low, narrowly avoiding the missile.

"What the—?" Tank ended up wearing the snowball on his jacket.

Rachel dropped to the ground. "Don't worry, Tank. I have you covered." She quickly scooped together enough snow for a decent snowball and aimed it at Bella and John. They were hiding behind the snowman, throwing a stockpile of snow-balls straight at her and Tank.

Tank fired two of his own snowballs across the yard. "I'm here for five minutes. After that, you're on your own. I have work to do."

Bella giggled as a snowball hit Tank's shoulder. He recovered quickly, picked up a handful of snow, and threw it straight at John.

While John and Tank traded snowballs, Rachel ran

toward Bella with a small snowball in her hand. She threw it at Bella's bright red jacket and smiled at the look of excitement on her face.

Bella picked up one of her own and threw it at Rachel, reaching for another snowball as soon as the last one left her hands.

Rachel was so focused on Bella, she forgot about John. By the time she realized where he was, it was too late. He'd snuck up behind her and dropped a huge handful of snow on her head.

She yelped as the cold snow melted against her skin, trickled down her back, and left a trail of goose bumps in its path.

Bella laughed as Rachel turned to face her grinning adversary. "Sneaky move."

"I thought so, too." John's blue eyes were alive with laughter. For the first time since she'd met him, he looked happy.

She felt the weight of the snowball that she still had in her hand. It wasn't big, but if she was quick and accurate, it could do what she needed it to do. She took a step closer to John.

He took a step backward. "You should know I'm an expert snowball maker."

"Really?"

"And Bella's coming up behind you with another snowball."

"You can't distract me that easily, John Fletcher." Rachel took aim, fired her snowball at him, then ran as fast as she could to miss Bella's snowball. She didn't get far.

John grabbed her around the waist and pulled her into his body. "Quick, Bella."

Rachel twisted in his arms. "Not fair," she laughed as his arms tightened.

"Everything's fair when you're having a snowball fight."

Bella's snowball landed on Rachel's shoulder, showering

her in soft, white powder. Another trickle of cold water ran down her neck, making her squirm against John's body. "I give up. The war is over."

Bella ran toward her and hugged her around the waist. Rachel felt John lose his balance. She tried falling sideways, but his arms kept hold of her and they all toppled backward. His grunt of pain was enough to let Rachel know he was hurt.

Bella was the first person to move. She slid off Rachel and sat in the snow, staring at her dad. "Are you okay?"

John took a deep breath and winced.

Rachel scrambled off his body. "Where does it hurt?"

He sat up. "It's nothing."

"Nothing doesn't make you go as white as the snow."

He slowly pulled himself to his feet. "I knocked my arm, that's all."

Rachel frowned. She'd landed against him hard and could have easily hurt him.

"Will you go back to the hospital?" Bella asked. Her little face was scrunched in a knot. She was worried about her dad.

Rachel leaned down and smiled. "Sounds to me like your dad needs a hot chocolate to make him feel better."

Bella looked at John. Her face relaxed into its normal smile when he nodded at her. "I'll tell Mrs. Daniels." She ran as fast as she could toward the house.

Rachel turned to John. Regardless of what she'd said to Bella, she was worried about him. He had enough to deal with over Christmas without aggravating the bullet wound on his arm. "How bad is it?"

"Nothing a painkiller won't cure."

She didn't believe him. "Do you need help getting back to the house?"

He looked cautiously at the hand she was holding out to

him. "You're not going to try one of your self-defense moves on me, are you?"

"Only if you misbehave."

He slipped his hand inside hers and stepped closer. "How bad would I have to be?"

Her heart pounded in her chest. "Are you flirting with me?"

John blinked. A deep red blush stained his cheeks. "No. I…"

For a split second, Rachel saw something so deep and real clouding his eyes that it made her sad. He was lonely and worried. She wanted to give him a hug and tell him everything would be okay.

He took a step backward and let go of her hand. "Thank you."

She pushed away the sadness and tried to smile. "For landing on your arm?"

"For making Bella's Christmas special."

"What about you?" she asked softly.

"My life's complicated." He looked across the yard. Tank was moving through the trees, talking on his cell phone. "I've forgotten what special feels like."

Rachel took a step forward and slipped her hand under his elbow. "One day you'll remember. But for now, how about we head inside for some hot chocolate?"

He looked down at her and brushed a wet strand of hair out of her eyes. "I'm glad I came home early from work."

"I'm glad you did, too." They started walking, arm-in-arm, across the icy ground toward John's home. Rachel breathed in the cold, crisp air and prayed he would find something special in his life. He was a good person and had so much to be thankful for.

He also had a lot of responsibilities and worries. "Do you

ever wonder what your life would be like if you hadn't become a billionaire?"

"All the time," he said with a sigh. "I probably wouldn't have met you. Just think how less complicated my life would have been."

Rachel smiled. "And less exciting. Who else comes home to find a blow-up Santa and reindeer in their living room?"

"Do you think Bella wants a snowman as well?"

"No. You gave her what she really wanted."

"What was that?"

"Time with you." She let go of his arm and opened the back door. "Your hot chocolate awaits, kind sir."

John walked inside and turned around. When she was halfway through the doorframe, he lightly kissed her lips. "Merry Christmas."

While she was dealing with the butterflies racing around her stomach, John pointed above her. Hanging from a green ribbon was a bunch of mistletoe.

"You kissed me."

"I know," he said with a shy smile. "I thought you might like a surprise, too."

CHAPTER 13

*J*ohn hauled another basket of wood into the living room and passed it to his brother.

"Tell me your new home will have a gas fireplace?" Grant started stacking the wood beside the pile he'd just brought inside.

"You're getting old."

"Not so old that I don't see what's in front of my face."

He wasn't sure he wanted to hear what his brother had to say. It was six days until Christmas. Bella was beyond excited, Rachel was driving him crazy, and someone was threatening to kill him.

"What are you talking about?"

Grant threw another log on the fire before going back to John's basket of wood. "Since Jacinta died, you've hardly put one Christmas decoration in your home. Now look at the place. With the number of lights strung outside, you can probably see the glow from the moon."

John cleared his throat. "We went overboard at Walmart. They had a sale."

Grant's eyebrows nearly shot off his face. "A sale?"

"Rachel wanted to go back there. The sale ends tomorrow, so we bought extra decorations for next Christmas."

"Next Christmas?"

He glared at his brother. "Would you stop repeating everything I say?"

"So there are more decorations packed away in your garage?"

"Not exactly," John muttered. "We got carried away and hung the extra decorations around the house. Bella wanted to put all the lights up, too, so we did."

"What about the blow-up monsters in your front yard? Were they Bella's idea?"

John knew they'd gone a bit far with the blow-up figures but, as Rachel had told him, Christmas only comes once a year. It was just as well no one could see his home from the street. Otherwise, they'd have cars and trucks parked along the sidewalk at all hours of the night, watching what was going on in his front yard.

"The decorations aren't monsters." He took a log out of the basket. The sooner it was empty, the sooner he could get away from his brother's scrutiny. "We'd already bought the Santa and the reindeer. The snowman, seven dwarfs, and Sleeping Beauty were last-minute additions."

"Who wanted Shrek?"

"That would have been me. It's Bella's favorite movie."

Grant shook his head. "Bella, huh? Are you sure it isn't your favorite?"

John zipped his jacket to his chin. "I'll fill one more basket. That should give us enough wood for the next few days."

"Not so fast, twinkle toes. I went into Angel Wings Café the other day. Tess was behind the counter talking to someone. They mentioned Rachel and the Christmas play. Your name came up in the conversation."

"Eavesdroppers never hear good things about themselves."

Grant snorted. "They weren't talking about me. Tess is worried that Rachel's getting too involved in your life. She thinks Rachel has taken more than a professional interest in Bella."

He glared at Grant. "Says Tess. There's nothing unprofessional going on here."

Grant's gaze sliced across all the Christmas decorations, the sparkling tree that stood taller than either of them, and the Christmas cakes sitting on the table, waiting to be boxed.

John picked up the empty wood basket. "Rachel normally makes food parcels for families around Bozeman. Bella and I decided to help her. We made a few Christmas cakes to go with the non-perishable items."

Grant counted the fruit cakes. "Thirty isn't a few."

"The families will appreciate it."

"You're right. If you need a hand to deliver them, I can help." He picked up two more logs and stacked them on the pile. "I still haven't met Rachel. What's she like?"

John knew how his brother's mind worked. He'd psycho-analyze what he said about Rachel, put two and two together, and come up with twenty. "You'll meet her on Christmas day."

"She's coming here? Isn't that going above and beyond what you'd expect a teacher to do?"

He hadn't told his brother Rachel was living with him. Grant only came around once or twice a month. By the time his brother came back, the people sending him death threats would have been caught and life would be back to normal. But, in all of his plans, he'd forgotten one thing. Christmas.

"Rachel's living here."

Grant dropped a log on his foot and said something short and not so sweet. "You want to repeat that?"

"She's not living with me. Well, she is, but not how you're thinking. I've been away a lot. I have a problem at work and Rachel offered to look after Bella. It made sense that she stay here instead of going back and forth between her apartment and my home."

Grant looked at him as if he'd just come up with the lamest story he'd ever heard. "Are you sure she doesn't want to be the next Mrs. John Fletcher? You have a few more zeroes behind your name now."

Someone cleared their throat. Someone who sounded like Rachel.

He turned around. Rachel stood in the doorway.

"I don't know who you are, but I'm not a gold digger," Rachel said frostily to Grant. She looked at John and her expression didn't change. "We're back from Safeway. I'll be in the kitchen sorting through the groceries if you need me." She spun around and left the room.

John rushed into the hallway. "Rachel, wait. Grant didn't mean what he said." The kitchen door slammed and he turned back to his brother. "Look what you've done now."

"She's pretty. All that blond hair and big blue eyes. A man could get lost in the girl-next-door thing she's got going on."

John clenched his jaw. "Keep away from her. Rachel's off limits."

"Because you like her?"

He closed the living room doors. "No. Because she's my employee."

"Oh, sure. Is that why you closed the doors? So your employee couldn't hear you?"

"Sometimes I wish you weren't such an idiot. You have no idea what you're talking about."

Grant sent him a wide-eyed look. "Yeah, but Tess does. And I'm telling you now, Rachel likes you. Although from what I just saw, you may not have any relationship to salvage."

"We're friends, that's all."

"If I had a friend who looked like her, she wouldn't be my friend for long."

John picked up the heavy-duty basket he'd been using. "That's why you're still single. I'll be back soon."

He went outside and headed toward the woodshed. He'd talk to Rachel later, try to explain his brother's overprotective streak. After what Grant had said about Rachel, he was glad he hadn't told him about what was happening at work. He'd end up with a neurotic brother following him everywhere.

His cell phone beeped. He looked at the screen before answering the call.

Tanner's voice echoed through the woodshed. "Rachel's here, boss. Apart from Tank getting an even bigger complex about being her personal shopper, everything went well."

"Thanks. I'll see you later." John ended the call. If Tanner had called ten minutes earlier, he could have stopped his brother from making an idiot of himself. Rachel wouldn't have heard his comments about gold-diggers and he wouldn't have another apology to make.

With thirty food parcels to wrap, and a brother who was staying for dinner, it would be an interesting evening.

RACHEL WATCHED John's brother as she ate the beef casserole Patty had made. The two brothers were so different that she was still having a hard time believing they were related. Grant's blond hair brushed the collar of his denim shirt and his blue eyes were even more secretive than John's.

She had a feeling their cautious nature was about the only thing the two men had in common.

Grant reached across the table for a bread roll. "You'd better put Rachel out of her misery, little brother. She can't work out if we're really related."

"Some days I wish we weren't," he said dryly. "But, for my sins, Grant Byers is my brother. Same Mom, different Dads."

"Uncle Grant lives on a ranch," Bella said proudly. "He has ten horses and lots of cows."

Rachel smiled at Bella. "That's impressive."

Bella nodded enthusiastically. "Uncle Grant said he'll teach me how to be a cowgirl."

"That sounds exciting. What are you looking forward to the most?"

"Going on a cattle drive. Tank and Tanner are coming, too."

Grant dipped his knife into the stick of butter in front of him. "Did you grow up on a ranch, Rachel?"

She shook her head. "No. My mom was a secretary and Dad was a mechanic."

"Must have been a busy life?"

Rachel cut a green bean in half. "It was, but I expect ranching takes a lot of time as well."

"Too much, sometimes."

She waited for Grant to tell her more about being a rancher, but he didn't. "What about you? Have you always been a rancher?" She was surprised when Grant shook his head.

"I tried other things for a few years. About five years ago, I came back to Bozeman. When our mom and my step-dad died, I took over the family ranch."

"Moving to Bozeman must have been a big decision?"

Grant shrugged.

It was a little too careless, as if he wasn't going to tell her the whole truth.

"John was overseas and ranching wasn't for him. It worked out well for both of us."

Rachel looked at Grant's hand. He wasn't wearing a wedding ring, so she assumed he didn't have a wife or family.

"Dad, can I leave the table? I want to finish something important."

John smiled at his daughter. "Sure, Bella. Remember to rinse your plate and leave it in the dishwasher."

Bella scrunched her nose up. "Do I have to?"

"Yes."

Bella pushed her chair back from the table and looked at Rachel. "I'll be in my room. You can come up later if you want?"

"I'll do that."

"But no boys," Bella said quickly as she looked at her dad and uncle. "It's a secret." She waited until John and Grant both agreed before leaving the table.

Rachel watched her head toward the kitchen. She knew all about the top-secret project Bella was working on and how much it meant to her. She just hoped it didn't bring back too many sad memories for John.

Grant put down his knife and fork. "I have an apology to make. I didn't completely mean what I said about being a gold digger. Some women get sidetracked when they know how much money John's worth."

Rachel had calmed down enough to know that his comments weren't entirely directed at her. She kept her gaze on Grant. If she looked at John, she'd blush beet red and never say what she needed to. "You don't have to worry about me. In another few weeks I'll be living in my own home, working at Bozeman Elementary. John's paying me to teach Bella and that's what I'm doing. Things became a little complicated and it was safer for me to stay here."

"Safer?" Grant's gaze shot to his brother.

John stopped chewing.

Rachel looked at each of the brothers. John hadn't told Grant about the death threats. She thought fast, trying to come up with something that sounded logical. "The weather. Driving on the roads isn't safe. It made sense to stay here."

Grant pushed his plate away. "What's going on?"

John clenched his jaw. "Nothing."

"Are you kidding? You have extra guards around the house, Rachel's living here, and whenever Bella goes outside she has a bodyguard with her. Something's happened and I wouldn't call it nothing."

Rachel cleared her throat. "Do you want me to leave?"

John shook his head. "You might as well hear the entire story." He glanced at Grant. "Someone found out about a surveillance project my team was working on. A group called the Oracom Corporation contacted me through their lawyers. They offered me a lot of money for a prototype of our security drone."

"When did you start making drones?" Rachel thought Fletcher Security specialized in keeping people and their property safe, not designing surveillance equipment. When John told her he was sent death threats, she'd assumed it was because he was rich. She couldn't have been more wrong if she'd tried.

"About four years ago. We haven't told many people about our technical development program, but somehow Oracom found out. I turned their offer down and created a new set of enemies I don't need. A few days ago they sent me an email. It explained just how far they were prepared to go to get their hands on what we've developed."

Grant's face became a blank mask. "Where's the drone now?"

"We sold it to the Department of Defense. The technology we used is more advanced than anything I've ever seen."

Rachel looked at John. "If you've already sold the drone, why are you getting death threats?"

Grant's mouth dropped open. "Death threats? Why didn't you tell me sooner?"

John ran his hand around the back of his neck. "I didn't want you to worry. You have enough happening in your life without me adding to your problems."

"You're my brother," Grant hissed. "The only one I'll ever have. It's my job to help you."

John scowled. "If I'd told you sooner, you would have left the ranch and camped in my front yard. I don't want you getting hurt."

"So that's why there's extra security guards around Bella and Rachel?"

John nodded. "I'm not taking any chances."

Grant didn't look convinced and Rachel agreed with him. If the drone was important enough to kill someone over, there'd be no stopping the people who were after it.

John looked between Rachel and Grant. "The chance of Oracom getting anywhere near the drone is almost zero."

"What about near you?" Grant growled. "You know as well as I do how easy it is to kill someone. If that's what they're intent on doing, a few extra bodyguards won't help."

"There are more than a few extra bodyguards in place."

"What about the people in your technical team?" Rachel asked. "Are they okay?"

"They have round-the-clock surveillance and bodyguards with them. I've done everything I can to minimize the danger everyone's in." John glared at his brother. "Let me send a security team to your ranch."

"No way," Grant muttered. "If I can't look after myself, there's something wrong. Is anyone looking for the people behind the threats at Oracom?"

John took a sip of water from his glass. "The CIA and the FBI are working on it. We've told the local police department. There isn't a lot we can do except keep everyone safe and wait for Oracom's next move."

"Or beat them at their own game," Grant said. "Who's in charge of the case?"

"Don't do anything stupid," John warned his brother. "We're not in the military now. There's a process that needs to be followed and it doesn't involve you going off on your own to stop Oracom."

"Someone needs to. Who do I speak to?"

John stared long and hard at his brother. "Dan Carter is my first point of contact. But I'm warning you, if you so much as interfere with what's going on, I'll never trust you again."

Grant pushed back his chair. "It's better than being dead. Mrs. Daniels mentioned she'd made cheesecake for dessert. Does anyone want some?"

John shook his head.

Rachel's stomach was churning so much she couldn't have eaten another thing. "No, thanks. I'll go upstairs and check on Bella." She picked up her dinner plate and headed toward the kitchen.

"Are you okay, Rachel?"

John's voice cut through what she was thinking. "I'll be fine." But she wasn't. Hearing what was actually behind the death threats was scarier than assuming she knew. If the people behind the threats weren't stopped, the risk of something happening to any of them could continue for a long time.

And that wasn't something she was looking forward to.

CHAPTER 14

*T*he next afternoon, John looked across his desk at Samantha Jones, his Technical Development Manager. "Did Harry get back to you?"

Sam shuffled through the folders in front of her, then passed him a stapled set of papers. "He's looked at the financial records and reports Oracom has made public. They have a diverse portfolio of interests, ranging from rice production to solar power technology. There wasn't an obvious reference to military weapons or equipment, but they did have an emerging technologies sector with a multibillion dollar budget."

"Were you able to identify who manages that sector?"

Tanner stepped forward. He'd been leaning against the back wall, watching the small group in front of John share what they knew. "That's where it gets interesting. Their organizational chart shows someone called Darshive Fredericks as being in charge. Except Darshive Fredericks died six months ago in a car accident. The executive secretary from another team told me they're recruiting for the role. What she wouldn't tell me is who's temporarily doing the job while recruitment takes place."

"Does anyone have anything to add?" John looked at Martin and Sebastian, two of his longest-serving staff. Both men had been in the military. They were loyal and reliable, two qualities John never took for granted.

Martin looked John in the eye. "The CIA won't confirm anything, but we think they've planted an undercover agent in the recruitment process."

"Maybe two," Sebastian said in his usual deadpan way. "I've tried hacking Oracom's digital network, but I'm not getting very far. The firewalls they've designed are some of the best I've seen."

"Did you talk to Dan Carter?"

Sebastian nodded. "He's increased police security at the airport and they're keeping a close eye on what's happening around town. It's not easy. The heavy snow has brought all the skiers and snow bunnies to Big Sky Resort. The population around Bozeman has doubled over the last month."

John tried not to be disappointed by the slow progress they were making. His brother wasn't the only person convinced the government wouldn't find the people responsible for the death threats. The Department of Defense's main concern was keeping the design of the drone safe from unwanted eyes. Death threats weren't high on the National Risk Register, unless you were the President of the United States.

He turned to Tank. "Did you find out who the ice skater was on Emerald Lake?"

"Mallory Fraser. She's a distant cousin of Tess Allen." Tank passed John a folder. "She's been working in Orlando as a physical therapist. According to the people I spoke with, she's heading home in another month's time. No prior convictions. Nothing that would throw a red flag in the air."

John opened the folder and looked at the picture of the pretty blond woman. "Is she staying with Tess and Logan?"

"No. She's boarding with the McFallon sisters in town."

John closed the folder and handed it back to Tank. "What's next?"

"I also did a background check on Franky Smith, the kid with red hair that's become Bella's friend." Tank waited for John to nod before continuing. "His family has had a tough few years. His dad hit a rough patch a couple of years ago and dropped out of sight. He lost his job, left home, and didn't contact anyone. There was talk about him living in the mountains, but nothing was ever confirmed. When he came back, his wife left him. He eventually found a job pumping gas."

"Does Franky have any brothers or sisters?" John asked.

"A younger sister. She goes to Bozeman Elementary School."

John leaned back in his chair and stared at the folder in Tank's hands.

"Franky's a good kid," Tank said softly. "He helps at The Lighthouse and with Pastor Steven's youth group."

John knew all about the good work Pastor Steven was doing. He ran a drop-in center for anyone who needed a hot meal and a safe place to stay. Tess Allen and Annie Bayliss supplied enough meals for everyone. Other people helped where they could.

John gave Pastor Steven a substantial donation each year. It filled the gap when it came to buying clothes, paying utility bills, or giving people a helping hand when they needed it.

He lifted his gaze from the computer. "Thanks, Tank."

"There's one other thing, boss. Franky's dad used to be in the Detroit Police Department. Something must have happened to send him over the edge."

"Has he been getting any help?"

"I don't know. Do you want me to find out?"

John picked up the papers Sam had left on his desk. "Bella and Rachel are your primary concern. But if you get the opportunity, ask Pastor Steven about Franky's dad. Keep it discreet. And find out if there's anything we can do to help him."

He flipped through the report about Oracom and stopped at the financial statements. "If we can't get evidence that Oracom is behind the death threats, maybe we can get them another way. Is Harry looking into any off-shore transactions where large amounts of money have changed hands?"

"Harry isn't the only person looking," Sam said. "The CIA has been delving into Oracom's financial practices as well. If there's anything remotely illegal, we'll find it."

"Hopefully before the CIA," Tanner muttered. "You know how those guys are—once they have some information they're not happy about sharing it."

John did know, but he wouldn't let that stop what they were doing. "We'll be one step ahead of them."

And, hopefully, they'd be one step ahead of the person threatening to kill him.

THAT EVENING, Rachel sat quietly in front of the open fire in John's living room. She pulled a fluffy blanket around her shoulders and leaned her head against the sofa.

Grant was back today, checking on the security system around the house. Even though Tank and Tanner hadn't said much at lunchtime, Rachel knew they weren't happy.

After Grant left, the wind picked up. It was howling along the shingle roof, sounding like a rattlesnake warning of danger.

Rachel had never been superstitious, but with everything

going on, even she was jumpy. She'd made sure Bella was safely tucked up in bed and double-checked all the windows and doors before sitting on the sofa. Tank had shaken his head at her, but he hadn't stopped her from checking each catch.

"You're still awake?"

Rachel turned toward the open doorway. John was standing just inside the room with a mug in his hands. "I couldn't sleep."

He looked down at the drink in his hands. "Do you want a hot chocolate? The kettle's still hot."

"Sounds good." She pushed the blanket off her shoulders and stood up.

"Stay there. I'll get it for you," he said quickly.

"I don't want to be a nuisance."

The frown on John's face was deeper and more concerned than usual. "You're not a nuisance. If anything, I'm the one who's caused you more grief than you deserve."

"You couldn't help what's happened."

John's gaze dropped from her face. "I'll be back soon." He left his mug on a cabinet and left the room.

Rachel sat down and pulled the blanket around her shoulders. She tried to imagine what she'd be doing now if she wasn't here. It was four days until Christmas. The stores would be full of last-minute shoppers all looking for the perfect gift. She would have been with the crowds, listening to the Christmas music playing over the speakers, humming along to *Snoopy's Christmas* and *Silver Bells* as if she'd never heard them before.

"You're smiling," John said as he walked into the living room.

"I'm thinking about Christmas. Did you know there are about 28 million real Christmas trees sold in America each year?"

"Really?"

"And there are close to 350 million Christmas trees being grown at the moment."

"Fascinating." John handed her a mug. "Be careful, it's hot. What other stupendous facts have you memorized?"

Rachel narrowed her eyes at his smiling face. "Don't be too quick to laugh. I'm a brilliant partner in a game of Trivial Pursuit."

"I'm sure you are." John sat beside her and took a sip of his drink. When she didn't say anything, he smiled. "Okay. Blow me away with more intriguing facts."

"Did you know the grizzly bear is the official state animal of California, but no grizzly bears have been seen there since 1922?"

"No, I can't say I did know that. Keep going."

Rachel went through all the trivia she'd filed away inside her head, looking for the oddest fact she could find. "In more than half of all US states, the highest paid public employee is a football coach."

"You're joking?"

"I kid you not," Rachel said with a smile. "And did you know there are 60,000 miles of blood vessels in your body? If you stretched them out in a single line, they'd go around the planet more than twice."

John held his hand out in front of him. "That has to be wrong."

"Nope. I read it in a science journal."

"You know not to believe everything you read, don't you?"

Rachel sighed. "There's a big difference between knowing something and believing in it. Take Santa Claus, for instance."

"I have no idea where you're going with this."

"You don't need to. All you have to do is listen." She

looked over her shoulder in case Bella had come downstairs. "Most adults know Santa doesn't exist. But if all those adults suddenly gave up *believing* in Santa, the world's economy would collapse. Last year, there were over three trillion dollars' worth of Christmas sales in America alone. People want to believe in the magic. They want their children to believe in Santa Claus. We make up stories about how Santa will still visit houses with no fireplace. We leave carrots and cookies on a plate by the Christmas tree and make sure there are only crumbs left in the morning. It's part of the magic."

"Blood vessels are different from Santa Claus."

Rachel sighed. "Of course, they are. But isn't it amazing to think that your blood vessels could stretch around the world, not once, but twice? Even though it's true, it's still magic."

"Not for the person who did the calculation. How do you think they worked it out?"

"I don't want to know," Rachel mumbled. "My imagination isn't painting a pretty picture." She blocked the images crowding her mind and focused on the fire in front of her.

Even though it was late, she was glad of John's company. When he wasn't busy working, there was a stillness about him that she appreciated. His sense of humor wasn't bad, either. And if she dug really deep, she was sure she'd find someone who still believed in magic.

John stretched out his legs. "Bella was born on a night like this. We'd had the worst weather anyone had seen in a decade. Snowdrifts were covering people's vehicles and getting anywhere was a nightmare."

"Did you make it to the hospital?"

"Jacinta delivered Bella in our apartment. I was on leave and Bella wasn't due for another six weeks." John's gaze settled on the fireplace. The orange and red flames danced in the grate, moving in time with the wind whistling down the chimney. "I don't regret many things in life, but not spending more time with Jacinta and Bella is one of them."

Rachel sipped her hot chocolate. She thought about her own mom and dad, the loneliness that had become as familiar to her as breathing. "My parents worked long hours. Even though we all lived together, there weren't many times when we were all in the same place at the same time. It was hard."

"Is that why you were worried about Bella being lonely?"

Rachel nodded. "I was an only child, too. I thought Bella wanted a mom because she was on her own all the time. I didn't realize Bella has friends who help fill the gaps. Mrs. Daniels loves her as if she was her own granddaughter."

"Patty is special, but you were right. It's too easy to think Bella has everything she needs. Even though she has people around her who care, it still doesn't replace me not being here."

"Will you be able to spend more time with her once the drone problem is over?"

"I'll make sure I do." John turned to her. "You never talk about your mom and dad. Do you see them very often?"

"I'm visiting them tomorrow night for dinner." John's gaze sharpened. "Don't worry. Tanner has drawn the short straw and is coming with me. Mom was excited when I told her I was bringing someone. She thought Tanner was my boyfriend."

"Was she disappointed when you told her he wasn't?"

Rachel wasn't sure whether her mom had been disappointed for the reasons John meant. "I've given up trying to understand my parents. I've taken a lot of boyfriends home and they're used to seeing people pop in and out of my life."

John's face became wary. "You date a lot?"

"I used to." Rachel sighed. "My mom told me I had no stickability. A couple of years ago, I was engaged and Mom couldn't have been happier. When I called off the wedding, it reinforced what she'd been telling me for years."

"Why didn't you get married?"

Rachel's face felt as hot as the fire in front of her. She didn't like talking about the stupidest thing she'd ever done. As well as being embarrassing, it had made her feel like a leper in her own town.

"Rachel?"

"I'd rather not talk about it." She could feel John's gaze drilling into her, trying to figure out what could have been so bad.

"Are you sure?"

"You did a security check on me before I started working with Bella. That should have told you everything."

John's lips twitched. "It told me you're not bankrupt, you have no criminal convictions, and you took a year off work. It didn't tell me why you decided not to get married."

"In case you're wondering, I didn't take time off work because of a broken heart. Dad had an accident and needed someone to look after him. He's better now, which is why I'm going back to full time teaching."

"Glad to hear it."

Rachel crossed her arms in front of her chest. "If I tell you, you can't laugh or say anything weird. Most of the town know why I didn't get married. They'll be stunned if I ever find someone who wants to walk down the aisle with me."

"It couldn't have been that bad?"

"I drank too many cocktails at my bachelorette party and I kissed a total stranger. It turned out the stranger was my fiancé's cousin. Everything went downhill from there."

"You called your wedding off because you kissed another man?"

"It wasn't just any man," she muttered. "It was Jeremiah's

cousin. And it wasn't just a peck on the lips. It was a full throttle, in your face, kind of kiss."

John clamped his mouth together and didn't say a word. The wind and rain lashed against the side of the house, the fire hissed and spat, and he still didn't say anything.

"You're the only person who hasn't judged me." Rachel rearranged the blanket around her shoulders and looked at John. "Everyone who heard the story was quick to take sides. It was either the luckiest escape I'd ever had or I'd turned into the biggest tease this side of the Rockies. No matter which way I looked at it, I was doomed."

John's lips twitched. "Doomed?"

"I stopped dating. I decided my girlfriends were better company than men."

"And now?"

"Now I date, but I'm more selective." Rachel had a whole set of criteria a man had to pass before anything became serious. She wasn't making the same mistake twice.

"Wise move."

"I think so. What about you?"

John cleared his throat. "Me?"

"Do you date?"

"Not much."

"Oh."

"That doesn't mean I'm not open to the possibility."

Rachel blinked. She glanced at John, blushing when she saw him looking at her. All the bad girl thoughts she'd hidden away were making a sneaky appearance.

John lifted his hand and pushed a lock of hair behind her ear. "If I were to date someone, she'd have to like Bella, have a good sense of humor, and not worry about what I own."

"There must be hundreds of women lining up to date you," Rachel said a little breathlessly as John's hand brushed the edge of her jaw.

"Maybe."

A heat that had nothing to do with the fire rolled through her body. John was her employer. She had standards. High standards. Standards that didn't involve jumping on top of her boss and kissing him senseless.

John's hand rested lightly on her shoulder. "For a few minutes, do you want to pretend we're two normal people in front of a roaring fire in the middle of a snowstorm?"

Rachel's gaze slipped to John's mouth and stayed there. "I'm not normal," she whispered. "I have issues."

John left his mug of hot chocolate on the floor, then took Rachel's mug out of her hands. "So do I."

"If I kiss you, it's because I want to. Not because of how much money you have."

"And if I kiss you back, it's because I want to, not because I feel sorry for you."

Rachel moved forward, then stopped. "You feel sorry for me?"

The grin on John's face melted her heart. "You think your girlfriends are better company than a boyfriend. You just haven't met the right man."

His lips nudged her mouth, dissolving the words she was about to say. She pulled him forward, wrapped her arms around his shoulders, and held him close.

His groan tore at something she'd buried a long time ago. Something so wonderful she never thought she'd feel it again. It was a sense of belonging, a rightness to what was happening. It settled deep inside her, warmed her from the inside out.

John buried his hands in her hair and devoured her mouth with an urgency that left her wanting more. She pushed the blanket away and straddled his hips, making them both moan as their bodies connected through layers of denim and wool.

"Have to slow down." He groaned as Rachel's lips nibbled his neck.

His hands found their way under her sweater, teasing and caressing her skin until she couldn't think straight. A tremor of need started in the center of her body. She'd never wanted anyone as much as she wanted John Fletcher.

That thought alone was enough to scare her senseless. She pulled her lips away from his mouth, slipped off his lap, and landed on the floor.

He looked down at her and frowned. "How did you get there?"

"Gravity." She took a deep breath and rested her head against his legs. "You were right."

John's hand stroked her hair. "About what?"

"Men."

His hand stilled. "Is that a good thing?"

"A very good thing. But I need to go to bed before I get myself into more trouble. Bella and I have a lot of things to do tomorrow."

"You're not going into town, are you?"

"This is the last time. We did some more baking for Pastor Steven and we've run out of craft supplies." Rachel knelt in front of him and ran her fingertips over his frown. "We'll be okay. Tank's coming with us."

John held her hands. "Be careful. Bella told me she's getting bored, but she's safer here than anywhere else."

"I know."

He leaned forward and kissed her lightly on the lips. "I don't want anything happening to you, either."

She looked into his blue eyes. "Nothing will happen to Bella or me. I'll call you as soon as we arrive at Pastor Steven's home and when we leave town. We won't do anything stupid." John nodded, but she could tell he was still worried. "I'm going to bed. I'll see you in the morning."

She felt John's gaze on her as she left the room. She didn't look back, didn't slow down. If she hesitated for one second, she'd spoil a good working relationship. He was her boss, the father of her student.

The man she wanted to keep kissing until they were both quivering wrecks.

CHAPTER 15

*B*ella slid the last box of Christmas baking onto Pastor Steven's table and smiled. "Rachel said Franky's helping you take our baking to other families. Can I help next year?"

Pastor Steven lifted a chocolate cake out of the box. "Of course, you can. This looks delicious. Could you put it in one of the baskets in the living room?"

Bella nodded and held out her hands. "We baked all sorts of cookies, too. I kept some peanut butter ones for Dad, but we brought chocolate, vanilla, cinnamon, lemon, and…what was the other flavor, Rachel?"

"Hazelnut. Has anyone seen the gingerbread loaf Mrs. Daniels made? It has a big Santa Claus tag attached to the wrapper."

Tank held a parcel toward her. "Is this it?"

Rachel took the parcel and smiled. "It is. This is for you, Pastor Steven. Mrs. Daniels knows you like gingerbread. It's a thank you gift for all the work you're doing to make people's Christmases special."

"She didn't need to make me anything, but thank you."

Pastor Steven picked up the box of cookies and smiled at Bella. "Let's take this baking through to the living room. I hear you've planned an exciting trip into town."

Bella walked out of the kitchen with Pastor Steven. She was chatting away, totally oblivious to the reason Tank went everywhere with them.

"It will be all right, Rachel," Tank said from behind her. "She's happier helping someone than being stuck at home."

"I know she is, but I can't help feeling uneasy about being away from the house. I think John was right. We need to be super careful."

"Nothing will happen while I'm looking after you."

"That's what you said last time we went shopping, and look what happened."

Tank looked affronted. "I wasn't the only person who thought the popping balloons sounded like gunfire."

"Not the balloons. The decorations. It took John two days to get used to all the tinsel and the blow-up Santa. You're a bad influence."

He grunted. "It didn't stop him from going back for more, though."

Rachel pulled three lemon cakes out of another box. "I think the Christmas spirit is growing on him."

Tank raised his eyebrows, but didn't say anything as he disappeared into the living room.

By the time he came back, Rachel had finished unpacking another box. "Do you think the people behind the death threats will ever be found?"

"I don't know, but everyone's doing their best to locate them."

Bella rushed into the room. "The Christmas baskets look amazing. What can I take into the living room next?"

Rachel passed her two containers of cookies. "Give these

to Pastor Steven. I'll be there soon." She picked up some more cookies and followed Bella.

The first task of the morning was well underway. She hoped Bella would be just as excited about their next stop.

TANK LISTENED to the person who was speaking to him on the phone, then hung up. "There's been a change of plans. We're not going shopping."

Bella's mug of hot chocolate clattered against the table. "But we have to. I haven't finished making dad's Christmas present."

Rachel looked up from the table. "What's happened?"

"Christmas is what's happened. Walmart is packed with people."

Pastor Steven bit into a slice of Mrs. Daniels' gingerbread loaf. "It happens every year. The week before Christmas is crazy wherever you go." He looked at Bella. "What do you need to finish your present? I might have some extra supplies here."

Bella leaned back and pulled a crinkled piece of paper out of her pocket. "I need pink foil, some double-dot jewels, sticky red jewels, glitter sticks, and more cardboard sleighs like the ones Rachel found the other day."

Pastor Steven frowned. "It sounds like fun, but I don't have any of those things. What if you visited one of the specialty stationery stores in town? They might have what you want without having to go to Walmart."

"We might not even need to do that," Rachel murmured. She looked at Tank. "I know a craft store that sells the scrapbook supplies Bella needs. Would you take us there?"

He looked at Rachel. His intense stare told her he wasn't impressed with her suggestion.

Bella walked around the table to Tank. "If I don't find what I need, I can't finish Dad's present. It will only take a few minutes. Can we please go to Rachel's store?"

Rachel looked through the kitchen window. "It's not snowing anymore. We can rush into the store, buy what we need, and be back in your SUV before you know it."

"John won't like it. I'm sorry, but the answer's no."

Rachel thought fast. Bella needed the supplies and this would be their last chance to do anything in town. "I know John wants us to be careful. I wouldn't have suggested the store if I didn't think it was safe. What if I went into the store and you stayed in your vehicle with Bella? I could phone ahead and order what we need. It will be twice as quick. All I'll have to do is pay for the scrapbook materials and leave."

Tank looked at Bella. She used her big brown eyes, silently pleading her case better than any adult Rachel had ever seen.

He looked at Pastor Steven, then back at Rachel. "Okay. But if we get there and it doesn't look safe, we leave straight away. Where's the store?"

"On Main Street, beside Angel Wings Café. It's called Crafty Crafts."

Tank raised his eyebrows. "You're kidding me?"

"It's a great name." Rachel had known the store's owner, Kelly Harris, since eighth grade. She was a good friend and loyalty ran deep in Montana. "Kelly turned a musty old building into the prettiest craft store in Bozeman. Scoff all you like, but a lot of people buy their supplies from her. But craft supplies aren't the only thing she sells. She has the best selection of local artists' work in Bozeman, and she runs workshops teaching people how to paint."

"She sounds like a saint," Tank grumbled.

"She's better than a saint." Rachel walked across to her

bag and took out her cell phone. "She sells what we need. You've just made a little girl very happy."

"The only thing that matters is that Bella's daddy is happy when we get home. Otherwise, both of us will be looking for new jobs." Tank looked across at Bella and his hard-as-nails face softened.

Rachel couldn't think about John at the moment. Kissing him last night had been the most reckless thing she'd done in months. And recklessness, she'd learned, always came at a price.

She turned on her phone and searched through her contact list for Kelly's number. "How did you know Walmart was busy?"

"I have my sources," Tank said as he pulled out his own cell phone. "I just hope they can get across town before we arrive at the craft store."

Rachel held her phone to her ear and waited for Kelly to answer. Buying the scrapbook supplies was important. Bella wasn't creating a run-of-the-mill Christmas present. It was a heart-wrenching, emotional present that might make John realize how his daughter felt about him.

And if that didn't work, Bella could always bake him his favorite cake and hope for the best.

"It's a parade," Bella squealed from the back seat of Tank's SUV. "It's the Christmas parade. Look…there's Santa!" Bella pointed to the merry man in red.

"There's no way I'll be able to park close to the store," Tank said. "You know what that means, don't you?"

Bella frowned. "You can't go back on your word. I need the craft supplies for Dad's present."

"I'm sorry, Bella. But a deal is a deal. I told you before we left Pastor Steven's house that if this didn't feel right, Rachel wasn't going inside for your supplies. It doesn't feel right, so we're going home."

"I don't want to go home. If we follow the parade down Main Street, we'll drive straight past the craft store. The floats are so slow that you wouldn't need to find a place to park. Rachel could jump out and then run along the sidewalk and catch up with us."

"Rachel would slip if she ran along the sidewalk. We'd end up in the hospital with a concussed teacher who should have known better."

Rachel glared at the back of Tank's head. "The so-called concussed teacher now has everything clearly spelled out. Thank you, Tank."

"Don't get angry with me. I'm just telling you no one is going anywhere." He stopped at a set of traffic lights.

Rachel watched the people on the side of the road. They were huddled in their jackets, with scarves and hats firmly attached to their bodies. The Christmas parade was a big deal in Bozeman. Most families made sure they were standing on the side of the road to see the long trail of floats moving down the street.

Tank would have to take a left-hand turn up ahead if he wanted to go anywhere. Main Street was closed to vehicles and, judging by the number of floats, it would be a long time before it opened.

Before Rachel could think of another craft store they could visit, Bella unclipped her seatbelt and jumped out of the SUV.

Rachel made a frantic grab for her jacket, but her seatbelt locked her in place. "Bella! What are you doing?"

Bella kept running, disappearing into the crowd of people walking along the sidewalk. "Tank, Bella's gone. I'm going after her." She threw off her seatbelt, slid across the SUV, and jumped out Bella's door. Dodging the other vehicles waiting at the lights, she hit the sidewalk at a run.

Even though this end of Main Street was less crowded, there were still a lot of people blocking her path. She stepped around strollers and preschoolers as she tried to see where Bella had gone.

Rachel crossed the street, slowed down as the slippery road made it impossible to keep moving fast. She made her way toward the craft store. It was still three blocks away. Three icy, snow-covered, blocks.

Bella hadn't been to the craft store before, but she had been to Angel Wings Café. Rachel had taken her there when they'd been in town.

Her phone rang and she pulled it out of her pocket. The callers' number was blocked. She looked at it again before answering. She hoped it was Tank and not John.

"Where is she?"

Rachel breathed a sigh of relief. "I don't know. She's probably heading toward the craft store, but I can't see her." Rachel looked at the buildings around her. "I'm just passing Pete's Emporium."

"Keep heading toward the craft store. Bella has a GPS chip in her coat. I can find her with that."

Tank ended the call and Rachel stared at the phone. A GPS chip? She had no idea John had gone to such extreme lengths to keep track of Bella. Usually, she'd be mortified, but not today. Bella had disappeared and she had no idea where she was.

IT SEEMED to take forever to get to the craft store. The middle section of Main Street was bursting with people, especially around Tess' café. With a wide porch hanging over the sidewalk, this part of the street was a popular choice for families to gather. Add in hot coffee and fresh baking, and you had standing room only.

Rachel used her body to push through the crowd, finally making it to the front of Kelly's store. Tank stood outside with his phone in his hand. "She hasn't moved for the last five minutes. Come with me."

"She's not in the store?"

"No."

Rachel hurried after Tank, following him into Tess' café. She looked at the people sitting at the tables, the line of cold and hungry people waiting to place their orders. She couldn't see Bella anywhere. "Are you sure this is the right place?"

Tank looked at his phone and nodded. "She must be in the kitchen."

Tess jumped a mile when Tank suddenly appeared beside her. "Tank? What are you doing behind the counter?"

"We can't find Bella. Have you seen her?"

Tess shook her head. "It's been so busy I haven't done anything except serve customers. Caitlin, Annie, and Kate are out the back putting orders together. Ask them if they've seen her. Is she okay?"

Tank didn't bother replying. He pushed open the kitchen doors and strode into the room.

Tess glanced at Rachel before turning to her next customer. They both knew it was the worst possible day for an eight-year-old to go missing. There were people everywhere, it was cold, and the weather forecast wasn't going to improve.

Rachel followed Tank into the kitchen. Compared to the café, it was a calm oasis of tranquility. Caitlin was busy making toasted paninis. Annie was beside a deep-fryer, churning out hot chips, and Kate was about to take a big order into the café.

"Has anyone seen Bella Fletcher?" Rachel asked. "She's eight years old, has curly brown hair down to her shoulders and big brown eyes. She's wearing a bright red jacket and blue jeans."

Kate balanced her tray on the edge of the stainless steel counter. "No one's been in the kitchen except us, and I don't remember seeing her in the café. How long has she been missing?"

"About fifteen minutes," Rachel said.

Tank moved toward the back of the kitchen. He opened the door to a walk-in storage room, quickly searching the large space. When he couldn't find her in there, he threw open the back door and walked into the staff parking area.

Rachel followed him outside. The cold air hit her face and made her eyes water.

"What's up here?" He was already walking carefully up a set of exterior stairs.

"It's Tess' old apartment. No one's living there at the moment."

He tried the door handle. It didn't budge. He glanced down at the snow and shook his head. "It doesn't look as though anyone's been here." He looked at the emergency fire escapes attached to the walls of the other businesses beside Tess' café. "She wouldn't have been able to reach any of those ladders. We'll take another look around the café and then I'm calling it in. We need more help."

The back door opened and Tess walked outside. "Have you found her?"

Tank walked down the stairs. "She's not here."

"I'll ask my customers," Tess said. "Someone might have seen her come into the café."

Tank re-checked his phone. "She should still be here."

"What do you mean?" Tess held open the door as they walked inside.

"Bella has a GPS tracking chip in her jacket." Rachel stopped in the middle of the kitchen and turned to Tank. "What if she took off her jacket? What if her jacket's here, but she isn't?"

"Then she's really in trouble." He ran into the dining area with Rachel and Tess behind him.

Tess pulled an empty chair out from one of the tables and stood on it. "Excuse me, everyone," she yelled over the loud conversations. "Can I have your attention, please."

The chatter came to a standstill. "Has anyone seen an eight-year-old girl with curly brown hair and brown eyes in the last fifteen minutes? Her name is Bella Fletcher. She's wearing a red jacket and jeans. Can you also look around your tables for a red jacket that doesn't belong to you?"

A lady at a table at the front of the café held a red padded jacket in the air. "Is this what you're looking for?"

Tank took the jacket out of the lady's hand. "It's Bella's."

"Thanks, everyone," Tess said.

"Do you need help finding her?" A man beside Tess picked up his jacket. "I was about to leave, but I could search some of the other stores on Main Street for you."

Tess looked at Tank.

He shook his head. "She won't go to someone she doesn't know. But thanks for the offer."

He tapped his phone and walked into the kitchen. The last words Rachel heard before the kitchen door closed behind him were, *Bella's missing.*

CHAPTER 16

*R*achel walked into Kelly Harris' craft store with a heavy heart. The last hour had been devastating. The police and John's security staff were everywhere, looking for Bella. An AMBER alert had been issued. All the airport, train, and bus stations had posted messages and signs, looking for her.

Tess followed her into the store. "I just heard from Billy-Rae at the radio station. They're broadcasting messages between every second song, asking people to look for Bella. He said all the digital signs across the Interstate have been changed and the AMBER Alert website has been updated with Bella's photo." She gave Rachel a quick hug. "Everyone's doing their best to find her."

Kelly walked out from the back room. "Still no news?"

Rachel shook her head.

"Bella's photo is on all the television stations. Someone has to know where she is." Kelly pulled out a stool from behind the front counter. "Sit down. You look as though you're about to fall to pieces."

Rachel sat on the stool and wiped her eyes. "She isn't wearing a jacket and it's freezing outside."

Tess put her hand on Rachel's shoulder. "The only thing we can do is pray hard that someone sees her. How is her dad?"

"I haven't seen much of him. He's really worried." While the police were interviewing Rachel and Tank, John had given the police a recent photo and description of Bella. They were using that information for their website and communication with the media.

John had barely spoken to her as they'd passed each other in the corridor at the police station. She couldn't blame him for being upset. He'd warned her to be careful, to stay at home rather than go into town. But she hadn't listened, and her mistake could be deadly.

Rachel's cell phone let out a shrill blast. She pulled her phone out of her pocket and deleted the message. "That's the third AMBER text alert I've had about Bella." Her eyes filled with tears. "What if she dies?"

Tess pulled a handful of tissues out of a box on the counter. "There's no point dwelling on things like that. Let's look for her." She passed Rachel the tissues. "I can't sit here and do anything."

"But John said to stay here," Rachel said with reluctance. "I've already made too many wrong decisions. If Bella suddenly finds her way here, she won't know what to do."

Kelly waved her hand in front of Rachel's face. "Hello? Earth to Rachel? I'm not exactly invisible. If Bella comes in the store, I'll keep her warm and call the police. I have plenty of things she can do until they get here."

"Are you sure?" Rachel asked.

Tess pulled Rachel off the stool. "Of course, she's sure. Kelly has six brothers and sisters. If anyone can look after an eight-year-old, it's her."

Rachel zipped her jacket to her chin. "Okay, but we have to get back here within an hour. If John finds out I've left the store, he won't be happy."

"I hate to break the news to you," Tess said. "But John probably won't care where you are. His main focus is on Bella. Kelly will look after her if she comes into the store. We've covered all the bases."

"Why don't I feel as confident as you are?" Rachel asked.

"Maybe because you're closer to Bella than I am?"

Rachel blinked back more tears. "Tank's meeting John at the police station. Where should we start looking?"

Tess buried her hands in her jacket pockets. "I vote for starting at the café. We can work our way back to where she left the SUV."

"I'll call you if Bella comes into the store," Kelly said. "Good luck."

Rachel knew they'd need more than luck. She just hoped Bella had found somewhere safe and warm to stay if she was lost.

The alternative wasn't worth considering.

JOHN SAT in a black plastic chair in the chief of police's office. If someone had kidnapped Bella, there was a high probability they'd contact him and demand a ransom.

And he knew exactly what they'd want.

Dan Carter walked into the room. "We've checked the security cameras on Main Street. There's no sign of Bella going past the craft store. Between your security guards and my detectives, we've gone into every store within half a mile of where she was last seen."

"If she was snatched off the street and bundled into a vehicle, she could be miles from here by now."

LEEANNA MORGAN

Dan looked up from the file he was holding. "We're doing everything we can to find her."

"I know. I feel so useless just sitting here."

"With the death threats you've already received, you need to stay here. If we haven't found Bella in the next couple of hours, you can go home. But, if I hear you're on the streets looking for her, I won't be happy." Dan sat behind his desk. "I know a detective has already asked you these questions, but I'm going to ask you them again. Does Bella have any places she regularly visits in town?"

John crossed his arms in front of his chest. "I've taken Bella to Angel Wings Café a few times. Mrs. Daniels, my housekeeper, takes her to Safeway when she does the grocery shopping, and Rachel has taken her to Walmart. She goes to the library for drama club and to Denise Walker's dance studio for her ballet class."

"Friends?"

"Poppy O'Sullivan is her best friend. Bella likes talking with Franky Smith at drama club."

"You didn't mention Franky's name before."

John's gaze shot to Dan. "Do you know something I don't?"

Dan stood up and walked around his desk. "I'll be back in a few minutes. If your cell phone rings, let Detective Adams know and we'll try to trace the call."

John watched Dan walk into the squad room and talk to one of his detectives. He glanced at the phone on Dan's desk, then at his cell phone.

He needed to speak to Tank, and he needed to do it now. John looked back at the squad room and leaned across the desk, lifting the police chief's phone off its cradle. He punched Tank's cell phone number into the handset and waited.

Dan was still talking to the detective.

"Tank speaking."

"It's John. I need you to look through the background check you did on Franky Smith's family. Pull everything you can on his father."

"Sure. Is there anything in particular you want me to check?"

"Find out why he left the police force." Dan was coming toward him. "I can't talk and my cell phone is out of commission. Call me on this number." John hung up and sat back down in his seat.

He might have been grasping at straws, but at least it was more productive than sitting here doing nothing. If Franky's father had anything to do with Bella's disappearance, he'd track him down and make sure he never hurt another child.

Dan walked into his office and frowned at John. "Who did you call?"

"Would there be any point telling you I didn't call anyone?"

"No. I traded my spare set of eyes for an eagle-eyed duty officer."

John looked into the squad room and a police officer nodded at him. "I called Tank. We've already completed a background check on Franky's family. I want to make sure we didn't miss anything. I'll make sure you get a copy of the information."

Dan nodded. "I thought you'd want to know that one of my officers saw Tess and Rachel in town. They're back-tracking through the places Bella could have gone."

"On their own?"

"I don't have any extra staff to go with them and neither do you."

John ran his hands through his hair. Today had turned into the biggest nightmare of his life. He only hoped it didn't get worse.

～

RACHEL LIFTED the lid on a large trash can halfway down an alley. The smell of rotting garbage made her stomach heave. "She's not here."

Tess looked behind a pile of old wooden pallets. She pushed her hat out of her eyes and frowned at Rachel. "If you were eight years old, where would you go?"

Rachel looked down the alley. "I wouldn't go here, that's for sure. I don't understand why she went into the café when she wanted to go to the craft store."

"What time did Bella jump out of Tank's SUV?"

Rachel wiped her hands on the side of her jacket. "At about half-past one. Why?"

"I'm trying to work out if there was another reason why she would have come into the café."

"She wouldn't have been hungry. We had a big lunch before we went to Pastor Steven's house. And even if she was hungry, Bella didn't have any money with her."

Tess started walking out of the alley. "Kelly bought a sandwich from me. It would have been about the same time Bella was trying to get into the craft store. Kelly doesn't usually close for lunch, but it was so busy with the parade that she didn't have much choice. What if Bella ran to Kelly's store and the door was locked? Would she come into the café to see me?"

"She could have. She likes going to the café and she enjoys spending time with you at The Bridesmaids Club. Bella would have known Tank and I would be upset with her. Maybe talking to you would have been her way of working out what she would do next."

Tess kept walking toward the café. "That still doesn't account for why she took off her jacket. She wouldn't have been in the café long enough to get hot."

Rachel looked closely at the stores they were passing. They'd already been in each and every one of them, asking about Bella, finding out if they'd seen anything out of the ordinary at the parade.

Tess stopped and picked up a red button that was lying on the sidewalk. "Is this Bella's?"

Rachel held the heart-shaped plastic button in her hand. "No. Her jacket had a zip and she was wearing a pale blue sweater underneath." She threw the button in the trash and looked farther down the street.

It was getting dark. In another hour, it would be impossible to see anything without a flashlight. By now, if Bella wasn't somewhere warm, she would be in serious trouble.

Tess hadn't moved from where she'd found the button. "You told me Bella had a GPS tracking chip in her jacket. Do the chips show you exactly where the person is?"

"Tank said it was accurate to within eight feet."

Tess' eyes widened. "Did you look in my old apartment above the café?"

"It was the first place we went to after we'd checked the kitchen."

Tess' shoulders slumped forward. "I was so sure we might have found her there. Out of everything we've talked about, it makes the most sense."

Rachel took a step toward Tess. A spark of hope flared inside her. "We didn't go inside the apartment. Tank tried the door handle. It was locked."

"The police asked me for the key. I told them where the spare key should have been, but they couldn't find it. They couldn't even find the magnetic box I keep it in."

"Why would someone take the key?"

Tess shrugged. "I don't know. The apartment's empty, so there's nothing to steal. And it's directly above the café, so I'd notice if someone was living there. I could understand the key not being there if I'd forgotten to put it in the box. But the box should have been there."

"How did the police get into the apartment?"

"I gave them another key that I keep on my key ring. It was still busy when they saw me, so I didn't go with them." Tess started walking as quickly as she could along the sidewalk. "We have to go back to my apartment."

Rachel joined her, getting more excited with each step they took. "The police officers would have searched the entire apartment. Why do you think Bella could still be there?"

"It's an old building. There are plenty of places where an eight-year-old could hide."

Rachel's foot hit a patch of ice.

Tess grabbed her elbow. "Are you okay?"

"I'm trying not to get my hopes up," Rachel said as they power-walked their way down Main Street. "How would she have gotten inside if the door was locked?"

Tess' stride didn't falter. "I'll tell you after we've looked in the apartment."

They kept walking, catching each other when they slipped on the ice, wiping soft snowflakes from their faces when fresh snow fell. Rachel assumed Bella had been kidnapped by the people who'd sent John death threats. But what if something else had happened? What if she'd gone to a place she thought was safe?

She knew finding Bella in Tess' apartment was a long-shot. If she was inside, it would be a miracle. But two hours after she'd first gone missing, a miracle was what they needed.

RACHEL FOLLOWED Tess up the back stairs to her old apartment. Her heart was racing and her imagination was working overtime. She crossed her fingers as Tess looked at where the magnetic box should have been.

"How would Bella have known where to look?"

"We talked about it when you came to The Bridesmaids Club with Bella. You told me not to leave it here."

"Even if the box was there, Bella couldn't have reached it," Rachel said anxiously. "It's too high."

Tess pulled a metal key ring out of her pocket. She chose a silver key and put it in the lock. "It's only too high if you're standing on the landing. If the magnetic box was there when Bella tried the door handle, she could have climbed on the rail and reached it."

Rachel looked over the edge of the landing at the parking lot below. It was a long way down. If Bella had climbed on the rail, she could easily have slipped on the icy wood and fallen onto the ground. "She must have been desperate to get inside."

"I suppose it depends on why she was up here." Tess opened the door and walked inside. "I left the electricity on, but the heating is switched off." She turned on the lights and looked around the living room.

Rachel walked into the center of the apartment. "Bella? Are you here? It's Rachel." She waited before moving into Tess' old bedroom. "Bella?" still no reply. She looked inside the empty closet, then opened the door to the bathroom. There was no sign anyone had been here. Apart from the sound of Tess moving around in the next room, the apartment was clouded in a silence as eerie as the snow flurries outside.

She walked back into the living room and watched Tess open a cupboard hidden in a wall. "I didn't know you had extra storage in here."

Tess knelt down and looked inside the small space. "I renovated the building a few years ago. Because of the slope of the ceiling, I ended up with a cavity running either side of the apartment. My builder suggested lining the space and turning it into storage areas. We hid the handles in the grooves of the wooden paneling."

Rachel walked farther along the wall and ran her hand along the same paneling Tess had touched. Another cupboard opened. It wasn't a huge space, but it was big enough for an eight-year-old to hide in. They searched each cupboard, but they were empty.

Tess walked toward what used to be her spare bedroom. "I'll look in this room, you take the other one."

Rachel walked back into the bedroom she'd left only minutes before. With the fancy wood detailing, she hadn't noticed the same grooves on the paneling in this room. "Bella?"

She opened the first door and sighed. The second cupboard was the same. Empty.

"Rachel? You need to come here."

Rachel ran into the spare bedroom and stopped in the doorway.

Tess was kneeling in front of an open cupboard. Bella was lying inside the cavity, sound asleep. "She's cold," Tess whispered. "Do you think we should move her?"

Rachel unzipped her jacket and slipped it off her shoulders. "We need to get her warm. We can't do that inside the cupboard. She knows us, so it won't be a shock when she wakes up."

Rachel gently shook Bella's shoulder. "Bella, it's Rachel. It's time to wake up."

Bella's big brown eyes fluttered open, then closed again.

"Wake up, Bella." Rachel nudged her arm again. She looked at the worried frown on Tess' face. "I'll lift her out of the cupboard. Can you hold her while I call for the police and an ambulance?"

Tess took off her own jacket and sat on the floor. "Of course, I can. We could use my jacket as a blanket, too." She held out her arms. "I'm ready."

Rachel leaned down and carefully maneuvered Bella until her head and shoulders were out of the cupboard. "Here we go," she said softly. Within minutes, Bella was sitting in Tess' arms with two jackets wrapped around her cold body.

Rachel pulled her cell phone out of her pocket and called 9-1-1. Bella's brown eyes opened slowly. As soon as she saw Rachel, she smiled, then closed her eyes and fell back asleep.

With the police and an ambulance on the way, Rachel had one other person to call. Her hands shook so much she could hardly hold the phone to her ear.

John answered his cell phone on the first ring.

"John? It's Rachel. We've found Bella. She's in Tess' old apartment above the café."

His gruff reply was instant. He was on his way.

Within minutes of her first call, Rachel heard sirens on the street below. She walked into the living room just as the first police officer came inside.

The small apartment quickly became full of police officers, paramedics, and John's security guards. After making sure Bella wasn't in any immediate danger, two paramedics gently lifted her onto a stretcher. They replaced Rachel and Tess' jackets with a foil survival blanket and made sure she was comfortable.

Rachel heard a noise on the back stairs and walked into the living room. John burst through the door, looking frantically around the room for his daughter. She pointed toward Tess' spare bedroom. "She's in there."

John looked as though he'd aged ten years since she'd last seen him. Deep creases lined either side of his mouth and his eyes were full of worry. He rushed into the bedroom and she heard the relief in his voice when he talked to Bella.

She walked past the police officers and guards, and stood in the doorway, watching John. The scene in front of her was heartbreaking. He held Bella's hand as the paramedics finished strapping her onto the stretcher. His eyes never left her face, never wavered as tears fell down Bella's cheeks.

"I'm sorry, Dad. I shouldn't have run away. Please don't be mad at Rachel and Tank. They told me to be careful and I wasn't."

John leaned down and kissed the top of Bella's head. "As long as you're okay, that's all that matters."

"Have you got Miss Snuggles?" she whispered.

John reached into his jacket pocket and pulled out an old soft toy. It looked as though the stuffing had been squeezed out of it years ago. "Here she is."

Bella's chin wobbled as she cuddled her small blue cat.

One of the paramedics glanced at John. "Would you like to travel in the ambulance with us? We're taking Bella to the hospital as a precautionary measure."

John nodded and followed the paramedics out of the bedroom.

Rachel moved out of their way, stepping straight into the path of a police officer. He waited until Bella and John were at the back door before talking to her.

"I'll take your statements at the police station. Are you and Mrs. Allen ready to come with me?"

John stopped in the doorway. He looked at the police officer standing beside Rachel, then down at her. "Will you be okay?"

Rachel couldn't look John in the eye. She'd let him down, and she'd let Bella down. She doubted she'd ever be okay again. "Can I visit Bella after Tess and I have spoken to the police?"

"Of course, you can. I'll text you if we leave the hospital before you get there. Tanner will stay with you."

"I don't need Tanner. I can look after myself."

"It wasn't a question. Tanner stays."

The paramedics wheeled Bella onto the landing. Two police officers helped lift her stretcher down the stairs. John looked at her once more before disappearing from sight.

Taking a tissue out of her pocket, Rachel blew her nose.

Tess wrapped her arm around Rachel's shoulders. "Are you really going to be okay?"

She shook her head and glanced at Tanner. He was leaning against the kitchen counter with his arms crossed, staring straight at her. "Bella could have died, John hates me, and Tank will never trust me again. My life is a mess."

"It could have been a lot worse."

"I don't see how."

Tess held both of Rachel's hands in hers. "We don't know why Bella hid in my apartment but she's alive. No one was hurt."

"I don't think John agrees with you."

The police officer stepped forward. "Ma'am, we need to leave."

Rachel pushed a lock of hair behind her ear and wiped her eyes. "Okay. I just need to get my—"

"Jacket?" Tanner had moved silently across the room. He held her jacket toward her.

"Thank you."

"Don't thank me yet," he said with a grim smile. "We don't know why Bella ran from the café. Until we do, you're not going anywhere without me."

Rachel followed Tess and the police officer out of the apartment. Tanner followed her down the stairs. He was so close he could have been mistaken for her shadow. "Where's Tank?"

"He's working on some information we received."

Rachel was halfway across the parking lot before a horrible thought crossed her mind. "He hasn't been fired, has he? It wasn't Tank's fault Bella left the car. It was mine. I should have locked the door and kept her beside me."

"With all due respect, you're not employed as a security guard. It's not your responsibility to look after Bella."

Tess opened the rear door of the police car. "Come on, Rachel. The sooner we give our statements to the police, the sooner we can get to the hospital. Tank will be all right."

Rachel wasn't so sure. Just like she wasn't sure she'd still have a job in the morning.

They drove down Main Street, passing vehicles with red noses attached to their front grills and reindeer ears attached to their windows. The boutique stores and restaurants were still open, happy to indulge the last-minute shoppers. It all seemed so normal.

Except this year was different.

She leaned her head against the cool glass of the police car's window. Thanks to Tess' quick thinking, Bella was safe. But if they hadn't found her when they did, today could have ended in tragedy.

CHAPTER 17

*J*ohn heard Rachel walking along the corridor outside the hospital's family room before he saw her. The heels of her boots clicked against the vinyl floor with the same speed she lived her life. Fast.

Until today, he'd enjoyed the challenge of not knowing what she'd say or do from one minute to the next. Today was different. Today, her impulsiveness could have killed Bella. His daughter meant the world to him and he wouldn't tolerate anything that could cost Bella her life.

Rachel slowed down when she entered the family room. He wondered if she had any idea what she'd done by convincing Tank to visit a different store.

"You wanted to see me?" Her hands twisted her knitted hat. She looked nervous, worried, and so unsure about what was happening that it made him forget what he wanted to say.

"John? Is Bella okay?" A panicked look replaced the worry.

"Bella's fine. She'll probably be going home in the next couple of hours."

Rachel sat down in the chair beside him. "I'm glad."

"So am I."

"I'm sorry. I never thought it would turn out like this."

He almost missed the softly spoken words, the apology he hadn't expected. "Did you think I asked Tank to go with you because he didn't have anything better to do?"

She shook her head.

"I received multiple death threats. Oracom threatened my family. I wasn't happy about you going into town, but Tank said you'd be safe. He had security staff in Walmart and a getaway car in the parking lot. When he was told it was too dangerous, you drove to another store that had no guards, no cameras, and no security clearance. Crafty Crafts was not an option."

"I realize that now. I shouldn't have pressured Tank into taking us to Kelly's store. It won't happen again."

John swallowed deeply. "You're right. It won't happen again because you won't be working with Bella anymore. I trusted you with my daughter's life and you let me down."

Rachel's mouth dropped open. "But it was one mistake. Tess and I found her and she'll be okay."

John's fingers tightened on the armrest of his chair. "Do you have any idea why Bella ran to Tess' old apartment?"

"No. Tess and I have just arrived. Tanner won't tell us anything."

"A man followed her down the street. The craft store was closed, so she went into the café. She thought she could hide in there. She took off her jacket and tried to look as though she belonged to another family."

John had to stop talking. The terror Bella must have felt was eating away at him. Part of that terror was of his own making. He'd never imagined starting his own company would put his daughter's life in danger.

He took a deep breath. "Bella heard Tess talk about her

apartment when she went with you to look at the brides-maids' dresses. When she went into the café today, she couldn't see Tess to tell her about the man. Instead of telling someone else, she ran into the alley and up the back stairs to Tess' apartment. She found the key and hid inside."

"Has she seen the man before?"

"No, but she identified him from images on the security camera in the café. The police, the FBI, and the CIA are looking for him now."

"Why didn't she call out when the police searched the apartment?"

"Bella doesn't remember hearing them. Her doctor thinks she may have fallen asleep. Because she was so cold, she would have been unresponsive to any noise or movement going on around her."

Rachel didn't move from the seat beside him. He'd expected her to leave, to say goodbye to Bella, then get on with her own life. But she didn't do any of those things.

She turned to him, placing her hand on the arm of his sweater. "I know how upset you must be, but telling me to leave now won't help Bella. I could stay another week, wait until she's feeling better. I don't want you to pay me. I could stay in my apartment and drive to your home each day."

He didn't have to think hard about his answer. Rachel was already more than Bella's teacher. He couldn't risk her getting any closer. "Bella will be okay without you. Tanner will take you home after you've seen her. He'll check your apartment is safe and continue as your bodyguard during the day. When the death threats have been resolved, he'll no longer be needed. If you want him to stay with you tonight, he'll be happy to do that."

Rachel took her hand off his arm and dropped her chin to her chest. "I don't need Tanner. I'm staying with Tess and

Logan until this is over. Logan installed an expensive security system when he moved into his home, so I'll be safe."

"That's good."

She glanced at him. "What else are you worried about?"

John leaned back in his chair. He didn't know where to
start. "Apart from a Technical Development Team that's now
on high-alert and under twenty-four-hour surveillance, and
the Department of Defense breathing down my neck, I still
don't know why Bella left Tank's SUV. She knows she has to
be careful. It's out of character for her to run away."

"It was important to her."

"Scrapbooking supplies aren't important."

Rachel sighed. "Have you asked Bella why she needed
them?"

"She said it was a surprise."

"It was for your Christmas present. She wanted to finish
it tomorrow so she could give it to you on Christmas morning. Don't be too hard on her, John. She's only eight years
old. We all make mistakes."

"Mistakes don't usually cost you your life." The words
were out of his mouth before he could stop them. His wife
had made a mistake the night she'd gone out with some
friends and taken Bella with her. She'd drunk a bottle of
wine and drove four miles before hitting a tree and killing
herself.

John didn't make mistakes and neither could Bella.

Rachel picked up a bag she'd brought with her. "I saw
Mrs. Daniels at the nurses' station. She thought Bella might
need some dry clothes, so she dropped these off. She said
she'd see you both when you arrive home."

For the first time since Bella had gone missing, he really
looked at Rachel. Her big blue eyes swam in her face, filled
with regret and so much worry that he felt as though he was
looking at a reflection of his own face.

"I'm sorry, Rachel. This isn't how I imagined saying goodbye."

Rachel wiped her hands on the knees of her jeans and stood up. "I enjoyed spending time with Bella. I'll say goodbye to her on my way out. Good luck with finding the man who followed her."

After Rachel left the room, he looked at the bag of clothes and tried to think of something positive that had happened today. But all he could see was the disappointment on Rachel's face when he'd told her she wouldn't be teaching Bella anymore.

His daughter was resilient and would soon bounce back from what had happened. She'd miss Rachel for a few days, then find something else to make her happy.

He didn't know if he could say the same thing about himself.

RACHEL WOKE up in one of Tess and Logan's spare bedrooms. It was still dark outside, but that was nothing unusual for this time of the year. The sun, when it remembered to peek its head out of the clouds, would be a welcome relief from the gloomy mornings and early evenings.

She wondered if that was why so many people strung Christmas lights around their properties. They brightened the streets, lightened people's hearts, and brought smiles to most people's faces.

The only lights she remembered from last night were the blow-up characters in John's front yard. The drive back to his home hadn't lightened her heart or made her smile.

After she'd left the hospital, Tanner took her to John's home to pack her bags and say goodbye to Mr. and Mrs. Daniels. It was a quick, tear-filled visit that made Rachel

191

realize how much of an impact people could make in your life. She'd miss Mrs. Daniels' baking, her wonderful sense of humor, and the joy she brought to John's home.

But she couldn't afford to dwell on what had happened. If she kept thinking about what was missing from her life, her heart would break all over again.

She looked at the time and sighed. It wasn't as early as she thought. With one last sigh, she rolled out of bed, opened the suitcase Tanner had carried inside, and looked for some clean clothes.

After she'd showered, she went downstairs to see if Tanner had arrived. He was sitting at the kitchen table, drinking a cup of coffee, and looking through the morning paper.

She smiled at her bodyguard. "Good morning. What time did you get here?"

"About five-thirty. The same time Tess left for work. She said to come to the café for breakfast. She'll cook a few extra pancakes for us."

"Us?"

Tanner's face moved into what could have been a smile. "There has to be some perks to the job."

Rachel poured herself a cup of coffee. She almost felt sorry for Tanner. Making sure she didn't hurt herself, get kidnapped, or even get killed, couldn't be the most satisfying job in the world. After yesterday, he definitely deserved a double stack of pancakes with all the trimmings. "Do you know how Bella is this morning?"

"She's doing okay. She left the hospital at eight o'clock last night and went straight to bed. Mrs. Daniels made her breakfast about two hours ago." Tanner closed the paper. "She asked where you were."

Rachel swallowed the lump in her throat. "Are you making that up?"

"No. Tank's looking after Bella. He wants to know if you're happy to call her. She misses you."

Rachel nodded. "I miss her, too. But I can't call her. John wouldn't want me to."

"I guess that's up to you, then."

Rachel looked sharply at Tanner. "You wouldn't be alluding to the fact that I'm a determined, independent woman, would you?"

"Who me, ma'am? I wouldn't dream of it. A determined, independent woman wouldn't worry about whether she was stepping on anyone's toes. She'd be more worried about making sure an eight-year-old was happy."

Rachel tipped the rest of her coffee down the sink. "That's good, because I wouldn't want you to think I don't care. I do, more than anyone realizes. But if John found out I'd called Bella, he'd send the National Guard to keep me away from his daughter."

Tanner stood up and rinsed his cup under the faucet. "The National Guard has nothing on us. Fletcher Security employs the best of the best, and I'm telling you now, some rules are meant to be broken."

As she pulled out her cell phone, Rachel bit her bottom lip. "I hope you're right," she muttered. "If John finds out about this, he'll complain to the school board. I'll be dismissed, have no job to go back to, and end up living on the street eating Tess' leftovers."

Tanner held her jacket toward her. "You don't need your bag. I'll bring you straight back here after breakfast."

Rachel stopped dialing Bella's number. "I'm on house arrest?"

"I wouldn't put it in those terms exactly, but bringing you back here isn't one of the rules I'm willing to break." He held the back door open. "After you."

Rachel pulled on her jacket. "You wouldn't have negotiated an early release for breakfast because you want to eat Tess' pancakes, would you?"

Tanner nodded at her cell phone. "I believe you have a phone call to make, Ms. McReedy."

Rachel redialed Bella's home number, hoping John was nowhere in sight. Tanner opened the back door and waved her through. She stayed where she was, waiting for someone to answer the phone. Tanner's stomach could wait a few extra minutes before they left.

Someone picked up the phone and said hello. "Tank? Is that you?"

"Rachel? How are you?"

"I'm fine. I'm staying with Tess and Logan. Tanner is here with me, but then you probably know that." Rachel clamped her lips tight to stop from rambling. "Could I speak to Bella for a few minutes? I just want to make sure she's okay."

"Sure, she's right here."

Rachel waited a few seconds for Bella to speak.

"Rachel?"

"I'm here, Bella. How are you feeling?"

"I'm good. Dad's gone into work early, but he's coming home soon. We're going to watch a movie and have popcorn and ice cream. Mrs. Daniels made bacon and eggs for breakfast and Miss Snuggles likes having me close."

"It sounds like you're having a great day."

"It would be better with you here. Dad said you're starting your other job sooner than you thought."

"It's something like that," Rachel said quietly. "Have a lovely day. I'll see you at school in the new year."

"But Santa is bringing a present to our house for you. I thought you'd be here on Christmas morning to help open our gifts."

"Maybe you could keep Santa's present safe and I'll see

you after Christmas? I'm visiting my mom and dad on Christmas morning."

"Oh."

Rachel heard the disappointment in Bella's voice, but she couldn't do anything about it. "I have to go now, Bella. Have a good day with your dad."

"I will. Rachel?"

Rachel felt the weight of the words Bella was about to say. "Yes?"

"I miss you."

"I miss you, too. Have a great time." Rachel ended the call, then looked at Tanner. "I guess this is what you call tough love?"

Tanner shook his head and reopened the back door. "Let's go to Angel Wings Café before Tess' breakfast deal expires. It might make you feel better."

Rachel followed Tanner outside. It would take more than her bodyguard's charming personality and Tess' pancakes to make her happier.

CHAPTER 18

*J*ohn leaned forward. Dan Carter had just told him the news he'd been waiting for all night. "You're telling me Bella wasn't followed? That the man running behind her wanted a coffee before he went home to his children?"

"Brian Tanner hasn't done a thing wrong in his life. No parking fines, speeding tickets, or tax evasion issues. It looks as though Bella panicked."

John stood and looked through the window. "I've been so paranoid about anyone getting close to her she must have overreacted. I don't know what to say."

"You don't have to say anything. I'm not sure if I'd act any differently if I were in your shoes. The CIA and the FBI are still working on the Oracom case. Until we hear from them, I wouldn't change what you're doing. It will be Christmas soon. Enjoy the time with your family."

"I will. Are you going to be here over Christmas?"

Dan nodded. "I drew the short straw this year. If I hear anything, I'll let you know straight away."

"Thanks, I'd appreciate that."

"Don't thank me. Thank your buddies in the FBI. If it hadn't been for them, the CIA would have cut us out of their communication channels before now."

"It didn't have anything to do with me. Oracom's reputation for getting what they want started long before our case. The only difference is that this time, they're up against the US Government."

"Have you heard anything more about the security drone?"

"Nothing I didn't expect. Thanks for what you're doing. It means a lot."

Dan shook his hand. "No problem. Call me if you need me."

John left Dan's office and headed toward his truck.

Tank was waiting for him on the sidewalk, talking on his cell phone. When he saw John he ended the call and moved swiftly across to their vehicle.

"Everything okay, boss?"

"Everything's fine. I want to head over to Angel Wings Café and thank Tess for what she did yesterday."

Tank opened John's door and walked around to the driver's side of the vehicle. "Tanner's there with Rachel. They're having a late breakfast."

John hesitated before sliding into the passenger seat. He wasn't ready to see Rachel. He'd fired her and called her irresponsible.

But it was the things he hadn't told her that made him feel worse. He hadn't called and told her Bella was safe at home. It wasn't until after he'd calmed down that he realized what an idiot he'd been. He'd woken up knowing Rachel wasn't the only person who'd made a mistake yesterday.

He pulled his seatbelt across his chest and locked it in place. "Forget the café. I promised Bella I'd come home early to watch a movie with her. Do you know if Mrs. Daniels has popcorn and ice cream in the kitchen?"

Tank turned on the ignition and moved into the traffic. "I'll call through to the house and ask. Are you sure you don't want to stop by the café first?"

"Positive." It was about the only thing he was sure about.

As they drove down Main Street, John checked his emails, but all the time his mind was on Rachel. Yesterday he'd been worried about Bella, angry Rachel and Tank had deviated from a plan he wasn't happy with.

Rachel had been as worried as he was about Bella, and all he'd done was tell her to leave. She was headstrong, beautiful, and intelligent. She deserved someone who appreciated and loved her as if she was the most important person in the world.

He hadn't been that person yesterday, but he wished one day he could be.

RACHEL LOOKED around The Bridesmaid Club headquarters. It wasn't where she thought she'd be on Christmas Eve, but then she couldn't have predicted anything that had happened over the last few days.

She handed a bridesmaid a purple organza dress. It had big, puffy sleeves and so many sparkly beads it could be used as a lighthouse off the coast of Maine.

"Cheer up," Tess whispered as all three bridesmaids walked into the changing room. "It's supposed to be the happiest day of their sister's life. You look as though you're dressing them for a funeral."

"Sorry. I'll put on my smiley face." Rachel plastered a fake smile across her face and turned to Tess. "Is this better?"

"A little. Now you look as though you've had too much Botox."

Rachel felt her smile droop at the sides. "It's no use. It keeps slipping."

Tess laughed so loud that she had to slap her hand across her mouth. "This is so not the Christmas Eve I imagined."

"You can't help it if the dresses the bridesmaids are supposed to wear never arrived."

"But I could have told them we're closed for Christmas. Who gets married on Christmas Eve, anyway?"

Rachel quite liked the idea. "I think it's romantic. They couldn't help the snowstorm." For the last ten days, the bride had been waiting for her bridesmaids' dresses to arrive from Italy. With all the airport closures and diverted flights, the dresses were somewhere in New York City.

Tess put one of the rejected gowns on a hanger. "No one could have predicted the storm, but they could have ordered their dresses earlier."

"When did you become so cynical? You're usually the first person to donate dresses to brides in distress."

"I'm not cynical, just practical," Tess whispered as the first bridesmaid came back into the living room.

Tess had called Rachel from the café at two o'clock that afternoon. She'd told her she had a desperate bride on the phone who needed three bridesmaids' dresses in the next two hours.

Rachel had been inside with Tanner for most of the day, getting more and more bored. Tess' phone call had given her an excuse to feel like a normal person. So she'd told Tanner four women were coming over to Tess' home to find the perfect bridesmaids' dresses.

He wasn't impressed, but he'd followed her into the loft, making himself scarce once the bridesmaids arrived.

An hour later, the only good thing Rachel could say about the last-minute dress fitting was that she wasn't bored.

She looked at the bridesmaid who was standing in front of her. "It's not the one." The petite redhead had chosen a hot pink, crinoline skirted dress. It looked like something Scarlett O'Hara would have worn in *Gone with the Wind.*

The bridesmaid twisted left and right in front of a full-length mirror. "Are you sure?"

Rachel walked across to the dresses in their Cinderella Collection. "Sometimes less is more. Why don't you try this dress? It still has a full skirt with little bows at the back, but it's a softer shade of pink. And there aren't too many sparkles to overshadow you."

"I'll try it, but we only have half an hour before we need to leave for the beauty salon."

"Come and see us after you've put it on."

Tess stood beside Rachel and watched the bridesmaid disappear into the changing room. "The hot pink dress would look better on her sister."

Another bridesmaid came out of the changing room and Tess sighed. "That looks perfect." The pale yellow dress hugged the bridesmaid's upper body and fell to the floor in soft pleats. It wasn't frilly or flouncy, and it didn't have a sparkly bead in sight.

The young woman smiled shyly at Tess. "I think so, too. Everyone else liked it, so I guess this is it."

"What did your original bridesmaids' dresses look like?" Rachel asked. Each of the bridesmaids had different ideas about what looked good on them and what didn't. Finding three dresses that not only looked good, but could be made in time for the wedding, must have been difficult.

"The other dresses were almost the same as this one, except they had lace overskirts and sweetheart necklines. They were made by a designer in Milan."

"Are you disappointed they haven't arrived in time?"

The bridesmaid shook her head. "This is the best thing that could have happened. My sister has been acting like bridezilla all week. At least it's given her something genuine to worry about." She looked over her shoulder at the changing room door. "I'll go and see what everyone's doing."

As soon as the door opened, Rachel heard the chatter of the sisters as they discussed the merits of each dress. While they were deciding what they'd do, she sat on a sofa and slipped off her shoes.

"I can't believe you're still wearing high-heels," Tess said with a dramatic sigh. "It's the middle of winter and Jimmy Choo was not made to be worn in the cold."

"I can't help myself. I bought them at a thrift store last year. We're not all six-feet tall." Rachel wiggled her toes against the thick rug under her feet. "I have a fascination with heels that are higher than four inches. But these shoes may be too high, even for me."

"Hold that thought," Rachel whispered as the three bridesmaids and their bridezilla sister emerged from the changing room.

The bridesmaid who'd originally worn the hot pink dress stepped forward. "You were right. The soft pink dress looks better on me. Carly has organized her dress. Do you like Lottie's?"

A woman with short black hair stepped forward. She was wearing a simple, pale blue satin dress. The only problem with the dress was the width of the skirt over her hips. It was way too wide and would need to be taken in at least three inches.

Lottie bunched the fabric in her hand. "I'm an awkward shape. I have no idea how I'm going to find a dress in time."

Rosalind Smith, the bride-to-be, pulled out her cell phone. "Don't worry. The dress looks almost perfect on you.

I have a dressmaker on standby to do any last-minute alterations." She pushed speed dial and moved away from her sisters.

Rachel looked at all three bridesmaids. "You couldn't have chosen better dresses. You all look beautiful."

Carly smiled. "We'll look even better after our hair and makeup are done. Let's get changed before Rosalind finishes her call."

The bridesmaids lifted the skirts of their dresses and hotfooted it back into the changing room.

"It looks as though bridezilla has them organized," Tess whispered.

Rachel laughed at the twinkle in Tess' eyes. "Shh. She might hear you."

"It's Christmas Eve. I'm allowed to be a bit naughty."

By the time Rosalind finished speaking on the phone, all three bridesmaids had their dresses hanging in white plastic bags, ready to take to the dressmaker.

"Thank you so much," Rosalind said to Tess as she gave her a hug. "We really appreciate both of you going out of your way to help us."

"I hope your wedding is amazing," Tess said with a smile. "We were happy to help."

All four women headed toward the back door. Rachel handed them their coats. "It was nice meeting you. Be careful of the ice on your way out."

After they'd gone, Tess put on the kettle. "I'm making a hot chocolate before I tidy up the mess in here. Do you want one?"

Rachel looked at the gowns lying over the backs of chairs and the spare shoes abandoned by the clothing racks. "That's the second best idea anyone's had all day."

"What was the first?"

Rachel grinned at her friend. "Pancakes for breakfast."

"I'm glad I could be of service," Tess said with a cheeky smile. "Do you think Tanner wants a hot chocolate?"

"I wouldn't say no, ma'am."

Tess jumped a foot in the air. "You did it again. For such a big man, you don't make much noise."

"Comes with the job. I've been admiring your husband's cars in the garage."

Rachel handed Tanner a bridesmaid's dress. "He's car crazy. While Tess is making the hot chocolate, you can help me hang up our bridesmaids' dresses. There's about a dozen gowns that need to be put away."

"Why did I know you'd find something for me to do?"

"Because you're wise," Rachel said as she handed Tanner a hanger. "Just think how dull and boring your life will be when you don't have to look after me."

Tanner lips almost made it into a smile. "I'm looking forward to it already."

Rachel sighed. So was she.

CHAPTER 19

*J*ohn's eyes snapped open. He lay perfectly still, trying to work out what had woken him. He glanced at his alarm clock and squinted at the neon green numbers. It was five-thirty. He had two guards on duty outside and another one inside. His hand reached for the panic alarm.

"Dad?" Bella's voice whispered across his room. "Are you awake?"

John relaxed as Bella tiptoed toward him.

"Dad?" She shook his shoulder and he pretended to snore. "Dad, it's Christmas morning. It's time to get up."

John opened one eye and peered at his daughter. Her curly brown hair was standing out at odd angles around her face. She was wearing her pajamas, the ones with blue cats that reminded her of Miss Snuggles.

"Do you know what the time is?"

Bella shook her head. "It doesn't matter. We're both awake so we could see what Santa left for us."

John looked closely at his daughter. "Have you already been downstairs?"

Bella ran her hands over the edge of his blanket. "I was only there for a little while. Mr. Daniels told me I had to go back to bed."

"What were you doing?"

"I thought I'd make it easier for us to find our presents. I sorted them into little piles."

John rubbed his eyes. "Uncle Grant wants to be here when we open our presents. He won't be awake yet."

"We could call him and wake him up. Uncle Grant won't mind."

John was certain his brother *would* mind. "What if we choose one present each and then make breakfast? We'll call Uncle Grant at seven o'clock." His brother would still be sound asleep, but if John had to get up, it was only fair his brother suffered the same fate.

"Can we call Rachel, too?"

John swung his legs over the side of the bed. "Rachel's spending time with her family today."

"But can I call her? Mrs. Daniels knows her number."

"Why do you want to speak to Rachel?"

Bella sat on John's bed while he looked for a sweatshirt. "I like Rachel. She's fun to be around and she teaches me really good things. I miss her."

"Rachel was never going to stay here forever, Bella."

"I know, but she's pretty and smart. She knows lots of amazing things."

John glanced at Bella.

"It's true. She told me otters sleep holding hands with their friends, and a baby spider is called a spiderling."

He smiled at the earnest expression on his daughter's face. "Rachel is smart, but she also has her own life. She came here to teach you, Bella, not spend Christmas with us."

Bella's mouth set in a stubborn line. "She's my friend."

"We'll talk about it later. Let's go and open a present."

Bella bounced off the bed and followed him downstairs. "Santa ate his cookies."

"Did Rudolph eat his carrot?"

"He ate most of his carrot. You can see his teeth marks in it."

John held Bella's hand as they walked through to the living room. The entire entrance was still smothered in glittery tinsel. It felt like they were walking through Santa's magic cave, especially with the Christmas music he could hear coming from the kitchen.

"Mr. Daniels thought you might want to hear my music CD when you came downstairs. It's the same carols we sung in our Christmas play."

John stopped inside the living room and stared at the Christmas tree. "Did Mr. Daniels turn on the Christmas tree lights, too?"

Bella shook her head. "That was me. Doesn't the angel look beautiful?"

"She does." John gazed at the tree. It reminded him of when he was a boy. Everything had been sparkly and bright. He'd thought Christmas would always be a happy, family time. It wasn't until his mom and dad died, and then Jacinta, that he realized Christmas could be one of the hardest times of the year.

This Christmas, for the first time in many years, it almost felt like it used to.

Bella sat on the edge of the rug under the tree. "This is for you."

John took the carefully wrapped present out of her hands. "Thank you. I'll find one of your presents."

Bella shook her head. "Open yours first. I made it myself."

He carefully undid the tape and peeled back the paper. Bella didn't say anything as he pulled an album out of the wrapping.

"I called it, *Christmas Memories*." Bella knelt beside him and pointed to the first photo. "Uncle Grant looked through his photos and found some of your old family ones. Rachel helped me copy our photos."

The first photo was of his family. He would have been about six months' old. Grant was sitting on the floor holding him in his arms. His mom and dad were crouched either side of them, smiling at the camera.

"It's your first Christmas," Bella said. "Keep going. It gets better."

John turned to the next page. Another Christmas photo appeared, but instead of a Christmas tree, Grant and John were sitting on Santa's knee, enjoying Christmas at the mall. The page was adorned with paper hearts and small Christmas pictures.

"I like the decorations on each page."

Bella smiled. "I had to make some. Rachel couldn't come here yesterday, so Mrs. Daniels helped me."

He turned to the next photo and frowned. "Are there photos in here of each Christmas?"

His daughter nodded. "That's why it's called *Christmas Memories*. Do you like it?"

He left the album on the coffee table and pulled Bella close. "I love it. Thank you."

Bella buried her head in his shoulder. "I wanted to make something special for you. Rachel took my photo at the mall with the elves. It was so much fun. That's when I decided to make you a Christmas album. I found two photos of Mom and me at Christmas, but we don't have any with you."

John swallowed the lump in his throat. He picked up the album and turned to the two photos Bella was talking about. Jacinta looked back at him, laughing at the camera with the same carefree spirit he'd loved. "I wasn't home when you were a baby, Bella. I was working overseas."

"I know. That's why I added your military photo." She pointed at the photograph she'd stuck to the page. "I put little flags around the edges."

John kissed the top of her head, then turned to the back page. "Is this empty page for this Christmas?"

Bella smiled. "How did you guess?"

"Oh, I don't know. It could be because we have the most amazing tree this year. And Uncle Grant hasn't stopped bragging about a new camera he bought last week." John leaned forward and whispered in Bella's ear, "He might be expecting to take the photo."

Bella threw her arms around his neck. "He *is* going to take our photo. He's got a tripod and a timer and everything. Do you think Rachel could be in the photo, too? It was almost her idea."

John's heart sank. "Bella, Rachel's busy and can't be part of our family photo."

Bella's arms dropped from around his shoulders.

John watched her bent head and tried to think of something to say. "You haven't opened your present from me, yet."

Bella's head shot up. She slipped off his knee and watched him walk across to the tree. "It must be here somewhere," he muttered, as he pretended to search through the gifts.

"I could help you look."

"It's okay. It's right here." John handed the present to Bella. "Merry Christmas."

Bella tore the paper off the present and threw her arms around his neck. "Oh, Dad. I love it."

John knew how much she enjoyed creating things, so he'd bought her a big paint set and four different sized canvases.

"Can I paint something now?"

John couldn't think of a reason why she couldn't. At least if she was busy, he wouldn't have to get his brother out of bed too early. "Let's go into the kitchen. You can paint while I make breakfast."

"Can you make pancakes?"

"Blueberry, cinnamon, or maple syrup?"

Bella thought long and hard. "Blueberry, please."

They walked through to the kitchen and John took some eggs and buttermilk out of the refrigerator. "You have nice manners."

"I know." Bella sighed. "Mrs. Daniels said I need to be extra good to make up for running away from Tank and Rachel. I got them into trouble, didn't I?"

"You shouldn't have run away, Bella. You could have been hurt."

"I won't do it again. Is that why Rachel doesn't live here anymore?"

"Some of the reason. Rachel has things she needs to do."

Bella's bottom lip wobbled. "Doesn't she like me?"

"She likes you. You'll see her at school in another couple of weeks."

"But that's a long time away."

"It's the best I can do. How many pancakes would you like?"

"Three." She smiled at John. "Please. Do you think Mr. Daniels would like a pancake? He's been awake all night, but he didn't see Santa Claus. Mr. Daniels thinks he must have been checking the garage when Santa snuck into the living room."

John listened to Bella as she told him what Jim Daniels had been doing all night. With all his hair-raising adventures, John was surprised Santa had risked landing on their roof.

Jim Daniels, as well as being a former SAS officer and his housekeeper's husband, was a good storyteller. And if John was lucky, his adventures would be enough to stop Bella asking about Rachel again.

～

JOHN WATCHED his brother flop onto the sofa. It was eight-thirty at night. Another Christmas had almost been and gone.

Grant sighed. "Bella is now happily sleeping after two chapters of *Anne of Avonlea.* She really has a thing for Anne Shirley. I'm surprised she hasn't dyed her hair red."

"Keep that observation to yourself," John muttered. "If she thinks red hair is a possibility, I'll never hear the end of it."

Grant snorted. "The trials and tribulations of being a parent."

John cradled his coffee mug in his hands. "Do you remember when Spiderman hit the shelves at the library? You wanted to climb down the side of Mr. Garvey's barn, just like Spiderman would have done."

"It didn't do me much good. You must have run like the wind to get home before I took my first step."

John could still remember the terror that had propelled him forward. "You're my older brother. You're supposed to have more common sense than me. Jumping off the side of a three-story barn wasn't smart."

"Tell me about it. Mom didn't let me take a Spiderman comic out of the library for a month after that. She couldn't have inflicted a worse punishment."

John thought about their childhood, the carefree days of living on a ranch surrounded by some of the most beautiful scenery in the world. He'd never fully appreciated what they'd had until he was halfway around the world, fighting in a war no one would ever win.

Grant stood and added another log to the fire. "Do you want to tell me why you've been trying so hard to smile?"

"I don't know what you're talking about."

"Sure you don't. Just like you don't know why you keep looking at the two presents that haven't been opened."

John narrowed his eyes at his brother. "It's none of your business."

"Where have I heard that before?" He walked across to the Christmas tree and took the presents out from under the branches. "Well, that's a surprise. One of the presents is for you, and the other is for Rachel."

"Bella made her something."

"And you didn't think to drop it off?" Grant frowned at him. "I get it now. You're scared of her."

John clamped his lips together. He knew what his brother was up to. He was trying to rattle him, get under his skin until he annoyed him so much that he'd tell him everything.

Grant left the two presents on the coffee table. "Are you going to open the present Rachel left for you?"

"No."

"Come on. It won't kill you to open it. It's Christmas. That's what people do."

"I fired her, called her things I shouldn't have. She must have left our presents under the tree after she came home to pack her bags."

"Bella liked her gift."

John knew that was the biggest understatement of the year. Rachel had given Bella an *Anne of Green Gables* T-shirt, a carry bag, and a coloring book. Bella hadn't taken the T-shirt off all day.

"So you're worried your gift might contain cyanide?"

John looked at the two presents. "I hurt her."

"Tell her you're sorry. She'd be the first person to understand."

"It's not as easy as that."

Grant picked up the present from Rachel. "Why do you

always make your life so complicated? Even when you were Bella's age, nothing was ever simple with you."

"I felt a deeper sense of responsibility than you did."

"Or a deeper sense of guilt. You can't change the past."

John closed his eyes. He couldn't remember much of his childhood, but he did remember the soldiers who'd fought alongside him, the ones who hadn't come home. He thought about Jacinta, the regret he felt for not spending more time with her. Even after Bella was born he'd disappeared for months on end, leaving her to cope as best she could.

"Punishing yourself won't bring Jacinta back. Don't you think it's time to move on?"

He wiped his eyes. "I don't know how."

Grant sat beside him. "You start by believing in yourself. You're worthy of being loved."

John smiled through his tears. "You've been watching too much TV."

"I read it in a book," Grant said with a sad smile. "You're not the only person with issues. I'm four years older than you are and I've never been married, haven't even been engaged. Do you think I have a *do not touch* sign tattooed on my forehead?"

John grabbed a tissue out of his pocket and blew his nose. "Are you worthy of being loved?"

This time, Grant's face broke into a smile. "Maybe. You don't happen to have the phone number of a woman who's willing to overlook a few personality flaws, do you?"

"I only have the number of one woman and you're not getting within thirty feet of her."

Grant nudged his arm. "Worried about a little competition?"

That was the last thing on John's mind. "She'd eat you for breakfast and spit out the bones. Rachel teaches nine- and ten-year-old boys. She knows the type of games you play."

"Used to play." Grant picked up John's present. "Open it."

"No."

"Why not?"

"I fired her. She hates me."

Grant sighed. "You told me you'd fired her and acted like a jerk *before* she left your present under the tree. Doesn't that tell you something?"

"Yeah. She's too nice to hold a grudge. She probably left it there because she didn't have anyone else to give the socks to."

Grant squeezed the parcel. "It's not socks."

"How do you know?"

"I know socks when I feel them and, I'm telling you, this isn't a pair of socks."

John glanced at the present. "It could be thick socks."

"It feels like there's a box under the squishy stuff."

"A box?" John looked at the carefully wrapped present, then grabbed it out of Grant's hands. "For Pete's sake, I'll open it and put us both out of our misery."

"At last." Grant sighed dramatically. "That has to be the most intelligent thing you've said all night."

"Very funny," John muttered as he pulled the tape off Rachel's present. He opened one end of the paper and looked inside.

"If you're trying to torture me with your slow unwrapping technique, you're succeeding. For once in your life, just rip off the paper."

John glared at his brother. "Whose present is it?"

"You wouldn't have opened it if I wasn't here." He looked over John's shoulder. "See...I told you it wasn't socks."

John pulled the last piece of tape off the present. "It's a book."

"If you tell me it's a first edition Spiderman comic I'm marrying Rachel tomorrow."

John undid the plastic bubble wrap.

"Don't keep me in suspense," Grant groaned. "Am I nearly betrothed or still unhappily single?"

"You could be both if you read this book after me." John felt a smile work its way across his face. "It's called, *The Dummies Guide to Finding the Perfect Wife.*"

"Are you sure you didn't tell her you have feelings for her?"

"What are you talking about?"

"The book—it's not the sort of thing you'd give to just anyone. Do you think she wants to be the perfect wife for you?"

John's smile turned into a full-throttle, bottom-of-the-belly kind of laugh.

Grant looked at him as if he'd gone crazy. "What's so funny?"

"Do you remember how I met Rachel?"

"Yeah. Bella wrote a letter to a club who give away brides-maids' dresses. She wanted to find you—"

"A wife," John said. "Now I have no excuse."

Grant looked down at the book, then back at John. "What does it say?"

"About what?"

"Finding the perfect wife. Not that I'm a dummy or anything, but it might have a few pointers I could incorporate into my life."

"Like talking to a woman for more than ten seconds before asking if they want children?"

Grant scowled. "There's nothing more ugly than a jealous man."

John opened the book to the first page. His eyes widened as he read the table of contents.

"What? It can't be that hard to find the perfect woman?" Grant leaned over his shoulder and swallowed. "Forty-five chapters? How am I supposed to remember all of that? I can only do one thing at a time."

"You and me both," John muttered. "Maybe we're lost causes?"

"We could always split the chapters and cover the highlights? I'll tell you what I learned and you can do the same for me."

"I knew there was a reason you're my older brother. Sometimes you can almost be brilliant."

"I'll go to the bookstore and get another copy," Grant said. "What will you do about the present Bella made for Rachel?"

"I'll give it to Rachel when I see her again."

"And when will that be?"

John didn't like the evil glint in his brother's eyes. "In about two weeks, when Bella starts school."

"It's a Christmas present. By the time you get around to giving it to her, it will almost be Easter."

"And your point is?"

Grant picked up the last unopened present. "Bella will be disappointed Rachel didn't open her present on Christmas day. Take it to her."

"I'm not taking it to Rachel now. It's nearly nine o'clock. She's probably in bed, fast asleep."

Grant rolled his eyes. "Only people with eight-year-old daughters are asleep by now. The rest of the world is just starting to party."

"I don't think Rachel is the partying kind."

"Why don't you call her and find out? I'll stay here with Bella and half the retired US military personnel. I could even read the first chapter of your book and tell you what it said."

John took his cell phone out of his pocket. He pulled up his contact list, then put down his phone. "I'll call her in the morning. Bella will want to come."

"Bella will understand. Rachel could visit Bella tomorrow."

John wasn't sure this was a good idea. He'd be lucky if Rachel spoke to him. The flimsy excuse of a Christmas present wouldn't work. She'd see through it, tell him she didn't want anything to do with him.

Grant grabbed his phone off the coffee table and ran across the room.

"Don't you dare," John hissed. "Put that phone down."

Grant pushed a couple of buttons and smiled. "Oops. My fingers slipped. It's ringing…"

He passed the phone to John just as Rachel answered the call.

"Hello?"

He glared at his brother. "Hi, Rachel. It's John. I've umm… I have the Christmas present Bella made for you. Can I bring it around?" The silence on the end of the phone wasn't reassuring.

"Did you mean now or another day?"

"Well…it doesn't really matter, but now would be good." Grant was busy making high-five actions beside him. John could have thrown his brother out the door.

"Okay. Now would be fine. I'm at Tess and Logan's home. I'll see you soon." Rachel ended the call before John realized what she'd said.

"Well?" Grant watched him carefully. "Did you hit a home run or strike out?"

"I'm going to see Rachel."

Grant threw his hand in the air and high-fived John.

And for the first time in a long while, it felt good to be alive.

CHAPTER 20

*R*achel ran downstairs and sat in a big, overstuffed chair in the living room. She glanced at the gas fireplace, the candles she'd lit on the coffee table. It was too much. It looked like she was preparing for a night of seduction, not a quick five-minute gift-giving exercise.

She blew out the candles and waved the thin line of black smoke away from the table. The rest of the room looked normal. The cushions were in the right place, sneakers were at the front door and not under the sofa, and all the magazines were where they should be.

She ran her hands through her hair and tried to look as though she hadn't just gotten out of bed. She glanced at her watch and the grandfather clock in the living room. John should be here soon.

She wondered if putting a plate of cookies on the table would be a normal thing to do. Bringing over her Christmas present from Bella didn't mean he wanted to say or do anything more than give her the present. But a plate of cookies was fairly neutral. It was good manners to offer your guest something to eat and drink. Except he wasn't her guest. He was her boss. Ex-boss. The man who'd fired her.

What was she doing?

The doorbell rang and Rachel leaped out of the chair. Tanner would have stopped whoever was there if it wasn't John.

Brushing her hands down the side of her skirt, she hoped the dress wasn't too revealing. She'd worn it to her parents' house for lunch, so it should be all right for John's unexpected visit. She tweaked the bodice before opening the door. It was better to be safe than sorry. Or maybe not.

John stood on the front porch in his thick woolen jacket. He looked incredibly sexy in the mountain man versus James Bond way that he had about him. Her imagination was rambling. She needed to say something intelligent instead of staring at him.

Squaring her shoulders, she opened her mouth and said, "Hi." John's shy smile made her breath catch. "Would you like to come inside?"

"Thanks. I appreciate you seeing me so late in the day. I mean…it's not that late, but I tend to go to…"

Rachel stared at him. He was nervous. John Fletcher, the man most likely to be poised and confident in front of anyone, was nervous. Of her. Of being here.

She shouldn't have left their Christmas presents under the tree. "It's okay. I was still awake." Not quite a lie, but enough to make her blush as red as Rudolph's nose. "Do you want a cup of coffee? We have hot chocolate or juice if you want something different?"

John looked relieved. "Coffee would be great. Where's Tess and Logan?"

"They left a few hours ago. They're visiting Logan's mom for Christmas."

"Oh." He looked at her dress and frowned.

She glanced at the red crossover bodice and full skirt. It was too much. She should have worn jeans, pretended this wasn't a big deal.

"I like your dress."

Rachel cleared her throat. "Thanks. I don't often wear dresses but, seeing as it's Christmas, I thought I might—" She stopped in mid-sentence.

"...wear one?" John finished.

Rachel sighed. "I'm nervous. I didn't want you to think I'd done anything special for—"

"I changed five times before I came here. My brother skim-read the first chapter of the book you gave me and summarized it so I don't mess this up. I nearly turned around twice before ringing the doorbell." John took a deep breath. "I'm nervous, too."

"You are? Why?"

"I said things I didn't mean. It wasn't your fault Bella ran away. She shouldn't have done that and she knows she made a mistake. You were only trying to make her happy and I guess that's as good a reason as any to be spontaneous. In case that all came out in a garbled rambling, what I'm trying to say is that I'm sorry."

"Thank you. Apology accepted." Rachel grinned at her ex-boss. Ever since Bella had gone missing she'd been so worried she'd felt sick to her stomach.

In the space of a few seconds, John had made her the happiest person alive. "You can take off your coat and come into the kitchen. I'll make us coffee."

John shrugged out of his coat and hung it on the stand.

"I like what you're wearing," she teased.

He looked at his jeans and white button-down shirt. "Grant told me it looked casual without being sloppy. The white shirt is supposed to make my chest look wider and, therefore, more appealing to the feminine eye."

Her gaze shot to his face. "Did Grant really say that?"

"No. I made it up. But if you like my white shirt, I'm happy."

She looked at his white shirt again. It did make his chest look wider. It defined his muscles and left her drooling on the spot. "Are you flirting with me, John Fletcher?"

He took a step forward. "It was the third bullet point in the book you gave me. Is it working?"

Rachel moved a step closer. She ran her hand down the front of his shirt and saw his pulse leap in his throat. "It's working. What were the other two bullet points?"

"Ring the doorbell and don't fall flat on your face when you see the beautiful woman waiting for you."

"Wow. The cover said it was a bestseller, but I didn't know it was that good."

John rubbed his nose against the side of her face. "Do you want to know what the fourth bullet point said?"

She was impressed he could remember what bullet point they were up to. Her brain had gone into melt-down mode when he'd mentioned his shirt. She licked her lips and let her imagination wander through different bullet point options.

John muttered something under his breath, then plastered his amazing mouth against hers. Wrapping her arms around his shoulders, she pulled him close and felt a rush of heat melt her common sense away.

His tongue slid along the seam of her mouth, dipped between her lips, and teased her until she didn't care what bullet point four, five, or six, said.

He lifted her into his arms and she wound her legs around his waist.

"I think we're skipping chapter one," he whispered against her ear.

Rachel nibbled on the sensitive skin under his jaw. She smiled at the groan rumbling out of his chest. "Do you want to call Grant and ask him to summarize chapter two? He did a pretty good job of chapter one."

John walked across to the sofa and sat down with her in his lap. "We could make it up as we go along."

"You want to be spontaneous?" She felt the smile on John's face as she kissed him.

"I have been known to act first and think later."

She leaned back. "You have?"

"Once or twice." He closed his eyes and moaned as she wiggled against him.

"Show me."

"Are you sure?"

Rachel nodded. "I've never been more sure about anything."

"It will change our relationship." He tugged at the zip on the back of her dress and ran his hand along her spine.

Her breath came out in little pants of need. "We could start a new one." He undid her bra and she nearly fainted with the heat building inside of her. "Can we talk about this later?"

John lifted her off his lap and smiled at her confused frown. "I'm going to show you how spontaneous I can be."

And he did. More than once.

And she wasn't disappointed.

JOHN STOPPED in the middle of the kitchen doorway. Grant was sitting at the table, munching his way through a gigantic bowl of cereal.

"I didn't think you'd ever wake up. Late night?"

John wouldn't get sucked in by the gleam in his brother's eyes. "I was home by three o'clock."

"So early? Must have been a good night. How's Rachel?"

John poured himself a hot coffee and leaned against the counter. "Good."

Grant's spoon paused halfway to his mouth. "How did chapter one work out for you?"

"Good."

"I suppose the smile on your face means you had a good night's sleep, too."

John sipped his coffee.

"The silent treatment doesn't work anymore."

Bella ran into the kitchen. "Hi, Dad. Have you seen the snow outside? Tank's going to build a snowman with me."

Tank walked into the kitchen behind Bella. "We'll build the snowman after breakfast." He helped himself to a coffee and looked closely at John. "Tough night at work, boss?"

Grant choked on his cereal.

There was a reason John hired top military staff, only now he was regretting it.

Tank's eyes narrowed. "Tanner called. Said you were at Tess and Logan's house when he finished for the night. Is everything all right?"

Bella put two slices of bread in the toaster. "You saw Rachel? Did she like my Christmas present?"

A smile pulled at Grant's lips. "Good question, Bella."

John ignored his brother. "She didn't open it. She wanted you to be there, too."

Bella looked suitably impressed at Rachel's thoughtfulness. John felt slightly guilty about stretching the truth for his daughter.

Grant wasn't fooled.

Tank touched the microphone on his headset. "A police car's coming through the front gates, boss. Connor said it's the chief of police."

Bella's toast popped. She opened the refrigerator and

found the butter. "Mrs. Daniels has some cake and cookies in the pantry."

John poured the rest of his coffee down the sink and rinsed his mug. "It's probably too early for cake, but thanks for the reminder. Make sure you eat your toast before going outside."

John looked at Tank before he left the kitchen. He knew Tank wouldn't let Bella outside until they'd heard what Dan had to say.

He stood on the front porch and watched the police truck park close to the house.

"I have news about the Oracom investigation," Dan said as he shook John's hand. "Is there somewhere we can talk?"

"Sure, follow me." John led the way into his office. "Have a seat."

"Thanks." Dan sat in one of the leather chairs and took off his hat. "We've heard from the CIA. At six-thirty local time, four top-ranking Oracom officials were arrested in Prague. They've been charged with conspiracy to murder, fraud, international espionage, money-laundering, and intent to harm. Your case isn't the only one the CIA has been investigating."

"What will happen to them?"

"The US Department of Justice has filed extradition papers with the Prague High Court. It's too early to know whether they'll be brought back to the United States for a trial, but that's the plan."

"Who has the final say in extraditing them?"

"The final consent can only be authorized by the Czech Justice Minister. The officials who spoke to us don't think it will take long to sort out, but we don't have a precise time line to work with."

John took a deep breath and tried to think rationally. "Are

the US officials sure the people they arrested are the same ones who sent me death threats?"

"Positive. They have evidence that links three of the four people to your company. You don't need to worry about extra bodyguards. You're safe."

John leaned back and closed his eyes. After more than a month of thinking every second person was about to kill him, he could finally relax. Sam and the Technical Development Team wouldn't have to live in fear of their lives, and Rachel could go back to her teaching job without Tanner following her everywhere.

It was the kind of outcome he'd dreamed about but, now it was a reality, he was having a hard time believing it.

Dan stood up. "It will take a while to sink in. You can go about your normal business and not worry about Oracom. The managing director of their company will release a statement this afternoon. As soon as I have a copy, I'll email it through to you."

"Thanks. I appreciate everything you've done for us."

Dan shook John's hand. "That's what we're here for. It's not often we get to work with the FBI and the CIA on the same case. It's been an interesting few weeks."

They might have been interesting for the chief of police, but John never wanted to repeat it again.

Dan put on his hat. "Are you comfortable updating your staff about the arrests?"

John nodded. "I'll do it now."

"What about Rachel McReedy? Would you like me to head over to Tess and Logan's home and tell her?"

"I can do that."

"Well, in that case, my job here is done. I'll send the email through from Oracom when I get a copy."

After Dan left, John sank back into his chair. The people who had threatened to kill his family were finally behind bars. He could breathe a little easier and not worry about midnight kidnapping attempts or carjackings that could go wrong.

He picked up the phone and called Rachel's number. She could go back to living a normal life. She wouldn't have to check every detail with Tank or Tanner.

She wouldn't have to spend time with him.

RACHEL TURNED off the timer and pulled another batch of shortbread out of the oven. She'd been making all kinds of cookies for the first drama club program of the year. Not that it was exactly the New Year. Christmas day had officially ended nine hours ago and she'd been baking for the last three of them.

She looked around the kitchen. Most of the baking would end up in zip-lock bags, stacked in the commercial freezer Tess used, ready to be taken out in the second week of January.

She was baking because she had a lot of things to think about, things that required careful consideration and an open mind. Instead of going for a long walk, a horse ride, or a swim, she preferred to bake. It cleared her mind, filled her tummy, and if she was lucky, helped her come up with a solution to her problem.

But, so far, after three hours of sifting flour, creaming butter, and rolling out cookie dough, she hadn't come up with any answers to her six-foot-two problem.

John had left Tess and Logan's home early in the morning. He'd wanted to be home before Bella woke up, which made perfect sense. She could understand him wanting to keep their personal lives separate to their professional relationship, she really could. But she wasn't Bella's teacher anymore, and she most definitely didn't want to feel like a billionaire's dirty little secret.

She had standards. Standards that she'd conveniently pushed to one side last night. She didn't regret what had happened. John was an amazing man, but he wasn't *her* amazing man.

"What did you expect?" she muttered to herself. "A pledge of allegiance, a proclamation of his utter devotion, a promise of something more than friendship?" She would have taken any of those options. But John Fletcher had tiptoed out of her bedroom like a thief in the night, hightailing it back to his own home before he was caught with his pants around his ankles.

A loud bang came from the front yard. She jumped and nearly dropped a baking sheet on the floor.

Tanner was supposed to call her if someone came up the driveway. She looked at the clock on the wall. It wasn't like him to break protocol.

Rachel frowned. She was even starting to sound like John. With a curse, she left the baking sheet on the counter and grabbed her cell phone and a sharp knife. She hit speed dial and waited for Tanner to answer.

"Sorry, Rachel. I've been speaking with John and wasn't able to call you. Tess and Logan are home."

The front door flew open and Tess yelled, "Surprise!"

Rachel dropped the knife and headed into the living room. She was so glad to see her friend that she nearly burst into tears. "You're home early."

Tess' smile disappeared. "What's wrong?"

"Something smells great," Logan looked between his wife and Rachel. "I'll get our bags out of the car."

"Then go and see Dylan," Tess said without looking at him. "He's been texting you all morning." She wrapped her arm around Rachel and led her into the kitchen. "You've been baking?"

Rachel sniffed back her misery. "It's for the drama club. I bought all the ingredients from Safeway, so there's still plenty of food in the pantry."

Tess waved away her shopping efforts. "I'm not worried about that. You only bake this much when you have things on your mind. Did something happen to John or Bella while we were away?"

Rachel shook her head. "They're fine."

"How are your parents?" Tess asked. "I know how hard Christmas lunch must have been. Did they have another argument?"

"No more than usual. Dad cut the turkey the wrong way. Mom made too much noise when we were washing the dishes. I didn't stay long." Rachel's mom and dad were always arguing. It was a running joke in her extended family that one of them would have to die before the bickering stopped. She'd moved out of home early to get away from the constant stress of not knowing what would set them off. Each time she went home, it was harder to return.

"So, if Christmas with your parents wasn't unusual, what's wrong?"

Rachel picked up a peanut butter cookie and bit into it. "I slept with John."

Tess stared at her. "What?"

"I slept with John and I don't know how he feels about us. About me."

"How do you feel about him?"

She left the cookie on the counter and sat down. "He's the most amazing man I've ever met."

Tess sat beside her. "Have you asked him how he feels?"

"Not yet. I'm worried about what he'll say."

"You think he was using you?"

"No. He wouldn't do that." Rachel glanced at Tess. "I have

a confession to make but, before I tell you, I want you to know we respected your property."

"You slept with him? Here?"

"I'm sorry. We didn't plan it. He brought me a present Bella made and it just sort of happened. It was spontaneous, and wonderful, and he left without telling me how he felt." She pulled some tissues out of a box. "What am I going to do?"

Tess gave her a hug. "Talk to him."

Rachel blew her nose and straightened her spine. "Okay. I think I can do that. But first I need to tidy the kitchen."

"I can give you a hand."

"You're not angry with me?"

Tess smiled. "I could never be angry with you. You're my friend and you've got me out of more than one tricky situation. John would be a fool not to fall head over heels in love with you."

"Thank you."

"You're welcome." Tess picked up a bowl and walked across to the sink.

By the time they'd finished stacking the dishwasher, Rachel felt a whole lot better. John wouldn't have slept with her unless he cared about her.

All she had to do was work out how much he cared, and then she'd be happy.

CHAPTER 21

*J*ohn drove through Tess and Logan's front gates. Instead of the deserted front yard he'd expected, Logan was busy unpacking his SUV.

He thought Logan and Tess were visiting family over Christmas, but something must have happened to change their plans.

He parked his truck beside the garage. "Need a hand?"

Logan put one of the suitcases on the ground. "You might want to reconsider that offer. News travels fast."

"You know?" How many other people knew about the problems he'd been having with Oracom? Logan must have found out through his newspaper buddies. It was a small world, and even smaller when you were a reporter.

"Of course, I know," Logan said with a glare in his direction. "Rachel was in tears in the kitchen. The whole house smells of cookies, and Tess said Rachel only bakes mountains of food when she's worried about something."

"She doesn't need to worry. She's safe now. No one's going to hurt her."

"Including you?"

John frowned. "What do you mean? I'd never hurt Rachel. As far as I'm aware, the ringleaders of Oracom are behind bars. The Department of Justice is trying to extradite them to the US to face criminal charges."

Logan looked at him blankly. "I have no idea who Oracom is."

John backtracked through their conversation. "Rachel was in tears?"

"Yeah. Maybe you should talk to her? Do you want to tell me about Oracom first?"

"I can't. Give Dan Carter a call." He was surprised when Logan didn't pull out his phone and call the chief of police straight away.

John picked up two suitcases and walked toward Logan's house. Before he took them inside, he wiped the snow off his boots.

"John? What are you doing here?" Rachel stood in the hallway. The smile he was so used to seeing was nowhere in sight.

"I came to see you." Something was wrong. He didn't know how he'd expected her to react after last night, but it was nothing like this. Her eyes were red and puffy, and she was trying really hard to avoid looking at him.

"I guess you've found me. You can leave Tess and Logan's suitcases in the entrance."

John put the cases down. "Can we talk?"

Rachel took a deep breath and nodded. "Sure. What do you want to talk about?"

He looked around the entranceway. "Not here. The snow has stopped falling. Do you want to go for a walk?"

Again, there was a hesitation, something that wasn't right. "I'll get my jacket. It's in my room." She walked upstairs and disappeared from sight.

John waited where he was. If Rachel regretted what had

happened, he'd feel like an idiot. Maybe that was it. Maybe she wished last night had never happened.

By the time he'd worked out what could be wrong, she was coming down the stairs.

"Let's go." Rachel wrapped a bright red scarf around her neck and zipped her jacket up to her chin. She walked one step ahead of him, avoiding anything that might be considered a conversation.

John opened the front door and breathed in the cold morning air. "Tess and Logan are home early."

"They caught an earlier flight home."

John stood on the porch, looking at the front yard. Tess and Logan owned a big property. Even from the street, the landscaped grounds and two-story home looked impressive. But he wasn't here to admire the scenery. He'd come to update Rachel on what had happened.

He followed her out of the house, worried about what would come next. "Dan Carter saw me this morning. The people responsible for the death threats have been arrested. The Department of Justice is trying to bring them to Washington, D.C. for a trial."

Rachel stopped walking and turned around. "That's great news. You must be relieved."

"I am." He didn't feel relieved. Not at the moment. "You don't need a bodyguard anymore. I'll reassign Tank and Tanner to other projects tomorrow."

She nodded. "It will make it easier for Bella when she starts school."

"What's wrong, Rachel?"

She stuck her hands in her pockets and looked toward the street. "You left while I was asleep."

"We talked about that. I needed to be home before Bella woke up." He looked at her face. "Do you regret what happened last night?"

Rachel glanced at him. "What did happen?"

He had a feeling the answer to her question wasn't as straightforward as he thought. "I don't regret one minute of last night. I'm sorry I didn't wake you before I left, but you were sound asleep."

Rachel bit her bottom lip. "Do you want us to see each other again?"

A sinking feeling hit him in the center of his chest. "Did you think last night was a one-night stand?"

"I don't know what it was. I don't—"

"Sleep around? But you thought I did?" His voice echoed around them. He took a deep breath and tried to control his pounding heart. "The only woman I've ever slept with, before you, was Jacinta. I don't sleep around. I never have. If you thought I had, you don't know me very well."

"And whose fault is that? You keep your feelings to yourself so much I don't know what's going through your head. When Bella went missing, you were quick to judge me. You couldn't stand the sight of me. Then last night, everything just exploded and we ended up together. And then you left. I don't know what's going on."

"I can't afford to tell people how I feel. The last time I did that, I ended up on the front page of a newspaper. I own a successful company and I have a lot of people who rely on me. I can't afford to make mistakes."

Her eyes opened wide. "You think I'm a mistake?"

"No. That didn't come out right."

"I think it came out perfectly right. And if that's the way you feel, then I guess I've answered my own question."

"What question?"

Rachel threw her hands in the air. "I don't believe you. For some hotshot in the security industry, you know nothing about people."

"I have no idea what you're talking about."

"I'm talking about us." Rachel took a step toward him and lowered her voice. "I want to know if last night meant anything to you?"

He stuck his hands in his pockets. "Of course, it meant something."

"What did it mean?"

"It meant we're friends. That I care about you. Isn't that enough?"

She looked up at the sky, then back at him. "I care about Tank and Tanner, but I wouldn't sleep with them."

John knew what she wanted to hear, but he couldn't say the words. "I'm not ready to be in a relationship with anyone."

"Why did you sleep with me, then?" Her eyes filled with tears and he felt like a complete jerk.

"I thought you understood. Everything I do affects Bella. I don't have time to be part of someone else's life. It doesn't mean last night wasn't amazing, because it was."

"That's the lamest explanation I've ever heard." Rachel pulled a tissue out of her pocket and blew her nose. "You've forgotten what it feels like to love someone. You're so busy making money you think it can replace what's missing in your life." She straightened her shoulders. "I'm going inside to help Tess. Say hello to Bella and thank her for the present. I'll see her at school."

"Rachel, wait." She didn't stop, so he walked beside her. "I don't know what you want."

"Yes, you do," she said sadly. "You've known all along, but you're too scared to do anything about it. Have a good life, John." She put her head down and rushed back to the house.

John walked back to his truck. Before he'd come here, he'd thought everything was okay. But it wasn't, and he didn't know if it would ever be right again.

〜

TWO WEEKS LATER, Rachel opened one of her student's workbooks. Emma had written a story about what she'd done during her Christmas vacation. Although it didn't involve death threats, international espionage, or the FBI, it sounded as though her family had enjoyed their vacation in Idaho.

It was more than Rachel could say. John had tried to contact her after she'd left Tess and Logan's home. After five days of ignoring him, he'd finally got the message and stopped calling.

She needed time to sort out her life. John Fletcher's allergic reaction to relationships wasn't her problem. She had a new job, great friends, and thanks to teaching Bella, a healthy down payment for her first home.

Someone knocked on the classroom door. Rachel looked up and smiled at Tess. She was wearing a beautiful bright red jacket with knee-high black boots and a fluffy hat. Whether she wanted to or not, she looked like the supermodel she'd once been.

"Are you nearly ready?"

"I'll be one minute and then I'm all yours." Rachel stuck a big yellow smiley face on Emma's workbook. "Does Logan know about his surprise birthday party?"

"Are you kidding? Logan is the typical Capricornian male. If I'd told him about the party, he would have wanted to organize everything himself. This way, it's still a surprise."

Rachel looked at the time. The cleaning staff would set the security alarm at six o'clock, so she could walk out of the school with a clear conscience. "Thanks for picking me up. This was the only day the garage could service my truck."

"It helped me, too. Logan didn't want to go anywhere tonight. At least this way I can say going out to dinner was your idea and not mine. If you need a ride to the garage in the morning, let me know."

"I'll be okay. Someone's driving my truck back to my apartment." Rachel put the workbooks away and grabbed her jacket and bag from beside her. "Let's collect the birthday boy before he gets suspicious."

"Have you worked out what you'll say to Logan?"

Rachel smiled. "I'll tell him the truth. You told me it was his birthday and I'd like to take you both out for dinner. It's my way of saying thank you for letting me stay with you."

Tess looked impressed. "I like it. I've been worried all day that someone will say something to him and ruin the surprise."

"At least he's still on vacation and away from the office."

"But he's still working. Dan emailed him some information about the company who sent John the death threats. The guys that were extradited were involved in some nasty stuff. They've kidnapped people before to get what they want."

Rachel stopped in the middle of the hallway. "I thought John was overreacting."

"Not even close. Kidnapping, extortion, and bribery were common practice among some of the executives. Dan said there'll be a lot more arrests before the case is closed."

Rachel took a deep breath and kept walking. "Is John okay?"

Tess put her hand on Rachel's arm. "What happened between the two of you? He came into the café yesterday and asked how you were."

"I haven't spoken to him since I left your house."

"But that was two weeks ago."

"He doesn't want a relationship with me. At least not one that involves any commitment." She opened the front door to the school and waved Tess through. "Where did you park your SUV?"

"It's over here." Tess walked toward her vehicle. "I don't know what John's thinking, but I can tell you one thing. The only time I've ever seen him smile is when he's with you."

"At least he was honest about not wanting to be in a relationship," Rachel muttered. "He could have strung me along for another six months before telling me. No one knows what happened between us, except you, and that's all that matters."

"Why?"

"Because I don't want to repeat what happened last year. My name was on the front page of the community Facebook page for over a week. If I thought kissing Jeremiah's cousin was bad, sleeping with a billionaire would be worse. Especially if I became the jilted girlfriend."

Tess unlocked her vehicle and they got inside. "Think about how John must feel every day of his life. You're worried about our city's Facebook page. If John shows an interest in anyone, it would probably make the entertainment section of the New York Times. Maybe it's not only himself he's protecting, but you."

"And Bella." Rachel sighed. "She's such a great kid. She painted me a picture and brought it to school today."

Tess started her SUV and drove out of the parking lot. "She likes you."

"I like her, too," Rachel said softly. But it wasn't enough. She missed John, but she knew he wouldn't change his mind.

He was an adult who knew what he wanted, and it wasn't her.

JOHN WALKED into Charlie's Bar and Grill, wondering what on earth he was doing.

His brother waved his arm in the air from across the room.

That was why he was here. Grant had told him he needed to get out more, meet people who didn't shoot other people for a living.

Even though Grant's description of what John's team did was over-the-top, he got the message.

Grant was standing beside Logan Allen, catching up on what John hoped had nothing to do with Oracom. "Glad you could make it."

"Are you reminding me I'm late?" John asked.

Grant looked at his watch. "Only by twenty minutes. Practically a world record for you. I bought you a drink."

John took the can of soda out of Grant's hand. "Thanks. I think. Is there something you're not telling me—like I'm the nominated driver for tonight?"

Grant shook his head. "I brought my own truck and I'll be driving safely home in it. The soda is a precautionary measure. You'll need all your wits about you tonight."

John didn't know what his brother was talking about.

Logan picked up his glass of beer. "Did you read the article in today's newspaper?"

John nodded. "How did you find out who the executives at Oracom were? The FBI and the CIA were supposed to keep those details confidential until the trial."

"It wasn't too difficult."

John popped the tab off his can. "Thanks for not mentioning my name."

"There were enough leads to make the story interesting. The other people were more than happy to talk."

John looked along the bar. "Where's your wife? Newly-weds are supposed to stick together like glue."

Logan smiled. "Scoff all you like, but I can highly recommend married life. And for the record, Tess is behind you."

John turned around and nearly choked on the soda he'd swallowed. Rachel and Annie were walking toward them. Rachel had a smile on her face until she saw him. She glanced over her shoulder and that's when he noticed Tess. She was carrying something in her hands that looked remarkably like a birthday cake.

"You have to be kidding," Logan muttered. He glanced at the smiling faces around the bar. Someone started singing happy birthday, and he looked as though he wanted to disappear.

Rachel and Annie moved away from Tess. The cake she was holding was covered in brightly lit candles.

Grant grinned at Logan. "Exactly how old are you?"

"Don't make too many jokes. Your birthday isn't far away, either. When did Tess have the time to organize this?"

Charlie, the owner of the bar, left a glass of wine beside Logan. "This is for Tess. She's been planning your party for the last three months. We were sworn to secrecy."

"Is there anything else she hasn't told me?"

Grant laughed. "I think you can safely rule out anything that might involve lots of beautiful women." He glanced at John. "However, as a single man who's about to turn thirty-nine, I wouldn't be worried if my brother decided to give me a surprise birthday party."

"Would that be with or without the beautiful women?" John asked.

"Either option works for me."

John didn't have any doubt it would. Except Grant had about as much hope of that happening as a drought in the middle of winter.

Someone put a small table beside Logan. Tess carefully slid the cake on top of it and ignored her scowling husband. John looked around the bar, trying to see where Rachel had gone.

"She's over there." Grant nodded toward the jukebox. "Go and talk to her."

"She doesn't want to see me."

"She can't ignore you if you stand in front of her."

John glanced back at the jukebox. If he didn't make a move now, he'd never get away from the crowd of people moving toward Tess and Logan.

"Go." His brother gave him a nudge. "You can cry on my shoulder later."

John took a deep breath and decided, for once in his life, to follow his brother's advice. It couldn't be much worse than pretending nothing had happened. That he might have messed up something that could have been amazing.

He walked across the room and stood beside Rachel. He didn't know what to say or how to apologize for acting like an idiot.

She stopped pushing the buttons on the jukebox. "I'm supposed to be selecting all of Logan's favorite music, but I can't work out how to use the new machine. Do you know how it works?"

John didn't have a clue, but it couldn't be rocket science. He was just grateful she'd asked him and not someone else. "It's probably like a food vending machine." He studied the buttons on the control panel.

"Here are the codes for the songs Tess wants me to select." Rachel flattened a wrinkled sheet of paper. "I, umm, got a bit frustrated and kind of screwed up the list."

John looked down at the paper and decided not to say anything. "Is that a P or a D?"

Rachel leaned forward. Her shoulder brushed against his arm and his heartbeat thudded in his chest. He held his breath, hoping she didn't notice.

"D14," she said softly. She stepped back, leaving enough room between them for an elephant to step through.

John had no idea how he got the jukebox to program the songs, but he kept pushing buttons and everything seemed to work. "It should be ready to go."

Rachel nodded and pushed a red button. The first vinyl record dropped into place and Nat King Cole started singing. "Do you think they're original vinyl records or imitations?"

"Considering they have songs from the Bee Gees and Taylor Swift, I'd say they're imitations. But good imitations," he added, in case his answer spoiled Rachel's appreciation of the jukebox.

He handed her back the list of songs.

"I didn't know you'd be here," she said as if she was apologizing. "I knew about the surprise birthday party, but not who was invited."

"Would it have made a difference?"

Rachel looked away. "Maybe. I guess I'm just really sorry about what happened."

John thought about all the things he wanted to say. Nothing would have made a difference to the awkward silence between them. "Can we be friends?"

"Friends?"

The surprise in Rachel's blue eyes caught at his heart. "I care about you. I enjoy spending time with you. But if you'd rather not, then that's okay, too."

Rachel held his hand and pulled him toward the back door. A fire exit sign glowed above a picture of the President.

She frowned at the photo before letting go of his hand. He flexed his fingers and wondered how her touch could affect him so much. He was back to the heart pounding, sweaty, Neanderthal he'd been a few minutes earlier. Did he mention nervous? Because he was. More nervous than when he'd given her Bella's present.

She looked at the people around them and moved a step closer to him. "Tess told me about Logan's article. She said the men who sent you death threats were doing a lot of illegal things. Why didn't you tell me everything?"

"I didn't know a lot about Oracom until we investigated them. When the FBI and the CIA told me we needed extra security, I didn't argue. It wasn't until we looked into what Oracom doesn't report on, that we realized what we were dealing with."

Rachel frowned. He didn't know what he'd done to upset her.

"Why do you confuse me so much?" She sighed. "One minute I'm annoyed with you, and the next minute I want to kiss the living daylights out of you."

John started to smile, then wiped it away before she saw it. He'd take Rachel's type of confusion any day.

"I saw you smile," she muttered. And then she smiled, too. "We're as bad as each other." She leaned against the wall and tilted her head backward. "What would the President of the United States of America do in a situation like this?"

John looked at the photo above Rachel's head, then down into her eyes. He took a step forward and her smile disappeared. "I don't know, but I know what I want to do."

"What if someone sees us?" she whispered. "Is kissing under a photo of the President even allowed?"

"It's better than the Pope."

Rachel grinned. "Or a picture of my parents."

"Or of Bella," John whispered.

Rachel pushed the handle on the door beside them. "We could always go outside?"

She froze as the noisiest, most shrill siren John had ever heard filled the bar. He looked down at Rachel. She stuck her fingers in her ears and looked up at him.

Oops.

The staff directed people out of the building. Charlie, the

owner of the bar, rushed toward John wearing a bright yellow hard hat and hi-visibility vest.

He used his clipboard to whack John on the arm. "You're too old to be using the fire exit. Get out of here before we're surrounded by firefighters and the police."

John didn't need to be told twice. Half the town's reporters were inside the bar wishing Logan a happy birthday. The other half would be waiting by their phones for a late night story. If photos of them made *The Bozeman Chronicle's* most wanted page, Rachel wouldn't speak to him again.

Holding Rachel's hand, he pulled her out of the bar, hoping no one noticed the guilty look plastered across their faces. As soon as they were standing in the snow, he looked for Tess and Logan. If they were with the birthday boy, it might give them some cover.

Grant tapped him on the shoulder. Or maybe not. "You wouldn't happen to know anything about the fire alarm, would you?"

John was saved from answering by the arrival of the fire trucks. Three fire trucks to be precise. And two police cars, four police officers, and an off-duty doctor who was asking if anyone needed help.

John hung his head in shame.

Rachel kept hold of his hand as she hid behind his back.

Grant kept his beady-eyed stare on him. "Well?"

"It didn't say the door was alarmed." John tried to whisper, but with close to two hundred people standing on the sidewalk, a fire alarm screeching through the air, and the engines of the trucks turning over, it wasn't easy to have a quiet conversation.

Someone finally turned off the alarm. The split second of silence was followed by the noise of a lot of people talking at once. They wanted to get back inside. The bright lights of the emergency vehicles pulsing around them didn't make up for the food, music, and drink waiting inside the bar.

John saw Charlie's yellow hard-hat move in front of the crowd. A team of firefighters, wearing face masks and oxygen tanks, disappeared into the building. He had a feeling the people standing outside would be here for more than a few minutes.

Tess stood beside Rachel. "I wonder what happened? We couldn't smell any smoke, but you never know with old buildings. It could be an electrical fault in the ceiling or anything. I hope the birthday candles didn't set off the smoke alarms."

"I don't think that was it." Rachel chewed her bottom lip. "Do you think the firefighters will be much longer?"

"I don't know. If this snow keeps falling, most of Charlie's customers will go to another bar. It won't matter how long the building is closed."

Rachel looked at John. "I'll be back in a minute." She let go of his hand and disappeared into the crowd.

Tess looked confused. "Where's Rachel going?"

"It's confession time," John muttered as he followed Rachel. He just hoped the fire chief had a better sense of humor than the owner of the bar.

CHAPTER 22

$\mathcal{T}$he next day, Rachel had barely walked into Angel Wings Café when Tess made the first Facebook comment.

"How does it feel to be a star?" Tess asked from behind the counter.

Rachel closed the door and ignored the curious glances being sent her way. "I thought you finished work at one o'clock."

"I do, but Kate couldn't come in, so here I am. Your photo has more than a thousand likes."

"Shh," Rachel whispered. "I don't want more people knowing about it."

"It's too late," Tess whispered back. "Everyone already knows."

Rachel looked over her shoulder. Half a dozen people enjoying hot coffee, delicious food, and a good helping of gossip, grinned back. "Hi, everyone."

Doris Stanley, one of the most influential cogs in the local gossip wheel, stood and walked across to Rachel. "Well, I for one applaud what you did. Telling the fire chief what you'd done took a lot of courage, especially after what happened the last time you made the headlines."

Doris winked at Rachel. She supposed that in a roundabout way it was meant to be reassuring, but Rachel found it a little unsettling.

"You were always too good for Jeremiah. And just look at what he's done with his life since he left you at the altar…"

Rachel felt morally obliged to remind Doris she'd been the one who'd left Jeremiah, but Doris wasn't leaving room for interruptions in her speech.

"…he married a girl nearly half his age and just as scatterbrained as him. He missed his chance with you, Rachel, but John will appreciate you. He's such a kind man. Do you know he sponsored the reading program at the local high school? And not a word to anyone about his generosity. That's the type of man any woman would want to go out a fire exit with."

There was a general murmur of agreement and a nodding of heads around the café. Rachel looked helplessly at Tess.

Doris must have noticed Rachel's discomfort, but not the cause of it. She gave Rachel a quick hug. "If you ever need advice about men, come and see me. My husband is one in a million, but now and then even Mr. Stanley and I have disagreements. Do you know we've been married fifty-six years this June?"

Rachel sat in a chair in case Doris gave her another hug. "That's wonderful. Congratulations."

"It's not all hard work, mind you. We have had some lovely times—"

Tess stepped forward with the coffeepot. "Would you like another cup of coffee, Doris?"

Doris' cell phone beeped. "Another coffee would be very nice." She glanced at the message and smiled. "Would you look at that? Mr. Stanley has just posted the most delightful photo of you on Facebook, Rachel."

Rachel's mouth dropped open. She fumbled in her bag for her phone, but Tess was one step ahead of her.

Leaving the coffeepot on the table, Tess pulled her cell phone out of her pocket. She frowned at whatever she was looking at, then handed the phone to Rachel.

Rachel took one look at the photo, then dropped her head into her hands. It was worse than the photo of her talking to the fire chief.

Her face had flamed redder than a ripe tomato when he'd asked why she'd opened the fire exit door. After stumbling her way through the feeblest excuse she'd ever heard, the fire chief let her off the hook with a warning. But more importantly, he'd let everyone back into Charlie's Bar and Grill.

The fire department was happy because they didn't need to investigate the alarm, Charlie was happy because he had a full bar again, and she was happy because she'd made everyone else happy. Except John, but they'd learned a valuable lesson. Stay clear of fire exit doors.

And now she'd learned another valuable lesson. Try not to look adoringly into a billionaire's eyes when you were surrounded by a room full of reporters. It was like putting a goldfish in a swimming pool full of sharks. Not a pretty sight.

She glanced back at the photo and winced. John was leaning over her, his gaze locked on her eyes, soaking in whatever she was saying. It was the kind of photo that would keep the gossip columnists happy for the rest of the year.

The doorbell tinkled and Rachel wiggled farther down into her seat, hoping whoever it was kept walking toward the front counter.

"Nice photo," Dan said. The chief of police was at Logan's surprise party. Rachel had assumed he hadn't spoken to John or her because he'd felt sorry for them. From his smile, she'd say it was more like he'd wanted to get back into the bar before he froze to death.

"I didn't ask what you were doing in front of the fire door. Thanks to Jake, I don't need to bother, now."

Rachel looked at the photograph and frowned. Doris' husband hadn't mentioned anything about why they were there. There wasn't even a caption, thank goodness. She closed her eyes, then opened them, pretending to see the photo for the first time.

Dan was right. The picture didn't need words to explain what was happening.

She was doomed.

The doorbell tinkled again. She didn't know Tess' cafe was so busy at this time of the day.

"I know what you're thinking," Tess whispered as she passed her table. "And it's not usually this busy at four o'clock. You're pulling in everyone who wants to see the woman who's captured the billionaire's heart."

"I haven't captured anyone's heart." Rachel's voice was as close to a hysterical whisper as anyone could get. This was ridiculous.

"If you need some peace and quiet, wait in the kitchen for me. I'll close the café in ten minutes."

Rachel took Tess up on her offer. She was almost at the kitchen door when Tess said something that made her run for cover.

"The love fest is over, folks. Drink your coffee and I'll see you tomorrow."

A collective sigh filled the café. As soon as she was through the doors, Rachel headed toward the coffeepot. If Tess was right, John's name would hit the headlines on more than the Bozeman Community Facebook page. She needed to see him and work out how they could fix everything before it got worse.

And based on what had happened with her ex-fiancé, she knew it could get a lot worse.

JOHN CLOSED the document on his computer. Even though the people responsible for the Oracom deal were in prison, they were still waiting for their trial. He wouldn't sleep well until they were convicted and permanently put behind bars. Until then, he'd assigned a new team of bodyguards to watch Bella and Rachel.

Tanner enjoyed working from Montana, but on Monday he would be delivering a senator's daughter to Washington, D.C. Sometimes, the contracts that seemed the most straightforward weren't, and this was one of those times.

Maddie Steinbar was eighteen years old, a perfect student, the perfect daughter. Her one indiscretion with another senator's son had caused a media frenzy six months ago.

She'd been sent to live with her cousins in Montana, and her father's strategy for, 'out of sight, out of mind,' had mostly worked. Until the senator's son joined his girlfriend in Montana.

Now Tanner had the unenviable task of taking Maddie back to her father. Maddie didn't want to go. Her boyfriend didn't want her to go. But the senator wasn't taking no for an answer.

A knock on his office door startled John out of his thoughts. Tanner stuck his head around the corner of the doorframe. "Did you want to see me?"

"Is everything in place to take the senator's daughter home?"

Tanner nodded. "Are you sure you don't want me to guard Rachel tonight?"

"You've been working long hours for the last couple of months. I appreciate everything you've done for us, but Connor will make sure Rachel's safe."

"Does she know you've kept a surveillance team on her?"

John shook his head. "And she won't know if Connor and Jeremy do their job well. Have a good night."

"I plan to." Tanner pushed away from the doorframe, then reappeared two seconds later. "Did you see the Facebook post?"

"Gloria showed me."

"They were good pictures. Pity about the room full of reporters."

John threw his stress ball straight at Tanner's smiling face.

Tanner caught it before it hit him. "You'll have to work hard if you want to get to know Rachel better."

"Do you know something I don't?"

"Tank and I guarded her for weeks. She's practical, down to earth, and cares about people. It will take more than a handsome face to make her see the possibilities."

John didn't want to ask Tanner what he meant. He didn't need to. "I'll see you when you get back from DC."

Tanner lifted his arm in a mock salute and headed down the corridor. His heavy boots echoed in the empty corridor, reminding John it was time to go home. Turning off his computer, he stood up. Bella would have made dinner with Mrs. Daniels. She'd be setting the table, waiting impatiently for him to walk in the front door.

"Hi."

John froze. Rachel's face was flushed a soft pink from the cold. Her eyes were a brilliant blue and gleaming under the knitted hat she'd pulled on.

"I'm sorry if I startled you. Tanner was coming out of the

building when I arrived. He let me straight in. I hope that's okay?"

John wasn't worried about Tanner. Right now, his only worry involved a steady stream of Facebook posts that had been appearing all day. And a small, but critical inability to say something intelligent to Rachel.

"Thank you for the daisies. They were lovely."

"I'm glad you liked them." When he saw the first Facebook post at six o'clock this morning, he'd gone online and ordered her a bouquet of flowers. It was supposed to be an apology for the media frenzy that would follow. By the time the next photos hit Facebook, he was beginning to think he should get down on one knee and propose to her.

Whoever took the photos had known what they were doing. They'd captured everything that had been left unsaid. They made him realize how much he wanted Rachel to be part of his life.

He moved from around the back of his desk. Tanner thought it was Rachel who needed to see the possibilities in their relationship. He was wrong. John was the one who'd refused to see what was staring him in the face.

Rachel pulled off her hat. "I'm sorry I opened the fire door."

"You don't need to apologize." John stared at the blond halo of hair falling around her shoulders. He stuck his hands in his pockets and refocused his brain. There were things he wanted to know. Things that would make a difference to what happened next.

He cleared his throat. "I have a question for you. Why did you tell everyone what happened? You could have kept quiet. The Fire Department would have investigated the alarm and found nothing. No one would have known we opened the door."

Rachel shrugged. "Friday night is one of the busiest at the

bar and grill. If half of Charlie's customers went to other restaurants and bars, it would have made a big difference to his weekly earnings. I couldn't let that happen."

John thought about what she'd said, the things that were important to her. "What about the Facebook page?"

"I heard about the photos before school started. Most of the parents of my students saw the images as they were posted. The flowers you sent to school fueled the gossip mill even more. And the final end to a perfect day was meeting Doris Stanley in Tess' café. She told me you, above all other men, would appreciate me."

"I always thought Doris was an astute woman."

"She winked at me and gave me a hug."

John ran his hand along Rachel's arm. "Responsive and caring. What more could you want?"

Rachel held John's hands before they could do any more wandering. "Committed and honest?"

"We're not talking about Doris, are we?"

"No. We're talking about us. I thought about what you said last night, and I want to be your friend. If you still want to be friends, that is?"

John shook his head. "I don't want to be your friend."

Rachel's eyes widened. "You don't?"

"I've changed my mind. I want more."

"How much more?"

"If you'd be my girlfriend, I'd like to be your boyfriend."

Rachel's hands tightened around his fingers. "Just so we're clear, what would a boyfriend and girlfriend status mean exactly?"

John didn't need his hands to show Rachel what the difference was. She was already standing close enough for him to kiss her. "Well, it might mean that you could be my Scrabble partner. Grant and Bella are competitive, so we'll have our work cut out for us. I could cook you dinner, rub your feet, and buy you extravagant gifts."

Rachel took half a step toward him. "That's an impressive list of opportunities. I can see the benefits for me, but what do you get out of the relationship?"

"This." He leaned forward and slid his lips along Rachel's mouth. With a soft sigh, her hands wrapped around his shoulders and pulled him close.

John had been thinking about kissing her all day. He would take it slow and easy, savor each touch and taste, show her how much he cared about her. But within seconds, he forgot about his plans, forgot about taking things slowly, forgot to breathe.

He stumbled backward when Rachel's teeth started nibbling on the skin below his ear. "My knees just gave way." He felt Rachel's breath against his neck as she laughed.

"You're either getting old," she whispered, "or you need more practice."

John had to hold back a groan that rumbled through his chest. Walking across the room, he closed his office door. "I vote for more practice."

"I like a man who knows what he wants." Rachel stood in front of him and held onto the end of his tie. "How long do we have?"

"Ten minutes."

She grinned, and his heart rate soared. "We'd better make the most of our time, then. Do you have any suggestions?"

"One or two."

Rachel stepped forward. "Show me."

He cupped the side of her face in his hand and kissed her with a hunger that left them both breathless.

Ten minutes might not be long, but they could make it memorable.

~

A WEEK LATER, Rachel looked at the color charts and fabric samples on the table. "You weren't joking when you said you were desperate for help."

The light in John's eyes made her smile. "If I don't tell the interior designer what I want, they'll find another client. Bella's color choices are all various shades of pink and purple."

"And yellow," Bella added from between them. "I like yellow because it reminds me of sunshine."

Rachel thought that was as good a reason as any to like a color. She glanced down at the house plans before picking up one set of colors. "Is this for your room, Bella?"

Bella nodded. "Princess pink for these three walls." She pointed to the walls she was talking about. "Mrs. Daniels helped me choose just the right yellow for this wall. It will look so pretty."

Rachel smiled. "You're right. They're beautiful colors. What other rooms have you helped choose paint for?"

Bella picked up the other color samples Rachel had left in alphabetical order. "The kitchen, my bathroom, the garage, and the mudroom." She pointed to the kitchen colors. "Mrs. Daniels likes yellow, too. So we chose a creamy yellow for the kitchen walls. My bathroom is purple. Dad's cars are all bright colors, so I chose white for the garage, and the mudroom is the same color as the kitchen. Mrs. Daniels said it would look really nice."

"That's a lot of great colors."

John ran his hands through his hair. "Do you think it will work?"

"I think it will look amazing." Rachel picked up the samples the kitchen company had left with him. "I like the stone counter you chose. I'd maybe go a shade lighter on the cabinets, so they're a warm white rather than a soft yellow."

John frowned. "There's a difference?"

Rachel picked up a color chart and showed him. "A big difference. If it were my kitchen, I'd want the counter to look fresh and sparkly. If the cabinets are too yellow, they might make the stone counter look yellow, too."

John pointed to the living rooms. "What about these rooms?"

Rachel looked at the colors John had short-listed. "What furniture are you putting in the rooms?"

John leaned against the table. "That's the other problem. When we rented this house, it was fully furnished. Apart from the beds and a few photos, the rest of the furniture will stay here when we move."

Bella was practically bouncing on the seat beside Rachel. "Do you want to come shopping with us?"

"For furniture?"

John sighed. "I know it's asking a lot. You probably have things you need to do. But I really need to get this sorted. We don't need to buy anything, but if we take photos of what we'd like, the interior designer will handle the rest."

"Why don't you ask the interior designer to help you? They'll know what will look good."

Bella looked up from the table. "Because we want you to help us. It'll be fun. Please."

Rachel looked between John and Bella. It was hard to say no when two pairs of eyes were pleading with her. "Okay, I'll do it. I just hope you can live with what we choose. What's your budget?"

John raised his eyebrows.

"No budget? Not even a little idea of how much money you want to spend?"

"Nope."

Rachel looked at the house plans in front of her. Walking into a store and choosing whatever you wanted, regardless of the price, would be most people's idea of heaven. But all it did for Rachel was stress her out. "I have one condition."

John smiled. "Only one?"

She narrowed her gaze and his smile grew wider. "We have to visit at least two second-hand stores. You can find some lovely pieces of furniture you wouldn't see anywhere else."

"Poppy's mom bought a chair from an estate sale," Bella said in her sing-song voice. "She stapled different fabric on the outside and gave it to Poppy for her room. It's pretty."

John stacked the papers in front of them. "It sounds like we have a deal. Our flight leaves in an hour. Does anyone want a drink?"

Rachel put her hand on his arm. "Wait. What do you mean? I thought we were shopping in Bozeman."

"Not enough choice. We're flying to Denver."

"Denver?" Rachel felt a little woozy. No one she knew flew hundreds of miles to go furniture shopping.

Bella patted her hand. "It's okay. We're going on a plane, not in a helicopter. You can't see the ground so much in a plane."

Rachel looked at John. "You'd already decided to go to Denver before you asked me?"

John cleared his throat. "We needed to register our flight plan. I booked the plane yesterday."

"What if I didn't want to go?"

"Bella and I would have gone on our own, but it wouldn't have been the same without you."

Bella leaned toward Rachel and whispered, "We've got tickets for *The Wizard of Oz*, too."

"The movie?" Rachel said weakly.

John shuffled some papers. "At the Buell Theatre," he mumbled.

"You bought theater tickets as well? Are we staying overnight?"

Bella opened her mouth to say something, but John jumped in ahead of her. "Why don't you ask Mrs. Daniels for a suitcase and choose a dress to wear tonight?"

Bella slid off her chair. "Okay. Will you and Rachel come and help me?"

John nodded. "As soon as we're finished in here."

Bella grinned at Rachel and left the room.

John's gaze followed his daughter. "I'm sorry about that. It was supposed to be a surprise."

"I just…I guess I'm a bit…overwhelmed. I was happy to help choose paint colors, even furniture from stores in Bozeman. But Denver? Today?" Rachel tried to explain how she was feeling. "Most people don't fly to another city to buy furniture. Except if they get cheap seats on an airline. But we aren't flying economy, are we?"

John shook his head.

If she hadn't known him as well as she did, his expression would have passed for neutral indifference. But she recognized it for what it was. He was trying not to push her, trying hard to let everything about his billionaire lifestyle soak into her budget sized brain.

She took a deep breath and looked around the table. "I guess we'd better hurry. We don't want to miss our flight."

John's face relaxed. "Thank you."

"Remember those words. Shopping for furniture is a painful process."

"Only if you don't know where to look," John said carefully. He pulled a piece of paper out of a folder. "Courtesy of the interior designer. We'll be met at the airport by a chauffeur-driven Hummer and taken to some of the best stores in Denver."

"You forgot my special condition."

"Only temporarily. I'll have a list of second-hand stores emailed to me before we land. Would auction houses count?"

"Okay. But we're not paying collector's prices for furniture we can buy cheaper somewhere else."

"The price doesn't matter. I could buy every auction house in Denver if I wanted to."

"Don't remind me." Rachel slid the last few color charts into a folder and handed them to John. "I bet Bella's already packed Miss Snuggles."

"And one of her *Anne of Green Gables* books," John added. "If we're lucky, she's remembered a dress for tonight."

Rachel sighed. "She's almost nine years old. I can guarantee she won't have forgotten."

John held her hand as they walked up the stairs. "It's just as well it's not my money you're attracted to."

"Why do you say that?"

"I'll have a little less after our new house is built."

Rachel frowned. "I don't think it will make much difference."

John kissed the side of her face. "Neither do I."

CHAPTER 23

*R*achel smiled as she walked out of the Buell Theatre. John had his arm around her waist and Bella was holding her hand. Tank followed a few steps behind.

After she'd seen Tank at the airport, John admitted that he still had a small team of bodyguards looking after them. Rachel was more relieved than annoyed. All week, she'd felt as though someone was watching her. But each time she turned around, she couldn't see anyone. At least she knew she wasn't going crazy and imagining things that weren't there.

Bella swung Rachel's hand high in the air. She hadn't stopped talking about *The Wizard of Oz* since the musical had ended. "I loved Dorothy's shoes," Bella said. "They were so pretty. What did you like the best, Rachel?"

"I liked the songs. The actors were so good I kept looking around the theater, wondering who was singing."

"What about you, Dad?"

"I liked the Tin Man," he said quietly.

"If only he had a heart," Rachel said as she gazed at John.

He smiled, and she felt a warmth seep through her body and settle in her own heart.

Bella hopped over a crack in the sidewalk. "But it was there all along. Do you think the Tin Man knew?"

John looked into the distance. "Sometimes you need someone to show you."

"The Wizard of Oz was scary before he showed Dorothy and her friends who he really was." Bella gazed up at Rachel. "He looked like Tank," she whispered.

"I heard that." Tank's gruff voice made Bella giggle.

Bella looked over her shoulder at her favorite bodyguard. "But you're more handsome."

Tank nodded. "Good save."

They continued walking along the sidewalk. The huge glass windows of the theater were lit from inside the building, making everything look bright and festive. They stopped now and then to look in the windows and take photos of their night out together.

When they arrived at their vehicle, Tank looked at John. "Is plan A still in place, boss?"

John nodded and a look of understanding passed between the two men.

Tank opened the door of the Hummer for Bella. "Your chariot awaits, Dorothy."

She clicked her heels three times and grinned. "There's no place like home."

He closed Bella's door and turned to John. "Good luck. I'll see you in the morning."

Rachel looked at the two men. "We're not going to the hotel together?"

Tank smiled and opened his door. "Enjoy the rest of your evening."

After Tank and Bella left, she turned to John. "Why haven't we gone with them?"

"It's a surprise." He put his hand in his pocket and pulled out a set of car keys. "Are you ready to see more of Denver?"

She looked at the car that had been parked behind the Hummer. "That doesn't look like a standard family sedan."

John watched her closely. "It's not."

"It's a pretty shade of red." She had no idea what sort of car it was. It was low to the ground, sporty, and expensive looking. She looked at the emblem on the front grill and frowned. It looked like a three-pronged spear that Neptune might have carried around with him.

She walked closer to the car and peered in the windows. "Leather seats?"

John pushed a button and the car lit up like a Christmas tree. Rachel stepped back and smiled. "Wow. Do that again."

He locked the car, then unlocked it.

Rachel smiled. "Can I sit inside?"

John opened the passenger door and she slid into the seat. The interior was every bit as luxurious as the outside. The sporty two-door model oozed sophistication. From the curved leather console, to the neon blue lights on the dashboard, it was the type of vehicle no one forgot.

John sat in the driver's seat. "You're sitting in one of the first production models of the Maserati Alfieri."

"It looks nicer than my truck." She laughed at the pained expression on John's face. "I'm no good with cars. As long as it gets me where I want to go, I don't care what sort of vehicle I drive."

John patted the dashboard. "Don't listen to Rachel. She hasn't driven in anything like you before."

Rachel waited for a computer-generated voice to answer him. "Does the car talk back?" she whispered.

His deep laugh filled the interior. "Not yet. Maybe when the next model is released. Are you ready for your surprise?"

Rachel pulled her seatbelt across her chest. "You mean

this isn't it?"

"Not even close."

She grinned at her partner in crime. "I feel like I'm about to do something amazing."

John's smile disappeared. "I hope so." He looked in the rearview mirror and pulled away from the curb.

If she didn't know better, she would have sworn he was nervous. "You don't have to impress me with fancy gadgets and expensive things. I'm happy just spending time with you."

"I know. Do you know how unusual that is?"

"Finding someone who likes spending time with you?"

A smile replaced his frown. "What would my life be like if we hadn't met?"

Rachel laughed. "Quiet."

John's smile grew wider. The Maserati's engine purred as they accelerated along the street. It felt as though they were driving on a cloud. A very expensive, super-comfy cloud.

Rachel might not know where they were going, but she knew one thing. She'd found her second favorite vehicle, after her truck.

JOHN DROVE SLOWLY past the State Capitol building on their night tour of Denver. Rachel peered through the window, trying to see as much as she could. The lights surrounding the building made the entrance look majestic, but it was the dome on top that made her gasp.

"Is it covered in gold?"

John looked at where she was pointing. "It is. We'll have time to come back tomorrow, if you want to?"

"That would be great." Rachel already wanted to go back to the City Park and the Denver Art Museum. Then there was Larimer Square, with plenty of colorful boutiques, restaurants and cafés. She smiled at John as he slowed for a set of traffic lights. "Thank you for bringing me here."

"You're welcome. I'm glad you're enjoying yourself."

"And thank your interior designer. The list of furniture stores she gave us was great. I didn't think it would be so much fun choosing sofas and tables."

John glanced in his rearview mirror. "There's more to visit tomorrow. By the end of the weekend we'll have an impressive list of furniture for her to look at."

Rachel thought about the stores they'd already visited. Bella was so excited when they'd found a chair with pink flowers on it. It would be perfect in her new room and give her a lovely piece of furniture to enjoy for many years.

John slowed for another set of traffic lights and she smiled. The first time they'd stopped for a red light, people had pointed at their car. Rachel was embarrassed, but after realizing they were genuinely interested in the Maserati, she'd started enjoying herself.

At another set of lights, she'd pushed a button and her window had rolled silently down. John had wondered what she was doing, until she started talking to the man in the car next to them. By the end of the thirty-second conversation, she'd found out the Maserati was the man's dream car.

John had pulled away from the intersection fast, muttering about carjackings and personal safety. Rachel had grinned and told him not to worry so much. He'd replied by locking her window from the control panel beside him.

Even with her window permanently closed, Rachel was still enjoying herself.

They drove for a few more minutes before John turned into a parking lot and stopped the car.

"Where are we?"

"Skyline Park. It covers three blocks in the center of

town." He climbed out of the car and walked around to Rachel's side of the Maserati. He held open the door, and she tried to get elegantly out of the seat. It wasn't as easy as she thought.

Rachel looked left, then right. No one except John was around. "Close your eyes."

"Why?"

"I'll have to scramble out of here."

"I can help you scramble."

"Okay, but don't laugh. It's not easy wearing a straight skirt and high-heels in a low sports car."

John held out his hand. "No laughing allowed." He hoisted her out of the car and Rachel almost fell into his arms.

"My truck is gaining points in the practical department," she muttered. "How do other women get out of a Maserati?"

"Very carefully," John said with a straight face.

Rachel buttoned her coat and looked around the parking lot. "There aren't many vehicles here. Are you sure the stores are open?"

He locked the car and held her hand. "At this time of night, it's mostly the restaurants that are open. Come with me."

"But we've already had dinner. Are we having coffee or are you still hungry?"

As they hurried across the snow-covered asphalt, John's hand tightened on hers. "I'm not hungry."

Rachel jogged to keep up with him. "Because if you are, I don't mind. You're a big guy and you probably need to refuel on carbs a lot more than I do. The average male needs 2,500 calories each day to maintain their energy levels. But you're not average, so another meal could always come in handy."

"Nice to know I'm not average."

Rachel squeezed his hand. "You could never be average. You're super amazing."

John stopped so quickly that Rachel nearly slipped on the icy ground. She held onto his hand and smiled. "Oops. That was—"

John's mouth connected with hers and didn't move. When they finally came up for air, Rachel smiled. "Your kisses are super amazing, too."

He gently touched her face before leaving another kiss on the end of her nose. "So are yours. Are you ready for your surprise?"

Rachel nodded. "It doesn't involve hot dogs or donuts, does it? I'm still full from dinner."

John held her hand and walked around the corner of a building. "No hot dogs or donuts, I promise."

Rachel stopped and stared at one of the prettiest sights she'd ever seen. An ice rink, as big as a football field, sat in front of a whole lot of buildings. Twinkling fairy lights were strung across the area above it, and soft music played from the speakers.

Rachel looked at the seats on either side of the rink. No one was there. It was completely deserted, apart from a lady standing at a ticket booth.

John pulled Rachel's hand toward the booth. "Have you ever been ice skating?"

"A couple of times. But we can't go on the rink. It's closed."

"No, it's not." John walked up to the lady. She smiled and handed him two pairs of skates. He thanked her and handed Rachel the smaller of the two pairs. "These are for you."

Rachel looked at the skates and then at John. "How did the lady know we were coming? Did you pre-book our tickets?"

"You could say that."

Rachel sat on a plastic chair and frowned. "Why is no one else here? It's such a lovely night and it looks like a great place to visit. There must be something wrong with their advertising."

"You'd better get your skates on before they really do close."

While Rachel was wondering about the ice rink's promotions plan, John had put on his skates and was waiting impatiently beside her. She quickly slipped off her shoes and pulled on the skates.

"How do your boots feel?"

Rachel stood on the special mat in front of them and wiggled her toes. "Perfect. How did you know what size I'd be?"

"Bella looked inside your shoes."

Rachel frowned. "How long have you been planning this visit to Denver?"

John cleared his throat. "A few days. Are you ready to skate?"

Rachel was getting a little suspicious about John's motives for bringing her here. "There aren't hidden cameras planted around the rink, are there?"

He looked nervous. So nervous that Rachel started to get really worried. She looked at the buildings around them and stepped closer to him. "You haven't been sent another death threat, have you? We don't have to go skating if it's too dangerous."

John took a deep breath and pulled her onto the ice. "No death threats."

"What are you so worried about? You're frowning worse than when I first met you. Your palms are all sweaty. You aren't coming down with a virus, are you?"

John wiped his hands on the side of his jacket, then grabbed hold of both her hands. He skated backward, pulling Rachel across the ice until her legs stopped wobbling.

He let go of one of her hands and skated beside her. "Are

you okay?"

Rachel looked up and smiled. "I think so. I still can't believe no one else is here. It has so much potential."

"Maybe someone booked the whole rink?"

Rachel laughed. "No one would do that. It would cost a fortune…" She stumbled on the ice. John's grip on her hand tightened, but it wasn't enough. She lunged for his arm with her other hand and landed bottom first on the ice.

"*Oww.*"

John knelt beside her. "Are you all right?"

Rachel rolled onto her side and rubbed her bottom. "I think so, unless you count wounded pride as an injury. Tell me you didn't rent the whole rink for the two of us?"

"I didn't rent the whole rink for the two of us."

Rachel breathed a sigh of relief. "Thank goodness for that."

"I…umm…booked it for the four of us."

"Four?"

John pointed to somewhere behind Rachel. She turned around and scrambled to her feet. Tank and Bella were skating toward them.

She looked at John and frowned. "Didn't they drive back to the hotel?"

"They did. Bella got changed."

Rachel looked more closely at what Bella was wearing. She'd changed out of her pink coat and into a pretty powder blue jacket. With her hair in braids and glittery red boots on her feet, she looked like Dorothy from *The Wizard of Oz*.

Bella stopped in front of Rachel. "Are you okay?"

"I'm fine. I slipped on the ice, that's all. You look lovely."

Bella grinned and spun in a circle. "I'm Dorothy."

Rachel looked at Tank.

"I'm not Toto."

"You'd look cute with pointy ears," Rachel teased.

John cleared his throat and lifted his arm. "Can everyone remember what we talked about?"

Rachel watched Bella put on her serious face. The background music rose around them, filling the rink with a soft romantic feeling.

Rachel watched Bella and Tank turn around and skate away. "Are we pretending to do a scene from *The Wizard of Oz*?" she asked John. "It could be like Disney on Ice. Did you know that—"

John shook his head. "I know your mind is buzzing with facts, but I don't need to know how many ice skaters Disney employed in the last year."

"Good. Because I don't know. But I do know how many Disney princesses have featured in their productions in the last ten years."

John put his hands over his ears and Rachel laughed. "I'll save that fact for later."

She looked at Bella and Tank. They were skating toward them with a silver tray in their hands. On the tray was a container covered with sparkly jewels.

"Do you know what they're doing?" Rachel asked. "I don't remember this scene from *The Wizard of Oz*."

"It's not from the play."

"It's not?"

"No. Listen to the music."

Rachel focused on the music coming from the speakers. "It's a Nat King Cole song. Tess played it at her wedding. It's called, *When I Fall in Love*." She still didn't understand what was going on.

Bella and Tank stopped in front of her. Rachel looked at John, hoping he'd tell her what they should do next.

He took an envelope out of the container Bella and Tank were holding. "This is for you."

Rachel looked at the envelope and smiled. "That's the

same one Bella sent to The Bridesmaids Club. You kept it?"

John nodded. His frown made her nervous.

"Read the card again," Bella whispered.

Rachel knew what it said. She'd memorized each word, looking for any clue about who could have sent it. Wiping her hands on her jacket, she took the envelope out of John's hand. She slid the flap open and pulled out the letter. *"Dear Bridesmaids Club. Can you please help my daddy find a bride?"*

John put the letter on the tray and held her hands. "When you came into my office and gave me Bella's letter, I didn't know what to think. I'd never met anyone who made me feel so much, so quickly. You annoyed me, intrigued me, and made me want to know you better."

He took a deep breath. Rachel's heart pounded and her vision got a little blurry. When her skates wobbled, John steadied her.

"I love you, Rachel. I've loved you from the minute you walked into my office. I can't imagine my life without you. You make me happy and you make Bella happy. I didn't expect to feel this way about anyone."

Rachel tried to think of something to say, but her mind was completely blank. John was looking at her with so much love in his eyes that she had to remember to breathe.

He glanced at Bella. "We wanted to take you to *The Wizard of Oz* for different reasons."

"I like Dorothy's shoes," Bella said with a grin.

"And I wanted to let you know you've changed my life."

Rachel let go of John's hands and blew her nose. "I don't know what to say."

John studied her face before reaching into the container. He handed her a piece of paper that was rolled into a tube. Someone had tied a pink bow around the middle.

"That's from me," Bella said with pride. "It's a certificate for being the best teacher in the world. The Wizard of Oz gave the Scarecrow a certificate, too. Except he wanted to be brainy. I'm happy with the way I am."

Rachel opened the certificate and gave Bella a hug. "Thank you. I'm happy with the way you are, too."

Tank reached into the container. With one hand he took out a medal attached to a bright blue ribbon. "And this is from all of us. For being brave when we were all scared, and for finding Bella when no one else could."

Tank put the medal over Rachel's head. "The Lion in *The Wizard of Oz* wanted to be brave." Tank looked at the medal, then into her eyes. "He deserved his medal as much as you do."

Rachel wiped fresh tears off her face. "Thank you, Tank."

Bella looked at her dad. "It's your turn," she whispered.

John put his hand inside the container and opened a small red box. "And this is from me."

He knelt on one knee and Rachel held her breath.

"Bella and I love you, Rachel. Will you marry me and be part of our lives?"

She looked at the beautiful heart-shaped diamond ring. "The Tin Man wanted a heart," she whispered.

John wiped his eyes and stood up. "He wanted to know what love felt like. Each day I've known you, you've shown me what it's like to be loved. I'd like to spend the rest of my life showing you how much I love you. Will you marry me?"

Rachel nodded. Tears slid down her face as Bella and John wrapped her in their arms. She glanced at Tank and smiled as he blew his nose.

Closing her eyes, she felt joy unfold inside her. Like Dorothy in *The Wizard of Oz*, Rachel had found what she was looking for.

And it had been right in front of her the whole time.

THE END

THANK YOU

Thank you for reading *Sealed with a Kiss*. I hope you enjoyed it! If you did...

1. Help other people find this book by **writing a review.**
2. Sign up for my **new releases e-mail**, so you can find out about the next book as soon as it's available.
3. Come like my **Facebook** page.
4. Visit my website: **leeannamorgan.com**

Keep reading to enjoy an excerpt from ***Playing for Keeps***, Sophie and Ryan's story in the *Emerald Lake* series!

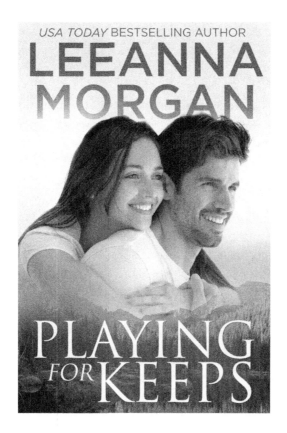

USA TODAY BESTSELLING AUTHOR

LEEANNA MORGAN

PLAYING FOR KEEPS

Playing For Keeps
Emerald Lake, Book 2

For the last five years, Ryan Evans has been riding the wave of country music super-stardom. He has everything he's ever wanted, more money than he knows what to do with, and a reputation that's been shredded to a pulp.

With a crazy ex-wife on the loose, he heads to Montana to hide from the media frenzy that's about to hit. But instead of finding blue skies that stretch into forever and more cows than people, he finds Sophie Elliott standing in the middle of a deserted road.

Sophie is in trouble. When Ryan finds her on the side of the road she has two choices – keep running or take a chance with a man who offers to solve her top two issues. She doesn't need to think hard about her answer. With a drug company stalking her and a sexy man offering her more than she expects, it's enough to make her scientific brain explode.

With more than his career at stake, Ryan has to convince Sophie that what they have is more real than anything either of them have known. But that means giving up a part of himself that he's never shared with anyone, and he doesn't know if either of them are ready for that. Especially when Sophie tells him the most deadliest secret of all.

Keep reading for a preview of **Playing for Keeps**, Sophie and Ryan's story in the *Emerald Lake* series!

CHAPTER 1

*R*yan sat in his truck, watching the people on the sidewalk. Downtown Bozeman wasn't exactly the center of the universe, but it was as close as he'd gotten in a long time. For the last few months he'd been building his dream house beside Emerald Lake and hiding from a past he wasn't proud of.

But that was all about to change. In ten minutes he was meeting his publicist, strategizing about the best way to deal with his crazy ex-wife and the media frenzy that was about to hit town.

Dorothy Patterson was nothing if not punctual. She strode along the sidewalk like the leader of a marching band; back straight, head high, and with the kind of serious expression that didn't bode well for a good meeting.

She'd made the journey from Nashville to Montana in record time. She had as much to lose as he did. If his ex-wife's photos hit any of the publications she was threatening to use, they'd both go down in flames.

Stepping out of his truck, he shut the door and prepared for one of the most important discussions of his life. By the time he made it inside Angel Wings Café, Dorothy had already found a table at the back of the room.

"You're late," she said with a forced smile. Dorothy looked like butter wouldn't melt in her mouth. But underneath the girl next door veneer, there was a woman with a heart of steel.

"I've been waiting in my truck. Have you spoken to her?"

"The only person Cindy's talking to is her lawyer. He called me four hours ago and told me her terms and conditions haven't changed. She wants half the royalties from the song you wrote when you were married. If you don't pay her, she'll release the photos. Sit down. I've ordered coffee."

He wasn't surprised his ex-wife hadn't changed her mind. "She's not getting any royalties from the song. My lawyer has already spoken to her lawyer. There's no way a judge will give her what she wants."

Dorothy smiled at the waitress as she left their drinks on the table. She leaned forward, her blue eyes boring into his. "You can't afford to let her release those photos. They'll kill your career."

"I divorced Cindy six years ago. She took half of what I owned then. There's no way she's getting more money. If you can't speak to Cindy, tell her lawyer she won't see another dime from me."

Dorothy pulled a folder out of her bag. "I thought you'd say something like that. I've been working on a plan to salvage what we can of your reputation. Are you sure she doesn't have more photos?"

"She sent me copies of all of them. They're so out of focus she'll be lucky if anyone believes her."

"It doesn't matter what they believe. What matters is that they'll be available for everyone to see. If Cindy can't get her hands on the money she thinks is hers, she'll take what she can. If that means destroying you in the process, she'll do it."

"She's not that calculating."

"I wouldn't bet on it." Dorothy turned the folder around and opened the cover. "Tell me what you think."

Ryan read the document but didn't get very far. Dorothy's suggestions for combating his ex-wife's demands were almost as bad as releasing the photos. "What do you mean, sing for a charity? I'm living in the middle of Montana, being hounded by my ex-wife, and you want me to give a charity concert?"

"I don't care how you do it or where you do it, but you need to generate some positive publicity. Hiding in Bozeman will make people think the photos are genuine."

It was his turn to lean forward. "They are true. I'd had too much to drink. I was twenty-one years old, and we'd been married for less than a year. I learned my lesson."

"It looks as though Cindy did, too. She's probably kicking herself that she didn't take more." Dorothy pointed to the list. "We need photos of you at your new house, with your clothes on and a tool belt around your waist. That will let people know you've got more than a pretty—"

"I get the idea."

"Let's hope everyone else does, too."

Ryan didn't bother looking for a smile on Dorothy's face. He'd given up years ago believing she had a sense of humor. Instead, he studied the list and frowned. Out of all the options she'd come up with, having his photo taken wearing a tool belt made the most sense.

He read the next bullet point on her list. "You're not asking for much. I haven't written any new material in the last six months. How do you expect me to write, produce and record an album in the next six months?"

"Your ex-wife was your inspiration for 'Sad Time Coming'. It made you an overnight success. Use that same energy to produce your next number one hit. Maybe you could call it 'Goodbye to Bad News'."

This time, he did look for a smile. Dorothy's mouth was tilted at the corners. "And here I was, thinking you didn't have a sense of humor."

Her smile disappeared. "I hide it well. Getting mad achieves nothing, but at least getting even makes you feel better. Cindy won't be impressed if her threats make you another million dollars."

"Especially if she can't get her hands on any of it," Ryan muttered.

He would have laughed at the next bullet point if it had been someone else's life they were talking about. "What do you hope to achieve by setting me up with another woman? The only thing I need is a good lawyer and a plan to keep Cindy away from me."

"A new girlfriend is my emergency option. After what happened with Cindy, you could be asking for trouble. But, after a lot of soul-searching, I believe it could be your saving grace." She reached across the table and pulled another piece of paper from the back of the folder. "She would have to meet certain criteria. You can't afford to make the same mistake twice."

He didn't bother reading what Dorothy had left in front of him. There was no way he'd date another woman to make his publicist happy.

Dorothy sipped her coffee. "You haven't had a serious girlfriend since you left Cindy. If you're not willing to do anything else, at least think about it. I might be a miracle worker, but I'm not Cupid."

"I'm not paying you to be Cupid," Ryan said. "I'm paying you to look after my career. I'll take the list home and read it. If I have any questions, I'll call you."

"I'll be in Bozeman until four o'clock this afternoon. I

have a meeting with your lawyer in half an hour. If there's anything else you need to tell me, call me on my cell phone." Dorothy left her coffee cup in the middle of the table and stood up. "If you hear anything from Cindy, call me straight away."

"Yes, ma'am."

She passed him her folder of notes. "At least promise me you'll read the other ideas. You're not the first musician to be blackmailed by an ex-wife."

Ryan didn't bother replying.

Dorothy sighed. "Why do I get the feeling that as soon as you leave the café, you'll put my notes on the floor of your truck and leave them there?"

"I guess we're both learning something new about each other. Cindy's not getting her hands on more of my money or ruining my reputation. I'll read your ideas and let you know what I think."

Dorothy left the café as quickly as she'd arrived.

Looking down at the folder, he frowned. Some days, being a country music superstar sucked.

SOPHIE ELLIOTT LIFTED one of her suitcases out of the trunk of her car. In both directions, the road was as straight as an arrow for as far as she could see.

Ten minutes ago she'd run out of gas. She knew she would have been lucky to reach Bozeman, but over the last two weeks she'd been in more difficult situations than a blinking fuel indicator. This time, she'd pushed her luck too far. About two miles too far.

Locking her car, she pulled up the handle of her suitcase. Bozeman couldn't be more than a thirty-minute walk from here. She'd buy more gas, walk back to her car, and keep looking for somewhere safe to stay.

As she started walking, she wondered how many people drove down this stretch of the interstate. In the last ten minutes, the only living thing she'd seen had been a hawk.

She'd driven from Chicago to Montana out of desperation. A friend who'd worked with her in the Department of Microbiology and Immunology at Chicago University had lived in Montana for six years. She'd told Sophie it was the prettiest place on earth. It was so quiet you could hear the wind whispering through the trees and, in the summer, it was so hot you could fry an egg on the asphalt. Even knowing all of that, Sophie wasn't used to feeling as though she was the last person on earth.

Her suitcase bumped over the stones, jarring her arm and slowing her down. At this rate, she'd never make Bozeman by nightfall. She pushed the handle back into the suitcase and carried it.

She kept reminding herself she was doing the right thing, that she could do more good by disappearing. Sharing what she knew with the wrong people could be deadly, not only for herself, but for her mom and sister.

A brown pickup truck drove toward her. Sophie put her head down and kept walking. The truck slowed to a crawl, and the driver rolled down his window.

"Looks like you could do with a ride?"

Sophie glanced at the cowboy. "Thanks for the offer, but you're going in the wrong direction."

"You're not from around here, are you?"

She didn't think her Chicago accent was that different from his, but she wasn't about to start a conversation with a stranger. Pushing a strand of hair off her face, she kept walking. It must have been ninety-five degrees, and it was barely eleven o'clock in the morning.

The cowboy turned his truck around and followed her down the road. "That suitcase seems mighty heavy," he said with a smile. "Looking at the car on the side of the road, I'd say you've run out of gas. I can easily drive you into town and bring you back here."

Sophie stopped walking. The cowboy's hat covered most of his face. She had no idea what he looked like, but there couldn't be many mass murderers and trained killers who wore plaid shirts.

His truck was covered in dirt. It had enough bumps and scrapes to pass for the real thing. "I don't want to inconvenience you. You've just come from Bozeman."

"It won't take long to drive back into town. Besides, you'll get there a lot faster in my truck than if you were walking."

She looked down the road once more before deciding what to do. It was hot and she was desperate. After two weeks of running like a scared rabbit, she was tired of second-guessing everyone. It probably wasn't the most logical thing to do, but logic didn't work so well when you were alone and thousands of miles from home.

"Thank you. I'd be grateful for a ride." She waited beside his truck while he climbed out. He was taller than she imagined. Taller and wider. The man had muscles that would have put her male colleagues in the science lab to shame.

Sophie looked into his deep brown eyes. "I appreciate you stopping."

"Happy to be of help," he said with a smile. Opening the back door, he took her case out of her hand. "Were you planning on staying a while or just passing through?"

Walking around the truck, she opened the passenger door and thought about what she could say; the half-truths and downright lies she could use to keep herself safe. "I'm not sure yet."

The stranger pulled on his seatbelt and started the ignition. "Montana's a good place to work out what you need to do. Have you been here before?"

"No, but I've heard some great things about Bozeman. Do you live here?"

He looked in his rearview mirror and moved onto the highway. "I move around a lot. I have family living in Bozeman."

She waited for him to say something else, but he kept his eyes focused on the road. "I'm Sophie." She held out her hand, wanting to keep the ride into town as professional as possible.

The cowboy glanced across the cab. "Hi, Sophie. I'm Ryan."

Their hands barely touched, but she felt the strength of his grip like a warning along her spine. "I thought I'd have enough gas to get me into town. I didn't pay enough attention to how quickly the fuel gauge was going down." Sophie closed her mouth. She was rambling. He probably thought she was a ditzy woman who didn't know one end of a car from the other.

"You must have a lot on your mind."

If Ryan knew what she had on her mind, he wouldn't have stopped to help. Sophie glanced out of the cab, suddenly feeling nervous. It was a bit late for that. She'd jumped into a truck with a total stranger. She was heading toward a town she'd never seen and had ninety dollars in her wallet.

As they drove closer to Bozeman, she thought about what she had to do next. After she'd refilled her gas tank, she'd look for a job. It wasn't what she'd planned on doing, but nothing over the last two weeks had been part of her plans.

Ryan glanced across the cab. "Where do you normally live?"

She didn't have to think hard about her answer. Before

she left Chicago, she'd made up a story that would protect her and the people she loved. "San Francisco."

"It's a big city. I've stayed there a few times. Did you ever go to Tony's Pizza Place? It's on Stockton Street."

Sophie felt her cheeks grow hot. "No, I don't think so."

"It's opposite Washington Square Park. It's well worth a visit."

Keeping her eyes on the passing scenery, she hoped Ryan got the message and didn't ask her any more questions.

"How long have you lived in San Francisco?"

"About three years." Sophie crossed her fingers, hoping the story she dreamed up sounded real. "I work in retail."

"What do you sell?"

She tried to look confident, as if his questions were the most natural thing in the world to answer. "Shoes. Ladies shoes."

Ryan looked down at her feet. He didn't need to say anything about her choice of footwear. Her sneakers were the most comfortable pair of shoes she owned. But they weren't the type of shoes a fashion-conscious twenty-nine-year-old would wear.

She pulled her feet closer to the edge of her seat. "I wore my old sneakers today."

"That makes sense."

As the first buildings in Bozeman came into view, she breathed a sigh of relief. The commercial properties were a mix of old red-brick buildings and newer retail outlets. The wide streets and almost empty parking lots were so different from Chicago. She felt as though she'd stepped back in time.

"There's a gas station down the road. They'll have a gas can we can use. When you get back to town, just drop it off to them."

When they pulled into the station, Sophie looked at the vehicles parked at the pumps. Everyone was going about their own business. They weren't worried about the brown truck that had parked at the side of the building.

As soon as Ryan stopped the truck, she had her hand on the door handle. "Thanks for giving me a ride into town. I really appreciate it."

He looked amused. "Anytime. It's nice helping a damsel in distress, but I haven't finished yet. I'll take you back to your car once you have a full can of gas."

Her eyes widened. She'd been in such a hurry to leave that she'd forgotten about getting back to her car.

"Just in case you need rescuing again, here's my phone number." He took a piece of paper out of a folder on the floor and scribbled a number on it. "Let's get some gas for your car."

Sophie didn't need to be told twice. She jumped out of the truck and headed toward a person working at the station. The sooner she bought what she needed, the sooner she could work on her other problems.

Running out of gas wasn't the best start to her arrival in Bozeman, but it was better than not getting here at all.

PLAYING FOR KEEPS
Available Now!

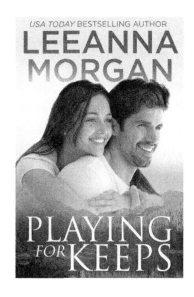

ENJOY OTHER NOVELS BY LEEANNA MORGAN:

Montana Brides:

Book 1: Forever Dreams (Gracie and Trent)

Book 2: Forever in Love (Amy and Nathan)

Book 3: Forever After (Nicky and Sam)

Book 4: Forever Wishes (Erin and Jake)

Book 5: Forever Santa (A Montana Brides Christmas Novella)

Book 6: Forever Cowboy (Emily and Alex)

Book 7: Forever Together (Kate and Dan)

Book 8: Forever and a Day (Sarah and Jordan)

Montana Brides Boxed Set: Books 1-3

Montana Brides Boxed Set: Books 4-6

The Bridesmaids Club:

Book 1: All of Me (Tess and Logan)

Book 2: Loving You (Annie and Dylan)

Book 3: Head Over Heels (Sally and Todd)

Book 4: Sweet on You (Molly and Jacob)

The Bridesmaids Club: Books 1-3

Emerald Lake:

Book 1: Sealed with a Kiss (Rachel and John)

Book 2: Playing for Keeps (Sophie and Ryan)

Book 3: Crazy Love (Holly and Daniel)

Book 4: One And Only (Elizabeth and Blake)

Emerald Lake: Books 1-3

The Protectors:

Book 1: Safe Haven (Hayley and Tank)

Book 2: Just Breathe (Kelly and Tanner)

Book 3: Always (Mallory and Grant)

Book 4: The Promise (Ashley and Matthew)

The Protectors Boxed Set: Books 1-3

Montana Promises:

Book 1: Coming Home (Mia and Stan)

Book 2: The Gift (Hannah and Brett)

Book 3: The Wish (Claire and Jason)

Book 4: Country Love (Becky and Sean)

Montana Promises Boxed Set: Books 1-3

Sapphire Bay:

Book 1: Falling For You (Natalie and Gabe)

Book 2: Once In A Lifetime (Sam and Caleb)

Book 3: A Christmas Wish (Megan and William)

Book 4: Before Today (Brooke and Levi)

Book 5: The Sweetest Thing (Cassie and Noah)

Book 6: Sweet Surrender (Willow and Zac)

Sapphire Bay Boxed Set: Books 1-3

Sapphire Bay Boxed Set: Books 4-6

Santa's Secret Helpers:

Book 1: Christmas On Main Street (Emma and Jack)

Book 2: Mistletoe Madness (Kylie and Ben)

Book 3: Silver Bells (Bailey and Steven)

Book 4: The Santa Express (Shelley and John)

Book 5: Endless Love (The Jones Family)

Santa's Secret Helpers Boxed Set: Books 1-3

Return To Sapphire Bay:

Book 1: The Lakeside Inn (Penny and Wyatt)

Book 2: Summer At Lakeside (Diana and Ethan)

Book 3: A Lakeside Thanksgiving (Barbara and Theo)

Book 4: Christmas At Lakeside (Katie and Peter)

Return to Sapphire Bay Boxed Set (Books 1-3)

The Cottages on Anchor Lane:

Book 1: The Flower Cottage (Paris and Richard)

Book 2: The Starlight Café (Andrea and David)

Book 3: The Cozy Quilt Shop (Shona and Joseph)

Book 4: A Stitch in Time (Jackie and Aidan)

Printed in Great Britain
by Amazon

26922621R00165